GINGER WALLS

This is a work of fiction. Names, characters, places, and incidents either are the product of the author's imagination or are used fictitiously. Any resemblance to actual persons, living or dead, events, or locales is entirely coincidental.

Copyright © 2025 by Ginger Walls

All rights reserved. No part of this book may be reproduced or used in any manner without written permission of the copyright owner except for the use of quotations in a book review. For more information, address: hello@gingeralana.com.

First paperback edition February 2025

Illustration and Book Cover design by Ink & Laurel

Copy Editing and Proofreading by Kristen at Kristen's Red Pen

978-1-962755-05-4 (paperback)

www.GingerAlana.com

Contents

CONTENT WARNING	VI
DEDICATION	VIII
PROLOGUE	1
1. SYDNEY	11
2. KOA	29
FICTION FORUM	39
3. SYDNEY	43
FICTION FORUM	55
4. KOA	59
FICTION FORUM	71
5. SYDNEY	75
FICTION FORUM	89
6. KOA	93
FICTION FORUM	105
7. SYDNEY	117
8. KOA	127

FICTION FORUM	137
9. SYDNEY	141
FICTION FORUM	155
10. SYDNEY	161
FICTION FORM	175
11. KOA	179
FICTION FORUM	191
12. SYDNEY	195
FICTION FORUM	209
13. KOA	213
FICTION FORUM	225
14. SYDNEY	229
FICTION FORUM	245
15. KOA	247
16. SYDNEY	263
FICTION FORUM	279
17. SYDNEY	285
FICTION FORUM	295
18. KOA	297
19. SYDNEY	309
20. KOA	321
21. SYDNEY	333
22. KOA	343

23. SYDNEY	359
24. KOA	375
25. SYDNEY	387
26. KOA	397
27. SYDNEY	407
28. KOA	413
EPILOGUE	421
THANK YOU	429
About the author	432
Also by	435

FOUL TERRITORY

Foul Territory is intended for adult readers only

It contains mature themes and sexually explicit content and is not intended for readers younger than 18 years old.

This book also contains a scene where the main female character is approached aggressively by a stranger while inside their car in chapter 22

FOUL TERRITORY

To all the book lovers in the world looking for a partner who appreciates and respects your interest in fictional characters finding their happily ever after, this one is for you. May we all find our person who'll listen to our book reviews and conspiracy theories with a smirk on their face and love in their eyes.

Until then at least we have Koa Mahina.

SYDNEY

HIGH SCHOOL GRADUATION NIGHT

(FOUR YEARS EARLIER)

Finally. I kick my shoes off and send them flying across the room. Diving face first into my bedspread, I inhale a deep breath of the fresh scent. The familiar smell mends a few of my frayed nerves.

After a long night of party hopping with my brother, Nash, and our best friend, Koa, I'm ready to slip into something more comfortable and escape reality for the rest of the night.

I need to occupy my mind with a good book instead of constantly thinking about *him* being a few feet away. I've been on edge ever since Nash asked Koa to stay the night on the way home. This isn't anything new. He's been staying over at our house almost every weekend since middle school. If he's not here, then they are both at his house or with our friend, Hart, who lives a few streets over.

I'm not sure which I like better: having him within reach but not being able to touch him or far away and wondering what he's doing. Neither choice feels right. *Nothing has felt right with him lately.*

"Are you okay?" Koa's voice filters through the air from somewhere behind me.

"I'm good," I mumble into my rose covered comforter. Flipping over on my back, I push up onto my elbows and find him leaning against the cream door frame, his arms casually crossed over his broad chest. A pair of deep brown eyes turn a shade darker as they rake over my body.

I stopped tracking the times Koa's looked at me with this much intensity months ago. It became depressing. Too many opportunities for him to make a move or admit he feels the same current of electricity flowing between us. I'd hold my breath waiting for him but I'm afraid death would come before he'd ever make a move.

"Did you have fun tonight?" he asks, his eyes focused on the wall above my head. I guess he had his fill. Not sure what else I can do to get his attention if laying on my bed in a mini dress isn't doing it for him.

"It was okay I guess. I didn't know very many people," I reply, sitting up on my bed and putting a pillow over my lap so I can cross my legs.

FOUL TERRITORY

The parties we went to tonight were hosted by different guys on the baseball team. Not exactly my crowd. I have a small selection of friends. None of which would be caught at a house party.

The truth is friends have always been hard to come by for me. I can count on one hand the number of true friends I have and they are all guys. I would be approached by girls at school who would pretend to play nice but were only talking to me to get closer to my brother and his friends. They treated me like I was their meal ticket.

If only they knew the truth. Sure the guys included me in things when they could, but I mostly felt like I was tagging along. Like I'm there by default—or worse, pity.

It wasn't always like this. I was Koa's first friend in town. I'll never forget the day we met. I'd just bought new roller skates with money I had saved up and was trying them out, skating up and down our long street.

At the very last house, he was there like a pot of gold at the end of a rainbow. Koa jumped off the back of the moving truck and his eyes caught mine. My knees buckled, making me almost lose my balance.

I didn't have the guts to stop and say something to him. I wanted to but I'd never talked to a boy as cute as him before. The next day he was outside playing catch with his brother. I skated by his house at least a dozen times. He never waved or anything but he would watch me. His eyes may have been hidden under his baseball cap but I've always been able to tell when I have his attention. My body lights up any time he looks in my direction.

On the third day, he was outside playing catch again. It seems to be the only thing he liked to do. His eyes followed me as I skated past his concrete driveway. He was so focused on me he missed the ball. I stopped it with my skate before it could roll into the street. I picked up the ball and handed it over to him. Our fingers touched and he shocked me. I felt his touch for days like a phantom limb.

One touch and a mumbled thanks was all it took for me to fall in love with the boy at the end of the street. That was a summer I'll never forget. We spent most days doing nothing but breathing the same air but it felt like so much more. I never wanted it to end. I wanted to be near him always.

I wish I was near him now. He's here in my room but he still feels far away. We never had another summer like that one. When the season changed and baseball started, he met Nash. Our duo became a trio and that changed everything. I'm usually pretty good when it comes to sharing, but I didn't like sharing him. *I wanted Koa to stay mine.*

I lean forward on the pillow, pressing my forearms into the soft cotton fabric and slouch my shoulders.

Koa shifts away from the door and curses under his breath as he scrubs a hand down his face. He's changed out of the jeans and button down shirt he wore to the party and into an old shirt and gym shorts. His muscular, tan thighs are barely contained in the mesh material and his white shirt is molded to his chest.

"Is something wrong?" I ask, not understanding why he's suddenly cursing to himself. He steps further into my room and closes the door behind him. He glances over at me before locking it. Sitting up straighter, I watch him as he paces the floor. "Koa?"

"Is that okay?" He tips his chin toward the locked door.

"Yes. I think so. What's going on? Nash is going to wonder where you are." I scoot back on my bed, stretching my legs.

I typically try to ignore my brother and his friends when they stay the night. During the day we hang out in the basement or in the living room. After dark, I know they don't want me around. I can say with full confidence this is the first late night visit I have ever received.

"He's distracted by his game. You know how Nash can get. He won't know if I'm gone for five minutes or five hours," he says, walking around to the other side of my bed and making himself comfortable.

Koa is laying on my bed. My palms are sweating and my pulse starts to race at a very unhealthy level. My heartbeat thuds louder, and I'm convinced he can hear it in my silent bedroom.

Play it cool. Be casual. I fluff the pillow behind my head and lay down beside him. "We graduated. It's hard to believe we're going to be at college in a few months. I'm scared," I admit, breaking the silence that's been building between us.

"You don't need to be scared. I'll be there with you," he says, taking my hand in his and lacing our fingers together. I stare dumbfounded at our hands as the hair on my arm begins to stand on end.

After the ceremony when we were taking photos, Nash asked him and Hart to keep an eye on me next year while we're at Newhouse. I acted annoyed but I'm grateful I'll have an excuse to keep Koa close to me. I was afraid I would lose him to baseball and other girls. *But he's holding your hand now.*

"You're not nervous?" I ask, my eyes dart from him and back to our hands. His thumb is making slow swipes back and forth over my skin like a metronome.

"No. I'm not nervous about going off to school." He squeezes my hand breaking the trance I was under watching his thumb move over my skin.

"What are you nervous about?" I ask.

He readjusts his position, bringing himself closer to the middle of the bed. *Closer to me.* "You looked really beautiful today. I like this dress. *A lot.*" He lets go of my hand and allows his fingers to skim the top of my thigh just under the hem of my dress.

Instinctively my eyes close as I savor the feel of his hand against my skin as it breakouts in tiny goosebumps. "You're not answering my question," I say, finding it hard to speak as he continues to toy with the hem of my dress.

His eyes travel up my body and latch onto mine. "I'm nervous about what you'd do if you knew how much I wanted to kiss you right now."

My eyes widen and I think I stop breathing for a moment. I've always wondered what it would be like to hear those words, or something similar, leave his mouth.

He's always been the boy that I wanted but could never have. I think he knew I liked him because by the end of seventh grade I was firmly put in the friend zone. He told me once that keeping everything platonic would be for the best. I wanted to ask for who? It didn't feel like what would be the best for me. But I already knew the answer. It's what was best for his friendship with Nash.

He didn't want anything to change, except it already had for me.

I was in love with him. I knew the moment he said *"we should stay friends"* I would be spending the rest of my life figuring out how to stop loving him. Is it too soon to start believing maybe now I won't have to know what it feels like to live a life loving him without him loving me back?

Hearing him say he wants to kiss me makes breathing difficult and my skin flush. It makes butterflies dance in my belly and my heart soar.

He places a hand on my back, encouraging me to move toward him. I drape an arm over his and clutch the top of his shoulder.

"I guess my reaction would depend on how much your much is," I say, grinning. "If your much is only this much." I raise my hand and hold out my thumb and pointer finger with an inch of distance between them. "I wouldn't be very interested. How much do you want to kiss me?"

"There isn't a unit of measurement large enough to adequately explain how much I want to kiss you at the moment." He palms the back of my head, pulling me until I'm a breath away.

"Then you better do it," I whisper against his lips. He closes the distance between us and fireworks erupt behind my eyes. Having his body pressed against mine lights up every nerve ending in my body.

The kiss is clumsy as if it's the first time he's kissed a girl before. But I know that can't be true. I've seen him hanging around other girls at school. I'm not the only person who's been crushing on Koa Mahina.

I wrap a hand around the side of his neck and slow the movement of my lips as they brush against his. I'm not ready for the kiss to end. If anything, I want to encourage him to do more. He dips his tongue into my mouth and swirls it around mine.

He shifts his weight and pushes me flat against the mattress. We both moan when he settles between my legs. The skirt of my dress shifts up and all that separates him from my body is a tiny thong.

His lips float down my neck and across my chest. "You are trouble," he says in between kisses. "Have been since the day I met you."

I grab his face and pull him back to my lips. I don't want to stop kissing the boy who makes me smile and laugh. The boy who's been one of my closest friends. Keeping our relationship platonic wasn't what I wanted but it was fine because he was still with me.

And now he's here holding me in his arms and kissing me like he needs them for survival.

I will never forget the way his lips feel against mine or the way his hand caresses up the side of my thigh and between my legs.

I will never forget the tender way he's looking at me or how shyly he asks if I'm sure I want him to be my first.

I will never forget the way he took care of me after and how he held me until I fell asleep. I will never forget the way it feels to make love to Koa Mahina.

I will never forget waking up knowing he was my forever.

But had I known the feeling wouldn't have lasted until lunch, I would have held him tighter and never let him leave my room before the sun came up.

Because now all I have is the memory of me standing in the hallway completely helpless while he broke my heart with one word.

1

SYDNEY

I am not in love with Koa Mahina anymore.

He has no effect on my life.

I am moving on.

I repeat my daily mantra as I rip the tags off my brand new pair of purple leggings a little more aggressively than I should. I bought them at the beginning of the year when Charlie had the terrible idea to start taking advantage of the exercise classes available on campus.

After another failed relationship, I thought what the hell. I will need something to do to fill my time and keep me from thinking about a certain someone. Why not work on myself in the process? *New year. New me. Blah blah blah.*

Sitting on the edge of my bed, I begin to stuff myself into the lycra fabric. As sweat begins to form around my hairline, I wonder if this counts as a warmup.

"What is taking you so long in there? We're going to be late," Charlie calls out to me through my bedroom door.

"I'm coming. Give me a minute," I yell back at her in between grunts as I yank harder on the leggings I'm struggling to put on.

I don't know how I let Charlie talk me into doing things like this. When I said yes to working out more at the beginning of the year, I meant yoga or maybe jazzercise.

Not joining a running club.

Who loves running enough to join a club for it?

A book club I can get behind. A club where you are required to bring a snack and beverage of choice sounds like a much better idea than one that is guaranteed to make me sweat and my muscles cramp.

I look longingly at the stack of books piled on my nightstand and on the floor by my bed. I think I would prefer to exercise my brain and stay home to read instead.

Bending my knees and swiveling my hips, I let out a deep breath when I finally get the pants on and positioned in the right place. I push my hair out of my face, and take a look at myself in my full length mirror. Not too bad. Working up a sweat to squeeze myself into these pants was worth it because my ass looks incredible. "You weren't kidding about these leggings," I shout.

The troublemaker in me wants to snap a photo and send it to Koa to irritate him. He always has something negative to say about where I work or what I'm wearing. It wasn't always like this.

I remember when my parents let me have my own phone. I would send him silly pictures and random updates on my day. That all stopped when I found out how he really felt about me. Now I text him to make sure he has information to report back to my brother and because I like to poke the bear.

If I was being honest with myself, I'm hoping that one day the bear might poke back. But not today. Because today I am not in love with him, I repeat over and over as I leave my bedroom.

"I told you. Now, let's go." She claps her hands. "We don't want to miss them warming up." Her smile stretches from ear to ear.

"What are you talking about? Who is them?" I ask, grabbing my water bottle and keys off the kitchen counter.

"You'll see," she says with a conspiratorial grin.

"You're up to something. I know it." I eye her over my shoulder as I lock the door to my dorm.

"This is all for my class project. I'm not up to anything," she says nonchalantly, leading the way out of our residence hall. This is a red flag. Nothing about Charlie is nonchalant. "If I am putting together a charity fun run, we need to actually be able to hold our own and run during the thing. Right?"

We use the paths behind our building to cut across campus toward the tracks and open soccer fields that are available to all students, not just student athletes. It would be faster to drive versus trudging along the paths on foot but Charlie claims it would look bad pulling up to running club in a car.

"I guess," I answer before taking a gulp of my water.

"If anyone knows how to make running fun, it's the members of this club." She hops like a bunny a few times while squealing. I've never seen Charlie this enthusiastic about exercising.

We've been going to Pilates classes when we can fit them into our schedule. They usually end with us in the last row lying flat on our backs counting down the minutes until we can reward ourselves with a sweet treat from the bakery.

Seemingly out of nowhere she's been going to boxing and jump rope classes and now she's springing a running club on me. It's odd behavior even for her. There has to be an ulterior motive somewhere because I'm not convinced she's jump roping for her cardiovascular health.

As I fight to get fresh air into my lungs walking up the hill, the muscles in my thighs burning with each step, I start to wonder if this is how I die. My brother Nash must have inherited all the athletic genes in the family because I am not cut out for this kind of life.

"Almost there. Come on babe. If you think your heart rate is pumping now, you are in for a surprise."

"You're really starting to scare me now. I know you do not like exercising this much." Yep, she definitely has something up her sleeve.

"It's not the running that I'm looking forward to. Don't worry. There's nothing to be afraid of. I promise you will be in good hands."

I follow Charlie as she giggles down the path until it connects to the sidewalk that leads to the student gym. We head left, passing the gym, and continue toward the track and field.

Charlie stops and applies two layers of pink lip gloss. "Here." She passes me the tube that is definitely not my color.

"I don't need this. We're going to workout. My hair is going to get stuck to my lips. It will be a mess," I explain. I mentally add *'develop a formula for a lip gloss with shine but isn't sticky'* to my product creation to do list.

She huffs in annoyance. "Fine. Just remember I offered."

As we get closer to our destination, I hold out my hand and silently ask for the lip gloss. Had I known running club equates to over thirty guys milling around either shirtless or in tank tops showing off well defined biceps and abdominal muscles I would have signed up months ago.

"Now you know why I told you to wear the good leggings," she says, tightening her high ponytail and smoothing down any stray hairs.

"I will never question you again." I'm glad I took the time to throw my hair into Dutch braids this morning. I can already tell the humidity is trying to mess with my curls. "What's our plan?" I ask as we get closer.

I've become Charlie's wingwoman as of late. I don't know if I'm helping her get a man or if this is her way of helping me.

I'm not convinced anything will help me but I keep trying my best. *Because I am not in love with Koa Mahina anymore.* Repeat. Repeat. Repeat.

"I'll talk to Trevor." She nods towards a tall, slender, but muscular guy with dark, wavy hair. "He's the genius who started this whole thing. *Bless him*." She presses her palms together and bows her head. "We'll introduce ourselves and see if there is anyone who wants to teach us a few things."

"About running? Isn't that obvious? You're walking but much faster."

"But there is technique and proper breathing," she says with a dramatic eye roll. "Just follow my lead."

Charlie sashays toward Trevor where he's standing with a few of his running buddies and I reluctantly follow. I do clock a few guys hanging on the fringe I wouldn't mind teaching me a proper stretch or two.

This is what I continue to tell myself at least. It's part of my process to retrain my brain and heart. What is it people say about the power of words? If you repeat them over and over, eventually they will become your truth.

That's what I'm hoping at least. I have been for years. If I keep saying I want someone different, eventually it will become a reality.

Maybe I should switch to reading more nonfiction books about women empowerment instead of filling my head with romantic fantasies. *Yeah, no. That won't be happening,* I think, laughing at myself.

"Hi there." Charlie beams at Trevor, flashing a flirty smile. "I'm Charlie and this is my friend Sydney." She grabs my hand and pulls me closer to the semicircle of men that surround us. I bump into her shoulder, which causes me to stumble over my feet.

My roommate, Lauren, would get a kick out of this. I understand how awkward she must have felt when I introduced her to all my friends when we went to The Warehouse at the beginning of the school year. I wanted her to come out of her shell a little but putting her on the spot might have been a bad call. This is awful.

Four sets of eyes roam over our bodies checking us out. One of the guys offers a shy smile. I grin back with a shrug and slight roll of my eyes over Charlie's enthusiastic introductions, making him snort a quiet laugh.

"Charlie, you're just in time. We're doing some stretching to warm up before we start our five mile run," Trevor informs us.

Five miles? That's a joke, right? He doesn't expect us to actually run around this track twenty times, does he?

"Don't worry," the guy with the shy smile from earlier says. "You can bail at any time. A lot of people don't get to all five miles before tapping out. I'm Joe," he says, stretching out a hand in my direction.

"Sydney," I reply, placing my sweaty palm in his. His grip is gentle and soft. Not at all what I expected.

"Come on. You need to get your muscles warmed up or you're going to get cramps." He gestures toward an open space on the grass where we'll have more room to spread out.

I glance over at Charlie. She gives me a wink before bending over at the waist to touch her toes with an attentive Trevor behind her. *I guess she'll be fine on her own.*

I ease myself onto the grass opposite Joe and begin to mimic his movements. Sitting with my right foot touching my inner thigh, I stretch my arms out to reach my left foot. I should have participated more in the Pilates classes we took. This would be a lot easier if I had.

"Flexibility isn't my forte," I explain, as I struggle with the simple act of touching my toes.

His eyes glide down the length of my leg making me feel exposed in my thin leggings. "What is your forte?"

"I excel at couch rotting," I joke.

"Couch rotting? I'm intrigued. What is that exactly?" he asks, pushing a lock of his brown hair off his forehead, revealing a pair of green eyes.

"It involves me, a cozy blanket, some snacks, and a good book while laying on the couch all day." Something I wish I was doing right now instead of straining muscles I didn't know I had. My mind drifts back to the brand new stack of books piled on my nightstand and I sigh.

He changes positions and begins to stretch his other leg. I do the same even though I'm not convinced my left leg is fully prepared for what's about to happen.

"And what qualifies as a good book?" The small lift of his lip lends me to believe he already knows the type of books I enjoy reading. I would blush but I'm not ashamed of the genres I read.

"Lately fantasy and science fiction have been my first choice but I'm not selective. I will try anything once."

"Fantasy," he muses over the word. "Are we talking wizards and schools of witchcraft or wolves, vampires, and fae?" he asks, leaning back on the palm of his hands.

I arch an eyebrow. "I like all things mythical and magical. How do you know so much about this genre?"

"I may have read a few books about fae princes and lords. The world building is incredible."

"Right. The world building," I joke.

He lets out a deep chuckle before standing. He offers me his hands, helping me get to my feet. "You don't agree?"

I swipe at the grass on my pants. "Oh, no, I agree with you. The world building is supreme. I'm a little surprised you're into it."

We walk toward the track that borders the field. All of the club members have started to gather for the start of the run. I make eye contact with Charlie in the crowd. She grimaces and gives me a thumbs up.

"It isn't my first choice but it's a nice break from medical journals and textbooks," he replies.

"Do we have a future doctor in our midst?"

"Athletic trainer. *Hopefully*. What about you?" he asks, guiding me to the back of the crowd.

"Chemist," I say. His eyes widen momentarily before he does a quick sweep of my body again.

"Beauty and brains," he mumbles more to himself.

Trevor blows a whistle garnering everyone's attention and prevents me from responding to Joe's comment, which is probably best. Knowing me I would have said something like *'thanks, you too.'*

After a quick announcement about how many laps we need to make around the track—about ten too many—and running safely in large groups, he blows his whistle again signaling everyone can take off running.

"Walk and talk with me?" Joe asks. While others speed past us we begin to stroll around the track side by side. "Tell me more about being a chemist."

"It's not as noble as it sounds. I want to be a cosmetic chemist and eventually start my own line of beauty products."

"Ambitious too," he says as if he's keeping a running list of my qualities to refer back to later. The thought makes me blush, and I can't recall the last time a man made that happen.

Oh, wait, it was at the club with Lauren when her neighbor Emilio whispered something about tying me to his bed. I honestly can't remember exactly what he said but it was filthy. And very hot.

"More along the lines of being tired of not finding what I need for my skin tone and type in stores." It was depressing going to the store and only seeing one or two shades of foundation for darker complexions. I started mixing my own foundation and other beauty concoctions when I was a teenager. I drove my mom crazy with all of my jars of homemade lotions and oils all over the bathroom.

"I'm not one who follows beauty and fashion trends," he says with a sheepish smile, brushing the hair out of his face again.

"What? Really? I never would have guessed with your choice of running attire," I joke. He's wearing a white Newhouse Athletics Department tank top and matching black shorts.

"Hey, I'll have you know all the cool kids wear Newhouse Athletics gear." He runs a hand down his chest.

"Those kids aren't as cool as you think," I grumble thinking of my brother and his roommates.

Good looking? Yes.

Popular? Also yes.

Cool? Up for debate.

"Oh yeah? Do you have first hand experience with the athletes at this school? Ex-boyfriend maybe?" he asks. Then with slight hesitation he adds, "Current boyfriend?"

"Do you think I would date someone who wasn't cool?" I joke.

"No, I don't. Lucky guy whoever he is."

A few runners pass, having already lapped us on the track. I glance around, quickly spotting Charlie jogging on the opposite side of the field. Her smile is forced and she is favoring her right leg. The lengths she will go for a date knows no boundaries.

"My brother, Nash Pierce, he's the one who isn't as cool as he appears. Not my boyfriend. I mean I don't have a boyfriend." The words fly out of my mouth as I correct my statement.

"You're Nash's sister?" he asks, with wide eyes and slack jaw. "He talks about his sister all the time but has never given many details. Now I know why."

"He talks about me? What does he say?" Having second thoughts, I raise my hand to stop him from speaking. "Actually, I don't want to know what he says about me."

We haven't always gotten along growing up. Being fifteen months apart kept us close but also at each other's throats periodically.

"Like I said he never gave many details. He would mention you being out at The Armory, a party, or wherever and warn the guys to keep their hands to themselves if they see you there."

"Ahh, yes. The threat of losing a limb if you touch me. I'm sorry about that. He's overprotective for some reason. They're empty threats. I promise. I've been touched many times and as far as I know those guys still have their hands attached."

The corner of his mouth lifts slightly. What did I say that was so amusing? *Oh...oh no.*

"Not that many guys," I reassure him. "A small amount really. Not even a full hand." I lift my hand to show how small the number is before grasping it behind my back to keep myself from doing it again.

"Regardless of the number because it doesn't matter if it was a lot, I'm a single woman free to do what I want with whoever I want. But for reassurance purposes, all of their appendages are still fully intact as far as I know." I let out a breath and risk a glance in his direction.

He is grinning from ear to ear staring at me with amusement. I've got to get out of here before I dig myself a bigger hole of embarrassment.

"Oh look. There's Charlie. It was nice to meet you. I'm just going to..." My voice trails off as I point a finger at a group of runners in front of us. I don't know if Charlie is with them. I don't really care.

I walk swift enough my thighs could start a fire with the amount of friction they're producing. I cannot believe I said all of that to him. Maybe this is the real reason why I'm single.

It has nothing to do with *him*. It's me and my ability to make things weird in less than ten minutes of meeting someone.

"Sydney! Wait up," Joe shouts from behind me. I stare at the trees pretending I don't hear him.

Maybe I should start running. I could probably make it to the gym without having to stop and rest my legs. I could hide in the bathroom for a few hours. A humorless laugh escapes me. "With my luck I would trip or gas out halfway there," I mumble.

All thoughts of escaping vanish when a soft hand grips my elbow. "You're quick when you want to be," Joe teases with an appeasing smile.

"I wanted to get the full running club experience while saving what's left of my dignity." With his hand still holding onto my elbow, Joe continues our walk around the track.

"Your dignity is still intact," he says, dropping his hand. I'm not convinced. The urge to Usain Bolt my ass out of here is still very strong.

"What I was going to say before you ran off is that Nash didn't give me any warnings about you. Even if he did, it wouldn't stop me from talking to you," he says. His eyes deliver the *'or touching'* part of the conversation.

My heart however gets stuck on the *'it wouldn't stop me.'* I've been waiting a long time to hear someone say that exact phrase to me. Too bad it's coming from the wrong guy. Or maybe Joe is the right one and my heart needs to get with the program. *We are over him, remember?*

I school my face in an attempt to hide all the damage Koa left behind. He was a tsunami on my heart. I don't think he fully grasps the destruction he left in his wake. It's been four years and I'm still sifting through the wreckage.

"Oh yeah? Even after all of my rambling?" I ask in a half hearted attempt to be flirty.

"Your rambling is adorable. I liked it. It was enlightening," he says. I snort a laugh. I would usually be embarrassed but I'm already past caring at this point. We are running full speed ahead.

"I'm glad I could educate you on the inner workings of my brain."

As we make our way around the track we chat more about classes, books, music, and my love for British television. He is easy to talk to. It doesn't feel like we've just met. I don't know if it's him trying to be likable or if we actually have a lot in common.

"Should we call it?" he asks, watching all the other runners finishing their five miles and gathering for some sort of post run debrief.

"Probably." I massage my thighs that are currently throbbing with every step. It seems a little cruel that my muscles are aching from a forty five minute stroll.

A group of runners a few feet away shout at Joe to let him know they're ready to leave. He holds up a finger signaling them to give him a minute.

"What are the chances you're free for dinner later?" he asks. "I want to know more about the fae underworld you were telling me about. You can't leave me hanging like that."

"I'm sorry to disappoint you but you'll have to wait until another day to satisfy your curiosity or read the book for yourself. I have to work tonight."

"Another time then?" The hope in his voice is endearing.

"Definitely. Do you have your phone?" I ask. He hands it over before I even finish my question, making me laugh. "Text me."

"I will. And I'm going to look into that book forum you told me about too. Maybe I'll see you online."

"Maybe." I rake my teeth over my bottom lip.

"It was nice to meet you, Sydney Pierce," he says, walking backwards toward his friends.

"Nice to meet you, too, Joe..."

"Clark," he says, answering my unasked question.

I wait until he is a speck in the distance before I hunt down Charlie. I find her laid out in the grassy field still catching her breath.

"Am I dead?" she asks between staggered breaths.

I lay down beside her. It feels good to be off my feet. "I'm not going to be able to get up," I tell her.

"I can't feel my legs. It's fine. Did you give him your number?"

"I did. How did it go with Trevor?" I lay my forearm over my eyes to block out the sun.

"Not good. Connor on the other hand has potential. Are you going to go out with Joe?"

I lift a shoulder even though she can't see me. "Maybe."

"You should. He's cute."

"He looks like the sixth member of a boyband," I joke.

"I see no problem with that. Give him a chance."

I've been giving other guys a chance for the last four years. I don't know what would make Joe any different than the others. Which is exactly why I should stay focused on myself.

"He has my number. We'll see what happens," I say, standing up. "I need to get ready for work." By get ready I mean, spend the next few hours doing nothing while I mentally prepare myself to be around people again.

"Help me," she says, holding up her arms. "Is he going to show up again ya think?" Charlie stumbles a little as she finds her legs.

"I would be less surprised if he wasn't there at this point."

FOUL TERRITORY

I always wonder if Koa showing up at the bar where I work is another errand Nash has sent him on or if he is choosing to do it on his own. And why does it make a difference to me?

He's been popping up at most of my shifts since the day I started working at Ray's. He never says hello. He barely acknowledges me. He sits in the back of the bar like a ghost haunting me. I'm not allowed to touch him. Sometimes I can't even see him. I can only feel him. And I feel him everywhere.

2

KOA

I pull into my parking spot in front of my townhouse and shut the engine off on my car. Releasing a long yawn, I rub my eyes attempting to wake up.

I keep telling myself this is the last time I'll go see her, that she doesn't need me watching over her every shift, and she can handle herself just fine.

I'm going to wear myself out giving 100 percent to my team, balancing classes, and keeping an eye on Sydney every other night into the early morning.

I don't know how to stop. I tried staying home once. I lasted all of thirty-six minutes before I was grabbing my keys and heading out the door to check on her. That's what I convince myself I'm doing and it has nothing to do with my need to be near her.

The television flashes through the curtains covering the living room window as I approach the front door. Which roommate will it be?

Wyatt and Wren bickering over who committed the crime on their documentary?

Nash and his buddy Eli or Gage playing video games?

Hart waiting for Lauren to come home from work?

The last scenario would be preferred. Hart and Wyatt both know where I go when we have a night off and she's working. Hart, however, won't give me shit about it. He said his piece months ago.

Wyatt on the other hand enjoys heckling me. My only advantage in this situation is he'll be with his best friend, Wren, and she doesn't let him get away with anything.

I open the door, drop my head, and inwardly groan when I see it's Wyatt and Wren on the couch. If I don't engage with them, maybe they won't notice me slip into the kitchen and then upstairs to my room.

"The son did it," Wyatt says, pointing at the television. He's sitting on the couch with Wren's legs draped over his lap. *Only friends? I call bullshit.* There is definitely something more going on there.

"He did not. What's his motive? He finds his father annoying? If that's the case, there would be a lot less people on this earth," Wren snarks as I walk into the kitchen.

"I don't like what you're insinuating. Who do you think it was? Colonel Mustard in the library with the candlestick?"

I quietly grab a bottle of water from the fridge and pull out fixings for a sandwich.

"You can't actually kill someone with a candlestick," Wren replies.

"How do you know? Have you tried?" Wyatt fires back at her.

"No. I haven't. A candlestick might be a blunt object but I doubt it's heavy enough to cause enough damage. Even with a significant amount of force, it would take several strikes. A number of things could go wrong in that amount of time."

"How would you kill someone then?"

I wish I could sit in the living room and watch the two of them while I eat. They are more entertaining than any reality show I've ever seen.

"Poison is a solid choice if done correctly. It would be easier to hide and less to clean up. I've watched enough of these shows to learn from their mistakes."

"It's scary how fast you answered that," Wyatt grumbles.

"There's nothing to worry about until I start insisting on making all of your meals," she says, as I tiptoe past them toward the stairs.

"And where do you think you're going so fast, young man? Do you have any idea what time it is? Your curfew was two hours ago," Wyatt says as soon as my foot hits the bottom step. *So close*.

"Upstairs to bed. Goodnight," I reply.

"Is all that lurking making you hungry?" He nods toward my plate of food.

"You have no right to question his habits. You followed me around campus for weeks," Wren tells him.

"We aren't talking about me right now, birdie."

"Your generosity to let someone else have the spotlight for once is inspiring," she deadpans.

"God, that mouth of yours," he says, then kisses her lips, forgetting I'm in the room. I will have to buy her some of her favorite sticky notes the next time I'm in the campus store to say thank you for saving me.

Once upstairs, I put my food on my nightstand then grab my laptop. After flipping it open, I easily navigate to my secret obsession.

The Fiction Forum.

Sydney describes it as a book lover's utopia. You can leave reviews, trade books, join local and online books clubs, live chat, and even chat privately.

I haven't made any posts yet. I hang in the background following her into chat rooms in anonymous mode. I read all her reviews and comments. If she says something on this app, I know about it.

Damn, she hasn't logged on yet. I check the time on my laptop. It's earlier than I thought. It typically takes her almost an hour before she settles in for the night.

Unless she went back out. I followed her home from Ray's—the bar she works at. It's a good twenty to thirty minutes from campus. I like knowing she's home safe. It gives me peace of mind. *Sue me.*

I haven't gotten to the point I'm tracking her. Admittedly, after what happened to Hart's girlfriend Lauren at the beginning of our season, it's tempting. When Lauren didn't show up at one of our games, Sydney was able to track her on her phone.

Without that...I don't want to think about what would have happened.

I set the laptop down and exchange it for my sandwich. I make quick work of my food while keeping an eye on her profile. Waiting impatiently for it to light up green to indicate she's active online.

When the dot on her profile finally flashes green, my shoulders slump. *She's home.* I put my computer down and slide off the bed. I have a few minutes to shower before she'll join a chat room.

Maybe tonight I will man up and leave anonymous mode. I'm always tempted but I've never pulled the trigger. I know once I do my addiction to her will rise to another level. It happens every time she talks to me. *She always leaves me craving more.*

I grab a clean pair of boxers and head down the hall to the bathroom I share with Hart. I'm glad he isn't home tonight but I'm jealous he gets to spend unlimited amounts of time at Sydney's place since she's his girlfriend's roommate.

I turn the knob on the shower, then brush my teeth and strip out of my clothes while the water heats up. It's been a long day. After baseball practice I spent too much time at the library working on a research paper, forcing me to rush across town to the bar.

I step into the shower and let the heat of the water seep into my overworked muscles as I grab the soap and start to lather up a washcloth. My mind drifts to thoughts of Sydney.

Fuck, she looked good tonight with her hair in a ponytail and a little red bandana tied around her head. She looked like a nineteen fifties pin-up girl with a little Southern flair in a concert tee, cutoff shorts, and cowboy boots.

I would have loved to drag her down the dark hallway or take her into the back office. My hand drifts down to my cock. Just the thought of her makes me hard. Getting myself off to the memory of her has been the only relief I've gotten from the self-imposed hell I've been living in the last few years.

Squeezing my erection tighter, I begin to stroke myself faster.

Sydney drops to her knees. Her brown eyes stare up at me. "I've been waiting for the day you'd let me get on my knees for you. I haven't stopped thinking about you," she says, as she takes my cock in her hand.

I rest a forearm against the cool tile—a harsh reminder this is all a dream. It doesn't stop me from closing my eyes and imagining her plush lips skating up and down my cock instead of my hand.

"That's it, baby. Show me what you can do with your sweet little mouth. Look at you. Taking all of me so well. You like sucking my cock. Don't you, baby?" She nods. Her eyes shine with a mix of lust and god I hope there's some love there too.

I push her hair out of her face and cradle the back of her head. She hollows her cheeks and sucks me harder. She doesn't stop until I'm...

"Sydney," I groan her name as ropes of cum hit the shower wall. "Fuck." I stand under the shower head to wash off the guilt. No, not guilt. I don't feel guilty for thinking about Sydney while I touch my dick.

Maybe a little guilty this shower has had more cum go down the drain than water since we moved in.

What I feel is resigned. My fate was slated a decade ago when I first saw Sydney roller skating down the street past my house.

My family had just moved into the neighborhood. After my dad left the military we moved to be with my mom's family in Hawaii. I loved it there. Spending time with my grandparents and learning about our Polynesian culture, surfing, and playing baseball. It was a dream.

But my dad's parents needed our help and we packed up everything and moved to Alabama. I was so angry about the move. I didn't want to leave my friends and join a new team not knowing if I would be able to start.

My attitude changed the instant I saw her. I was pulling boxes off the back of the moving truck and she skated down the middle of the road with two braids in her hair wearing a worn pair of overalls.

It was her smile that took my breath away. It was big and bright. That's all it took to make me a goner. I spent the whole summer that year chasing after her doing whatever she wished.

I shut the water off in the shower and drop my head. It's hard to think about that summer. It's the only one we had, just the two of us. I met Nash, Hart, and the other guys that fall playing baseball.

Sydney was still part of our little crew of friends, but I had to share her. I would never label myself as selfish but I was the king of greed when it came to her.

I towel dry the best I can and slip into my briefs. I'm dying to see what Sydney is up to.

The wood floor creaks beneath my feet when I step into the silent hallway. Wyatt and Wren must have given up on their show and gone to bed for the night.

I prop myself against my headboard and place a pillow on my lap, making myself comfortable. I need to put the finishing touches on the paper I started earlier today and turn it in before I go to bed, but I won't be able to focus on anything until I get a little taste of her.

The small green dot flashes in the bottom corner of her profile picture. "Where are you, baby?" I click around to a few of her favorite chat rooms. Interesting. She isn't in the conspiracy theory chat. That is the one she likes the best and spends most of her time in.

Sydney loves dissecting books word by word looking for clues that will tell her what is going to happen in the next book, and it's rare she gets it wrong.

The corner of my mouth lifts. "There you are," I mumble to myself. I should have known she would be in the fantasy romance chat. She's been binge reading a new series for the past few weeks.

It's all she can talk about when she's in the forums. I think she even called it her Roman empire once or twice. *Whatever that means.*

I login to the chat anonymously and try my best to follow along with the conversation. I've been reading the books along with her when I can but I've fallen behind this week thanks to my busy schedule.

I can't fight the grin on my face as Sydney goes into great detail explaining her favorite characters and scenes of the book she is currently reading. Her passion and enthusiasm for this imaginary world bleeds through the computer screen.

When she compares one of the characters in her current read to a character in a book we read together that first summer, it's a sucker punch I didn't see coming. Images of her laying down on a blanket under the canopy of willow trees in my backyard flood my mind.

We spent hours in an imaginary world of our own creation. It was a place where only the two of us existed. Hours would pass while she read her books and I hit baseballs into a net.

I move the mouse to hover over the button that will change my name from anonymous to my actual screen name. Am I really going to do this? I've been anonymous for over three years communicating with her under the radar.

Yes I am. It's been long enough.

My pulse quickens as I type in the chat box. I keep it simple with a joke about that dude's hair. It always made me laugh the way it was described in the book as velvety and supple.

A few people agree. Others welcome me to the discussion. I don't care about them. *What does she think?*

My foot bounces in anticipation of her reaction. Her screen name pops up and I grin.

FaeAtHeart

> What are you talking about? You mean that description doesn't make you want to run your fingers through his hair?

I picture her smiling on the other side of the screen. I miss being the one to make her smile. I used to be able to do it with ease. I was the one she would come to when she needed a serotonin boost.

Then I fucked it up. I made a decision that altered the trajectory of our relationship and it's never been the same since. *She hasn't been the same*. I'll never forgive myself for that. If only I could go back.

Ignoring the others in the room, we begin to chat. Easily slipping back in sync like when we were younger. Volleying jokes and commentary back and forth. A piece of myself I thought I lost feels restored from this one conversation.

Ten years ago I fell in love with Sydney Pierce and my world was permanently altered. I didn't see things the same way anymore. The only thing I could see was her.

Then I let her go.

I let her slip through my fingers.

That is an error I will *never* make again.

FICTION FORUM

NotYourAverageJoe19

> How long are we going to have to wait for the next book in the series you think?

FaeAtHeart

> The last one took almost a year and a half.

NotYourAverageJoe19

> You're lying. Seriously? I knew I should have waited to start reading it.

> I'm going to have to reread the first two books to remember what happened.

FaeAtHeart

> I'll probably reread too. I normally do with all of my favorite series.

NotYourAverageJoe19

> Why?

FaeAtHeart

GINGER WALLS

> Because I love the characters. It's fun to watch them fall in love again knowing how it ends.

> I like finding the hidden clues to their relationship. Things they may not even see yet because they are blinded by pride, ego, or maybe circumstance.

NotYourAverageJoe19

> Do you think that ever happens in real life?

FaeAtHeart

> What? Missing important details?

NotYourAverageJoe19

> Yeah. Like looking over crucial signs that could potentially change your life.

FaeAtHeart

> I'm sure it happens all the time.

NotYourAverageJoe19

> Kind of frustrating to think about.

FaeAtHeart

> I would suggest not thinking about it.

> Sounds depressing to dwell on missed opportunities.

NotYourAverageJoe19

FOUL TERRITORY

> Especially if you're the one trying to leave the hints.

FaeAtHeart
> Maybe you aren't leaving the right ones. I obviously don't know what you're trying to accomplish but maybe you need to try a new tactic.

NotYourAverageJoe19
> I'm beginning to realize that. I have started a few new things.

FaeAtHeart
> I hope they work.

> If they don't, will you stop or keep trying?

NotYourAverageJoe19
> I'll never give up.

FaeAtHeart
> It must be something important. Why don't you take the direct approach?

NotYourAverageJoe19
> They are the most important person in my life.

> I don't think they're ready for direct.

FaeAtHeart
> Then for your sake, I hope they're good at reading between the lines.

3

SYDNEY

This is the last time I'm checking his online status and then I'm shutting my computer down for the day. I have been doing homework, but also flipping over to the forum and refreshing his profile every five minutes.

It's fine that he hasn't messaged me today. Not everyone has the same addiction to the forums like I do. I know this. I've accepted it.

Most people have lives. I shouldn't expect him to be online every time I am, despite how much I want him to be.

I found the forum the summer I graduated high school. After everything happened with Koa, I couldn't talk to him anymore. He was my only friend who didn't make fun of me for all the books I read which meant he got all of my daily reading updates. He never complained once. Sometimes I think he even enjoyed all of my rambling.

"And we're done thinking about the past," I mumble to myself. It needs to stay in the casket I buried it in. I don't need to be dredging up old feelings. "I am moving on." I nod in half-hearted agreement.

Sighing, I close my laptop and plug the charger back in. "I'm not going to look for him again until tomorrow." Grabbing a few clothes I have draped over my desk chair, I walk over to my closet to put them away. It's a failed distraction attempt. "*Maybe* not tomorrow. Tonight. I'll check later tonight."

Now I just have to keep myself occupied until then. It's not like I don't have plenty of things to do. I can go to the lab and work on some assignments. I can read the book I just downloaded. Or maybe I'll spend the day with Lauren. It's been awhile since I've visited with everyone in her neighborhood for Sunday dinner.

Or...I could stay here and get caught up on my reviews. And if he happened to show up, it would be a lucky coincidence.

My addiction to the *Fiction Forum* is even more out of control than before. It's not my love of books that has me searching the chat rooms for good conversation.

It's him. NotYourAverageJoe19.

Ever since he made me laugh with his comment about Viren's hair, I have intentionally sought him out online. I've gotten lucky a few times over the last week. I either found him in a room already chatting with other people or he would show up at some point before I logged off for the night.

I'm used to striking up conversations with strangers on *Fiction Forum*. It's easy to feel a connection to a fellow book lover. I can't tell you how many times I've typed the word '*same*' after someone posted an opinion about a character, book, or author they love.

I rub at my sore jaw thinking about how much he's been making me smile. There is something about this man that feels different. I have absolutely no idea how or why. His name appears on the screen and my heart starts pumping a little bit faster.

I wish I knew more personal details about him. It's a little concerning that I have no idea who he really is and I already feel a deep connection to him.

One night he left the chat saying he had to do homework. Does that mean he's in college? God, I hope he's not in high school.

Or maybe he's a psychopath or a kidnapper looking for their next victim. I think I would prefer this to some kid in high school.

"You look like you're spiraling," Lauren says, her voice laced with concern.

"Huh?" I glance at her as I walk into the living room. She's frozen in the kitchen holding a slotted spoon in one hand. "I'm fine."

"You don't look fine," Charlie says from our couch.

"What are you doing over here?" I ask.

"I'm bored and lonely," she admits. "Wren went home for the weekend. Lauren said I could come over and help with Sunday dinner."

"How are you helping cook dinner in the living room?" I ask.

"She's helping by staying out my way," Lauren says.

"Exactly. Now tell us why you're spiraling." Charlie pats the empty couch cushion. I exhale a long sigh, before taking a seat.

"I met someone."

"Joe. I know. I was there. You've been texting, right?" Charlie asks.

"We have," I say tentatively. Joe and I have exchanged a few texts. His schedule is just as busy as mine. He's currently traveling with the baseball team as their athletic trainer. If he was here on campus, we might have hung out this weekend.

"He seems nice," Lauren chimes in as she works her magic in our small kitchen.

"He is nice but I'm not talking about him." I spare them both a quick glance. Charlie leans forward desperate for me to continue my confession. "I met someone online in the *Fiction Forum*."

"Oh," Charlie says, void of emotion.

"Oh? That's all you have to say."

"Syd, you meet people in those chat rooms every day. You talk about your different book friends you've met online all the time. You know, *your friend who's not really your friend but the friend you know online*," Lauren says, while waving the spoon around in the air.

"Right. But this is different. *He* is different."

"He? Ooooh. How? Tell me more." Charlie crosses her arms over her chest.

I shrug. "He just is. I can't explain it. He reads a lot of the same books I do and he's actually into them. He picks up on all the little details that a lot of people gloss over. But even more than that he pays attention to me."

"Do you know anything about him? Where he lives? How old he is? What he looks like?" Lauren fires off questions at me. "You could be getting catfished."

"Better to be catfished than capfished," Charlie says.

"Capfished?" I question. "What is that?"

"It's when you meet a hot guy while he's wearing a hat. Particularly a baseball cap. Forwards, backwards, doesn't matter. Then he picks you up for your date without one...and well, he's not as hot. Capfished." She shudders.

"But his face is the same," Lauren says, slightly confused.

Charlie twists her body to face Lauren in the kitchen. "Picture Hart's face," she says. Lauren's mouth curls. "Now imagine him wearing a hat."

Lauren sways in place and flicks her tongue over lower lip.

"I rest my case," Charlie says, turning to me and sitting back down in her original spot on the couch. "I won't be deceived again by another man in a baseball cap. My grandmother always said fool me once, shame on you. Fool me twice, shame on me. Fool me a third time, he had a big dick," she says, with a shrug.

I bark a laugh. "She did not say that."

"She still says it. That woman is an icon." Charlie shakes her head. "Tell us more about this guy. When did you start talking?"

I readjust myself in my seat. "Last Saturday night after I got home from work."

"What's his name?" Lauren asks.

"I don't know." I nibble on my lower lip. "His username is *NotYourAverageJoe19*. Other than his interest in the same books as me, I don't know anything else about him. I realize it's silly to like him. He could live somewhere across the country."

"Or he could live right here in Montgomery." Charlie's eyes go wild with excitement. "Did you tell Joe about this forum?"

"I did," I draw out the word. "You think it might be him?"

"It's a possibility. What are the chances you meet a guy named Joe in person and online on the same day?" Charlie asks.

"Joe is a popular name. Wouldn't he have said something in one of his texts? Or in the chat?" Lauren questions.

"Maybe. Unless he's assuming she already knows it's him and doesn't feel it's necessary to bring it up," Charlie counters.

"You should ask him," Lauren says.

"Ask which him what?" I'm getting confused.

"Ask the Joe you know here on campus if he's the same Joe online," Lauren explains.

"And if he's not?" Charlie asks. "That could ruin everything."

"Or solve the mystery completely," Lauren replies.

"You need to go out on a date with Joe. Then you can casually bring up a topic you and online Joe talked about in a conversation. If he acts like this is new information, then you know he isn't the same guy," Charlie says.

"That could work," I agree.

Except for the whole date part. I haven't been on a date in years. Not a real one anyway. I dated Seth last semester but we didn't go out. We studied, did lab work, met up at the gym, and grabbed a pizza with classmates on occasion. Nothing serious. Nothing that would allow us to get too close.

The concept of getting dressed up and making small talk with someone new makes me feel like a phony. I know exactly what will happen. We will start off having a good time. We will talk and maybe flirt a little. But that's where the night ends. No matter how many guys I date, or attempt to date, they will never be him. *They will never be Koa.* It's like I'm cursed.

"We've talked about getting coffee but he hasn't asked me out to anything official," I say.

Charlie slaps her head. "That was him asking you out. You need to text him back and get something setup."

Lauren catches my eye in the kitchen offering me a sympathetic smile. She may not know how deep my feelings for Koa go, but she knows me.

She's seen me come home after every date I've been on over the past four years. When she would ask how it went, I would hit her with the *'he's nice, but there's no spark.'* It doesn't take a genius to figure out a standard has been set.

If you can't surpass the bar set by the man that ripped my heart to pieces, how can I trust you will be enough to put me back together?

The thought of Joe being my mystery guy online excites me. While I didn't feel an intense attraction to him in person, the way he makes me laugh and smile when we chat online makes up for it. There is potential there.

"Alright, I'll text him and set up a date." I need to know for certain if they're the same person.

If they are, this might be my chance to finally get over Koa Mahina once and for all.

"Scoot over, bro. I need to sit there to balance my plate." Nash kicks Koa's shin, forcing him to move to the middle of the couch.

I almost didn't come over today but I was bored at home. Lauren was occupied with Hart since he just got home from the road. Joe was busy with school assignments and there were crickets on the *Fiction Forum* from my mystery man.

Nash texted and asked if I wanted to hang out for some brother-sister time. I didn't expect Koa would be here, too, but I should have known. Those two will always be together if given the opportunity.

My plans for world domination and getting over him will have to wait another day.

Koa shuffles over and tries his best to stay within his designated cushion space. It isn't a small couch, but he's a big guy. I'm sitting with my legs tucked under me in my usual spot. I like propping my book up on the arm of the couch.

The familiarity of the current seating arrangement isn't lost on me. Nash on one side of the couch, me on the other, and Koa in the middle. We spent many nights and weekends just like this growing up.

"Sorry," I say when I accidentally kick his thigh. I can't seem to get comfortable now that he's sitting so close. Amazing what two feet of personal space can do for a girl. It was bearable being in the same room with him when he was on the opposite side of it.

"You're fine." His arms stay crossed over his chest and his eyes glued to the baseball game on the television. He's just as thrilled as I am to be sitting so close together.

I wonder what that is like. To feel absolutely nothing for a person you've shared some of your most vulnerable moments with. I must have embellished everything in my head. It's easy to do when you read as many books as I do. Everything feels like a romantic gesture.

After the night we shared, I realized I was a fool for ever reading into any kind gesture he made toward me. A door being held open was simply that. Same with him serving me food or getting me something to drink. It meant nothing. *We* meant nothing.

"Did you ever get a call back from your agent?" my brother asks. I attempt to keep my mind focused on the pages of my book even though I am more interested in hearing what Koa has to say about his agent.

I turn the page even though I didn't read it. I will have to come back to this part later. It's not like I'm comprehending much of it anyway with Koa invading all of my senses. How is anyone supposed to think clearly when he smells so good?

"I talked to him while we were on the road. I have a few options available." Koa drops his arm onto my calves, putting a significant amount of weight on them to keep me still. I didn't realize my legs were bouncing.

"Who's looking at you?" Nash asks, with his mouth full of his sandwich.

"Uh, I think he said Colorado, Texas, and maybe Chicago."

Nash lets out a low whistle. "Damn those are some good teams. Do you have a favorite?"

"I don't know. Nothing feels right. None of those cities feel like home to me," Koa says, looking down at his hand on my leg.

"The contracts are good though?" he asks, meaning the money.

"Yeah. I wouldn't be starving."

"What about you, Sis? Do you have your post graduation plans squared away yet?"

He knows I've applied for a few paid internships. One of which I'm really hoping I get. The company is doing exactly what I want to do—a Black woman owned beauty company specializing in developing products for people of color.

If I can learn the ropes under these women, I know it would have a big impact on my own company when I'm financially able of starting everything. That is the end goal.

"Not yet. I'm still waiting to hear from everyone. For now you're stuck with me this summer." I grin at him.

"I won't complain about that, although I hope you hear from them soon. I'm going to be busy with football anyways," Nash says, standing from the couch. "I have a feeling preseason is going to be a bitch."

"You'll be ready. You haven't let up since the season ended," Koa tells him.

"I don't want to be the weak link on the team this time. My career is on the line too. I've got to do whatever it takes to get teams looking at me."

"They will. I bet they already are. We got close to the championship game this year," I say.

"No thanks to me," he grumbles

"You're being too hard on yourself," Koa says. Nash glances back and forth between the two of us before nodding and going into the kitchen.

I divert my attention back to my book, trying hard to ignore the way Koa is slowly invading more of my personal space. It isn't easy to do.

"I'm going to go study," Nash says, walking back into the living room. "I'll order some pizza for dinner in a few hours. You'll stay, Syd?"

"Yeah, I can stay," I answer hesitantly. Does Koa want me to stay, too, or am I being the third wheel like usual?

"Cool. See you later." He grabs a textbook he left on the coffee table and then heads downstairs to his room in the basement. Typical Nash. Always asking me to come hang out and then bailing on me. He's been doing this more and more lately.

This isn't awkward at all. Maybe I should go home. I can pick up dinner from the cafeteria and do my laundry. My room is a disaster and I should really clean up the bathroom before Lauren gets home. I left a few experiments out on the counter.

"What are you reading now?" Koa asks gruffly. The question is a direct hit on my heart. His tone is different but it's the exact same question he would ask me almost daily in high school. For a time, I thought he enjoyed reading as much as I did but then sports took over his life.

I close the book and hold it up so he can read the title. He grunts, acknowledging he's seen enough. And with that, I've had enough. I start to push off the couch.

"Stay," he commands, tightening his grip on my leg. My eyes flutter and I let out a slow breath. For a moment my heart jumps in my throat at the thought that maybe he wants me to stay for him but I know better than that.

Wishing and hoping is a dangerous game. One I don't like playing. Yet, here I am rolling the dice and allowing myself to get comfortable with him again.

FICTION FORUM

NotYourAverageJoe19

Do anything fun today?

FaeAtHeart

Not really. Hung out with my brother and his roommate.

NotYourAverageJoe19

You don't like his roommate?

FaeAtHeart

It's complicated.

NotYourAverageJoe19

I've got time.

FaeAtHeart

You probably won't want to hear about this. We should stick to books and music for now.

NotYourAverageJoe19

GINGER WALLS

> Try me. Maybe it will help you by talking to someone about it.

FaeAtHeart
> There is a lot of history between the three of us. Not all of it is good.

NotYourAverageJoe19
> But there were good things?

FaeAtHeart
> Yes. That is half the problem.

NotYourAverageJoe19
> What's the other half of the problem?

FaeAtHeart
> I'm the only one who seems to remember them.

NotYourAverageJoe19
> How do you know they don't?

FaeAtHeart
> It's pretty obvious.

NotYourAverageJoe19
> Maybe you are missing those clues we were talking about the other day.

FaeAtHeart
> I can't read into those things. Not with this person.

FOUL TERRITORY

NotYourAverageJoe19
> Why not?

FaeAtHeart
> If I did, then I would start to think he might actually be in love with me.

NotYourAverageJoe19
> And that is a bad thing?

FaeAtHeart
> I fell for that trap once before. I would be an idiot to do it again.

> I don't want to talk about them anymore. I want to talk about you. How was your day? I hope it was better than mine.

NotYourAverageJoe19
> How do all of my best days wind up being your worst?

FaeAtHeart
> I don't know.

NotYourAverageJoe19
> I wish there was something I could do to change that.

FaeAtHeart
> You're making it better now. That has to count for something.

GINGER WALLS

NotYourAverageJoe19

> I'll take what I can for now.

4

KOA

Nash snickers beside me as I throw a medicine ball against the wall.

"Why are you here again?" I ask, as I wipe the sweat off my face with the bottom of my shirt.

He's sitting on a workout bench scrolling through his phone. "To workout. I still need to train during the off season."

"But you aren't working out. You're annoying me laughing at videos on your phone."

Nash rises from the bench and walks over to the rack of weights, keeping one eye on me. He grabs a thirty pound weight and brings it back over to the bench.

"Happy now?" he asks, doing a few bicep curls with a smirk.

"Asshole," I murmur, making him chuckle. "Are you going to tell me why you're really here this early?" He's normally getting to the gym when I'm leaving. I know he isn't here just to get on my nerves.

"I have an agility training session with Clark. I thought I would come early and hang out with you since you're so busy these days."

"I'm busy? You're the one bailing on me to go do homework." Not that I'm complaining he left me alone with Sydney for the rest of the afternoon.

The moment I dropped my arm on her leg I didn't move an inch. It's a risk every time I touch her but I sneak them in when I can. A hand to her back when we're walking, a quick hug when we say goodbye, or bumping my leg against hers when we're eating.

It hurts to do it—to touch her—because I know she's not mine to do it freely. Not yet, not the way I want. The pain is similar to that of getting a tattoo. Temporary pain for a permanent brand on my skin. She leaves one behind every time.

"You're also the one doubling up your workouts and going out several times a week. Where are you spending all your free time? Ever since you became the starting quarterback you forgot about us little people," I joke with him.

He hasn't let anything about being a starter go to his head. If anything, the pressure has done a number on his mental health. The team ended the season with a winning record but Nash refuses to take any of the credit with his below average stats.

"If I remember correctly, you were the one blowing me off the last time I asked you to hang out with me," he accuses.

I turn my back to him and begin throwing the medicine ball against the wall again. "I had school stuff I needed to take care of." By school stuff I mean go to Ray's while Sydney was working.

I did make notes for one of my assignments while I was there. Technically I'm not lying to him. It's something I always battle internally over. We were young when Nash first said he didn't want any of his friends to date his sister.

It was a request I wanted to honor but the more time I spent with Sydney the harder it became. Maintaining a friendship with both Pierce siblings has been emotionally trying to say the least. Every choice I make seems to be the wrong one.

Nash sighs and shakes his head as if he's disappointed in me. "Next time you head up to The Armory I'll be there," I reassure him.

"Sure, man. I'm going to hold you to that." He smiles but there is tension in his brow. I'm about to ask him what else is bothering him when Joe Clark approaches us with a clipboard in his hand.

"Mahina." Joe nods a greeting to me. Joe's a good guy. He knows his stuff especially when it comes to recovery and injury prevention. He mainly works with the football team but has been traveling with us for our away games during their off season.

He's probably my favorite of the student trainers on the staff. He'll be an asset to whatever professional team hires him if that's the direction he goes after college.

I nod back but continue working out. I need to finish and get out of here. I usually meet up with Sydney and walk with her to our first class on Thursday mornings when I can.

"What's the plan for today?" Nash asks, rubbing his hands together.

"I thought we would start with some drills. Are you warmed up?" Joe asks him.

"Yeah, I'm ready to go." Nash grabs his water bottle and towel he has sitting on the floor by the bench. "See you back at the house later?" he asks me.

"I'll be there after practice. Hart said the girls were bringing dinner over if you're going to be around," I reply.

"I would never turn down Lauren's cooking. My sister's on the other hand..." He scrunches his nose and makes a gagging noise in the back of his throat.

"Sydney doesn't know her way around the kitchen?" Joe asks, butting into our conversation. "I'll have to remember that."

The twenty pound medicine ball I'm holding falls to the ground with a thud. Why the fuck does he need to remember anything about Sydney?

"You know my sister?" Nash asks, his eyes traveling over Joe's shoulder to me. I attempt to mask my face into something that borders intrigue instead of a possessive caveman. I'm afraid I'm failing miserably.

"We met a couple weeks ago at running club," he explains. Nash laughs.

"You must be confused. My sister isn't a runner. There is no way she would have joined a club where you go running. Unless..."

"Charlie," Nash and I say in unison.

"The redhead?" He chuckles. "She was definitely the ring leader in their duo."

"She usually is," Nash says with a deep sigh. Charlie may be the most unpredictable in their friend group but Sydney has always walked the line when it came to staying out of trouble. I've never seen her back down from a dare in the ten years I've known her.

"Charlie definitely made an impression on some of my friends," Joe says.

"Sounds like my sister made one on you too," Nash prods while I try to act disinterested even though I'm hanging on every word of their conversation.

"She did. Sydney's great," he admits.

Great? Great is how you describe your day when you want people to leave you alone but also be polite. That is not how you describe Sydney Pierce.

She's a hell of a lot better than fucking great.

"We've been texting," he continues. I give them my back otherwise I'm going to bite my tongue in half from holding in all the words I want to say. "We're going out on a date this weekend."

Releasing a quiet breath, I retract every nice thing I've ever said about this guy. I'm not jealous of him. I'm jealous he can say those words to Nash without any hesitation. It's infuriating that he makes taking my girl out on a date look easy when I can't do the same.

"Oh yeah?" Nash raises an eyebrow. I wait for him to tell Joe he's not good enough for Sydney.

"I've heard your warnings about Sydney being off limits. I know you don't want any of your teammates dating your sister. I'm not looking for permission. I'm just letting you know," Joe states.

"You don't need my permission. Sydney makes her own choices. All I ask is you treat her right. She deserves the best," Nash says. My body tenses as I absorb the impact of his words.

His little spiel shouldn't surprise me. He's only ever told the people closest to him that Syd is off limits. Or maybe it was a rule set specifically for me. Either way I've heard him loud and clear.

"I agree. She's a cute girl. I enjoy talking to her," Joe says.

The muscle in my jaw ticks. Nash doesn't miss the change in my demeanor. It's getting more difficult to hide lately.

"Sydney does like to chat. I need to refill my water bottle. I'll meet you in the other room," Nash tells him.

"Sounds good." Joe nods and walks toward the football annex where we have an indoor field.

"You're going to let him take Sydney out?" I ask as soon as he's out of sight.

Nash shrugs. "I don't control her life. She can date whoever she wants."

I scoff. "Right. That's why you've threatened all of us within inches of our life for even thinking about it." I swallow all the bitterness like a daily vitamin.

"He isn't my best friend. He's got nothing to prove to me. It's all on Sydney if she wants to date him or not."

It's bullshit. That's what it is. What does that even mean? *He's got nothing to prove.* What do I have to prove to Nash? My loyalty? I'd say I've done a pretty good job doing that. I've picked loyalty to him over my own happiness the duration of our friendship.

"Also, I know that guy is not the one for her. He might last a week and she'll be done with him just like all the rest," he says.

"She dated that Seth guy for over a month."

"She tolerated him for a month. You never hung out with them together."

"No, I didn't." I couldn't. It looked like they were getting serious and that was hard to watch.

"He was basically friend zoned day one. He just didn't know it. I have a feeling the same thing will happen with Joe."

I nod in agreement but it still feels like the grains of sand are slipping faster through the hourglass and I'm running out of time. "Like you said, Sydney can date who she wants." I try to act casual but my words are terse.

The idea of Sydney being with anyone but me is a knife to the heart every time I think about it.

"Exactly." He slaps my shoulder. "I'll see you tonight."

I finish my workout, throwing the ball a little bit harder each rotation. I might have imagined tossing it at Joe's head for a few rounds. I wonder if we could put together a friendly game of dodgeball. The athletic department gets together for a bowling night every month. Maybe we could do this instead. It would be a lot more satisfying.

By the time I'm done showering and ready for class, I have to run to reach Sydney or I'll miss her exiting her residence hall.

As I make my approach, she's scanning her surroundings before taking the first step onto the sidewalk. *Was she looking for me?*

Her dark brown hair bounces with every move she makes. Tight spirals of curls graze over the top of her bare shoulder. My lips crave to do the same thing. Her loose fitting cream blouse exposes just enough of her dark brown skin to tease me.

Her body relaxes as soon as she realizes I'm close by. "You're running late this morning," she says as I slow my pace and fall in line with her shorter stride.

She smells like warm vanilla and whatever essential oil she's testing this week. I try to figure it out but I'm usually unsuccessful. Raking my teeth over my lower lip, I stare at the side of her neck. I wonder if she tastes as sweet as she smells.

"Good morning to you too." I swallow down the term of endearment that begs to be said. I haven't called her anything other than Sydney or Syd in years. Not to her, but God do I want to. I want her to know exactly what she is to me. She's my girl, my baby, my little trouble maker.

She peers at me from the corner of her eye. "It doesn't sound like a good morning. Is everything okay?"

Everything is great. I met the new guy you're dating. He's nice. I hope you break his heart. "Yeah."

"Why are you late?"

That's better than her asking why I'm here. It makes me think she might not mind me walking with her even if she acts like she hates it. "Are you tracking me now?" I ask. My question is comical considering what I've done to her the past few years. She knows it, too, as she snorts a laugh.

"No. I don't care what you do. You're going to do what you want anyway," she says, readjusting her backpack on her shoulder. "Like walking me to class. I told you I didn't need you to do that. Yet, here you are anyway."

"I thought you were walking with me," I joke. We both know I'm the one who goes out of their way to see her. It would be much faster for me to go straight to my class from the gym, but I can't seem to stay away. "If you must know I was late because I got caught up talking to Nash and one of our athletic trainers, Joe Clark. Do you know him?"

Sydney bristles at the mention of his name. *Interesting*.

"I know him," she says matter of fact.

"He's a nice guy," I remark. Sydney narrows her eyes. "What? He is. But I'm not telling you anything you don't already know."

"What is that supposed to mean?"

I'm edging near dangerous territory with her. I don't comment on her dates. I have plenty of thoughts about them but I've never voiced my opinions out loud.

Unlike all the other guys she's dated, this one runs in my circle. Not exactly out of sight out of mind. I thought maybe she was avoiding all athletes. Turns out she's only avoiding me.

"Nothing. I overheard him talking to Nash about your date. That's all." I shrug.

"Let me guess. Nash told him he couldn't date me."

"No. He got the green light." Nash might as well have rolled out the red carpet for the guy.

"Good. Like you said. He's nice. We have a lot in common."

The vice on my heart tightens with every word. Does she even care how it makes me feel seeing her with other guys? I don't blame her if she doesn't give a fuck. It kills me that we're living in this emotional battlefield with each other.

I don't want to hear about Sydney and this guy but she's talking to me. It's a rare event especially with half a smile on her face. I'm going to pretend she's smiling because she's aware she's making me jealous. Not because she's looking forward to her date with Joe.

"Right, like running club."

She smacks my arm. "Shut up," she says laughing. My brain starts recording the sound so I can replay the melody in my head the rest of the day. "It wasn't that bad."

"Did you actually run?"

"What else would you do at running club?"

"Pick up guys apparently," I grumble. "Maybe I'll go to the next one. I need to see you in action."

"Do you think you could keep up with me?" she teases. The challenge in her eyes reminds me of the old Sydney.

The girl who would push me to try new things and to be more adventurous. It's one of the things I love about her. She may enjoy staying home and reading but she's also not afraid to try something new.

I miss her teasing me. This is how our relationship was in high school. Every now and then when I see a glimpse of it, a tiny bit of hope enters my heart making me believe we can get things back to how they used to be.

"I'd give it my best shot," I reply as we reach the steps leading to the life science building.

Shaking her head she silently makes her way up the steps. Once again, leaving me to watch the best thing that's ever happened to me walk away.

FICTION FORUM

FaeAtHeart
> If your power allowed you to transform into a mythical creature, which one would you want to be?

NotYourAverageJoe19
> Probably a wolf.
>
> I like the idea of running free.

FaeAtHeart
> Do you need to run away from something?

NotYourAverageJoe19
> I've already been running from something for too long.
>
> It's time to start running toward something instead.
>
> What about you?

GINGER WALLS

FaeAtHeart
I've always been drawn to fairies and pixies.

NotYourAverageJoe19
Why?

FaeAtHeart
The cute little dresses of course.

NotYourAverageJoe19
Of course. I bet you look hot in one of those dresses.

FaeAtHeart
You're right I do. I wore one for Halloween and it did not disappoint.

NotYourAverageJoe19
I'm sure there was at least one guy who went home alone very disappointed.

FaeAtHeart
I went home alone that night too.

NotYourAverageJoe19
No boyfriend back then either?

FaeAtHeart
Um, well I was seeing someone but it was kind of fizzing out.

FOUL TERRITORY

> Honestly, I'm not sure if there was even a real connection. Not the kind I'm looking for that is.

NotYourAverageJoe19

> What else do you like about fairies? It can't just be about the clothes.

FaeAtHeart

> Hmm…I also like them because they appear delicate and small, but they have power.

NotYourAverageJoe19

> Is that you? Small but mighty?

FaeAtHeart

> I'm not sure about small but I like to think I have a little bit of power.

NotYourAverageJoe19

> If I were with you right now, you would have power over me.

5

SYDNEY

"Why do you think Nash doesn't care that I'm going on a date with Joe? He's friends with him too," I ask Lauren as she preps a variety of vegetables for the sheet pan something or another she's making.

We let ourselves into the guys' townhouse a half hour ago and she's been busy in the kitchen ever since. I offered to help but we both know that I would make a mess out of boiling water.

"I think you're asking the wrong question. You should be asking why he's keeping a certain person out of your reach," she says, spreading potatoes and peppers onto the pan.

Lauren checks the temperature on the oven before opening the door and placing two sheet pans loaded up with vegetables, potatoes, chicken, and steak inside. "Nash is protective. I've experienced that side of him too. When it comes to you, he seems to only be warning one friend. Why?" she asks, taking a seat beside me at the dinner table.

"I don't know." I sigh. "It doesn't matter anyway. Koa and I are never going to happen. We've both moved on." I dig my fingernail into a crack in the table.

"Is that what all this dating business has been? You moving on?" she asks with a smirk and raised eyebrow.

"This is me trying." The truth is I don't think I will ever be able to move on. Does it make me pathetic because I can't get over my first love? I like to think I'm more of a realist. Being with Koa ended up hurting me more than I thought possible. Yet, he's still the one I think about.

Lauren drops her elbows on the table and leans forward. "Koa doesn't look like he's trying very hard. I've never seen him give another female a second glance. Let alone date one."

"That's because he got over me a long time ago. Or maybe he was never really into me to begin with and it was all in my head." I tap the side of my forehead a few times with my index finger. "You don't see him dating anyone because he keeps that part of his life to himself."

I should know better than anyone. I was one of his secret conquests. My throat tightens to the point swallowing is difficult. I never wanted to be a secret fling. I never wanted to be his secret anything.

I'm beginning to think we weren't even a fling. I only had him for one night. That was all I got. One night and then it was over.

We were over.

It doesn't feel like it's over but it's what I need to tell myself every day in order to move on. A little illusion I trick myself into believing. Except it never sticks. I wake up every morning with my heart still hurting and my head making up lies to ease the pain.

I know my brother asked Koa and the guys to look after me. He did it when we started high school and again when we left for Newhouse. While I appreciate Nash's need to make sure I'm taken care of, it's left me very confused.

For a short period of time I thought Koa's protectiveness was because he cared about me. The truth is, he was there because Nash couldn't be. It was never about me but his friendship with Nash.

"Koa doesn't seem like the kind of guy who would lead you on. He's pretty straight forward. If he gave you the impression he was interested, I think you can trust that," she says.

I want to believe she's right. Even if she is, it's over now. The feelings he had for me are long gone. I need to get with the program and get over him too.

Resting her chin on her hand, Lauren purses her lips and narrows her eyes in my direction. I can tell she has put on her little detective hat.

"What? Go ahead and say whatever it is you're thinking." I take a sip of my water.

"I'm trying to understand what happened between the two of you that got you to this entry level friendship. I'm guessing you weren't always like this?"

I check the time on my phone. We still have twenty minutes before the guys get home.

"No we weren't." From the first day I met Lauren, I knew we would be close friends. She has always been there to listen to whatever was on my mind or my heart. There isn't much she doesn't know about me.

Except my history with Koa. We both kept our share of secrets despite our sisterly relationship. Some things are too painful to share. It wasn't until last semester that I found out about Lauren's past and who she really is.

I guess it's my turn to open up and do the same. Part of me has always thought if I never spoke about what happened between me and Koa then it would remain preserved in the back of my mind however I wanted to see it.

Sharing my past relationship with Koa brings everything to the surface again. It's not just the bad memories I try to forget. It's the good ones too. They're the ones that hurt the most.

"Koa moved into our neighborhood when we were twelve. I remember it was the summer before seventh grade. I saw him and immediately got a little crush, but he wasn't interested in more. He said he wanted to be friends." I shrug.

Lauren sighs and offers a sympathetic smile. "If you took Nash out of the equation, would that change anything?"

I've thought about this before. "Honestly I don't know. Nash isn't the only problem. Koa hurt me in high school. It wasn't Nash who messed up our relationship. It was him." I inhale a deep breath and let it out slowly. "He was the one who didn't pick me."

"Is that what you want?"

"I want to move on," I say as convincingly as I can. I want to stop hurting. I want to be happy. I want to have another man touch me and not compare it to the way *his* hands felt on my skin.

"I have a good feeling about Joe." Lauren grins. "Ever since you've started talking to him in your forums you've been happier. A little lighter on your feet."

"I don't know if it's him yet. Whoever this mystery man is, I do like talking to him. It would be nice to know if I'm picturing the right face behind the screen."

"And if it's not him?"

"I'll get my best friend who loves hunting down a good story to help me figure out who I'm really spending all my free time talking to." I bat my eyelashes at Lauren dramatically.

"Whatever you need. You don't even have to ask. I'm in." Lauren stands and walks over to the kitchen drawer by the sink. "We should make a list of questions you can ask online Joe." She holds up a small notebook and pen.

"Where do I even begin?"

"I guess being straight forward and hitting him with the name, birthday, location is too much?"

"I could but I don't want to run him off. What if he's shy? If I come at him hard, he could log off and be done with me."

"You haven't talked about anything personal yet?"

I shake my head. "Not really. We've talked about a few personal things but nothing that would make me think he's Joe Clark. We've mainly talked about books, music, movie adaptations—" I stop talking when I notice Lauren's smirk.

"He sounds perfect."

"He does. It's concerning," I admit. "Do you think it's Joe trying to impress me? Saying all the right things to get me to like him?"

"Could be. It is quite the coincidence that he pops up online the same day you tell him about the forum. But also it could be some random guy or girl in another part of the world."

"Your need to be pragmatic is annoying."

"You can call Charlie to fill your head with romantic fantasies. You have me and Wren to keep you safe and sound in reality." She pats my arm. "You should at least ask him what he looks like."

"I'm sure that will be an accurate description and not exaggerated at all." I roll my eyes.

"I doubt they would lie outright. Stretch the truth maybe, but why lie about your hair and eye color?"

"True." If he has dark hair and brown eyes, I'm out. There's a reason I've tried to only date blonds the past few years.

"Can you video chat in your forum?"

"I am not doing that," I say, shaking my head.

"Why? Whoever is on the other end would lose their mind when they see you on the screen."

"You think? Even when I'm wearing my face mask and reading robe?" I joke. Reading in my bright pink robe is like being wrapped up in a fuzzy blanket. It's helpful when you get to a part of a book that requires pacing the floor. You can focus on the book and not holding your blanket in place. It's honestly life changing.

"Yes, because that's your thing. It makes you happy. And if it makes you happy then whoever you're with will like that too."

I drop my head into my hands and groan. "I'm so pathetic. I'm a senior in college and the highlight of my day is putting on my pajamas and reading a book."

"I said it makes you happy. You are also happy when you're at work, hanging out with the girls, or working on your latest experiment in our bathroom and making a mess everywhere," she teases.

"I cleaned it up," I grumble.

"My point is you are not pathetic. You're incredible. And Joe and whoever this online guy is will see how amazing you are too. Do you know what you're doing for your date?"

"Maybe dinner or coffee and dessert. Somewhere we can talk." I shrug. He didn't give me any details. He only said to dress casually.

The front door creaks as it opens. Hart, Koa, and Nash enter the living room laughing. Hart drops his bag by the stairs and heads straight for Lauren.

"Smells good in here, *cariño*," he says, giving her a quick kiss on the lips.

Nash pops open the oven and Hart smacks him on the arm. "What? I just wanted to take a look. Damn."

"Be patient," Hart scolds him.

"It's almost ready." Lauren stands and offers her seat to Hart. "You can hang out here with us to wait or come back in a few minutes."

Koa and Nash choose to sit in two of the empty seats at the table, while Hart heads toward the closet in the hallway and grabs an extra folding chair for himself. We shuffle the chairs around the table to make room for everyone.

Somehow I end up sitting next to Koa. His thigh brushes against my knee, and while it was an accident the results are the same. My skin grows hot to the touch and heat slowly travels throughout my entire body.

Pressing my palms on the table, I begin to stand. Koa's fingertips graze over the top of my thigh, halting my movement.

"What do you need?" he asks. His warm brown eyes meet mine.

I need to get away from you because every time you're close to me, I want you even closer and I can't allow myself to want you again. "Water. I need more water. Do you want something to drink?"

"I'll get it." Koa stands and I'm gifted a moment to breathe.

"What's this?" Nash asks, pointing across the table. His eyes focused on the notebook Lauren was writing on. I snatch it off the table before anyone can read it.

"Nothing," I answer swiftly.

"Uh, a story I'm working on," Lauren says at the same time as me.

I glare in her direction. She's always getting after me about giving away more information than necessary. She should know better. I can't help it. I'm a Southerner. It's in my genes to overshare. It's what we do. I have to work hard not to tell my life story to strangers.

"For class?" Hart asks.

"Something for my dad. I'll tell you about it later," she says, giving Hart a look that only he could interpret.

I run out to the living room, throw the notebook in my bag and pray no one calls out the fact that I'm the one taking the notebook home and not Lauren.

"You two are terrible liars. It's about my birthday, isn't it?" Nash asks with a full grin on his face. My feet catch on the floor. *His birthday?* I glance at Lauren. She gives me a slight shrug and a nod.

"I'm not saying anything. I don't want to ruin the surprise," I reply.

"We aren't having a party here," Hart declares.

"It's my twenty-first birthday. You can't deny me a party if the girls want to put something together for me," Nash replies.

Hart's body goes rigid. Lauren stands and places her arms on his shoulders. "We can keep it small. And if it gets out of hand, we'll leave." She attempts to slide past him but he grabs her hip and pulls her back into his chest.

It only lasts a moment but it's long enough for me to feel a twinge of jealousy. There have been plenty of times when the shoe was on the other foot and Lauren watched me with my boyfriends.

She was never jealous. Never once did she wish she had what I had. Maybe she knew I was putting on a show. That those guys were nothing but stand-ins and wouldn't make it past the starting line. I wouldn't have been jealous of me either. They were never the real thing like her and Hart.

"Is everything okay?" Koa asks. His forearms rest on the table and he leans into my personal space. I attempt to put some distance between us but it doesn't seem to matter. His large frame crowds me regardless.

"Of course. Why wouldn't it be?" I plaster a smile on my face.

"I don't know," he says. "It's not like you to want to plan a party for Nash. That has never been your thing," he adds, leaning back in his chair.

Lauren brings dinner to the table while Hart passes out plates and silverware to everyone.

I hate that he's right. I am not a planner or event organizer. It is actually something that stresses me out. I find all the details from the food to the invitations cumbersome and overwhelming.

"Yeah, well, that was the old me." It's a lie but it irritates me to no end that he thinks he knows me anymore. Basic civility is the extent of our relationship. Even that has a time limit. It usually ends the moment he starts dictating how I should live my life.

It took an entire summer before I could even stand to be in the same room as Koa. I only did that because Nash begged me to try. He didn't want me going to Newhouse without knowing I would call Koa if I needed help. I agreed for his sake but it wasn't without reservation.

Koa grunts then picks up my plate to serve me food, frustrating me further as he leaves off the peppers because he knows I don't like them.

"Wren will help us," Lauren says. "She'll have the whole event mapped out in ten minutes. If you have any requests, you might as well tell us since the surprise is ruined now."

"Why would Wren need to plan the event? Didn't you two already have it started?" Koa asks. His eyes flicker with mischief and his lip twitches in amusement.

"We were throwing ideas around. We didn't have anything concrete yet if you must know everything," I explain.

"You should help Syd," Nash suggests, nodding in Koa's direction. "Who better to throw me a party than my best friend and my sister."

"Your sister and *her* best friend." I wave a hand between me and Lauren. "We don't need his help. We've got it handled." The last thing I need is to be stuck with Koa planning a party that never existed until two minutes ago.

"What kind of friend would I be if I didn't help plan his party?" Koa asks. I zone out, staring at my plate of food. I shove a bite in my mouth to keep myself from saying something I'll regret.

I enjoy the burn of the potato on my tongue and the roof of my mouth as a steady drip of rage begins to flow through my veins. This is how it always is with them. Their friendship takes precedence over everything else. Over *everyone* else.

"Your loyalty is commendable," I snark. Then stuff more food in my mouth. My fury is almost blinding. Everyone is a blur as I continue to eat in silence as they discuss potential party plans.

My anger doesn't stop me from feeling the occasional tap of Koa's leg against mine or the sweep of his eyes over my face.

It is hard not to smile at my brother's enthusiasm. I didn't realize he wanted a party so badly. I figured he was going to go to The Armory with his friends and have a few shots. Maybe meet someone new. He's been so focused on football he could use a night to let go.

"That settles it then. Do you think you can pull everything together in a few weeks?" Nash asks.

"Shouldn't be a problem," Koa replies.

"Whatever you do, don't ask Wyatt for help," Hart grumbles.

"Why? I figured he would be the go to guy for throwing a decent party." Lauren sips on her drink waiting for Hart to say more.

"Last year he was in charge of getting invitations printed. Somehow they got printed with clothing optional instead of costumes optional," Koa explains. I vaguely remember Nash mentioning this party but I opted to stay home with Lauren.

"People didn't," Lauren says, eyes wide in shock.

"They did." Nash grins.

"I'll handle the invites," I assure Hart.

"I'll do them. I know who to invite," Koa says.

"You don't think I know who my brother's friends are?"

Koa's eyes slide from me, to Nash, and then back to me. "I'm sure you do, but—"

"Then I'll handle it," I say, cutting him off. "Thanks for making dinner, Lo." I stand and take my plate to the sink, rinsing it off, and putting it in the dishwasher. "I'm going to get out of here and get ready for work."

Koa's hand grips tighter on the fork he's holding. His shoulders tense and he cranes his neck, twisting until it cracks.

I hug my brother and Lauren goodbye and squeeze Hart's shoulder as I pass him. Is it rude to say nothing to Koa as I walk out the door? Absolutely, but I've stopped caring if I make him mad.

Join the club. We're all mad here.

FICTION FORUM

FaeAtHeart
> Do you ever wonder what I look like?

NotYourAverageJoe19
> Are looks important to you?

FaeAtHeart
> No they aren't important. I won't deny that I'm curious about what you look like though.

NotYourAverageJoe19
> Would knowing what I look like change anything?

FaeAtHeart
> No. I would still want to talk and get to know you.

NotYourAverageJoe19
> We should focus on that.

> On the things that matter.

FaeAtHeart

GINGER WALLS

> Okay. What are you currently reading?

NotYourAverageJoe19

I should have known that would be what you'd want to know first.

FaeAtHeart

> It's important.

NotYourAverageJoe19

If you must know, I'm reading The Magic of Fire and Bones.

FaeAtHeart

> You are? I'm reading the second book in the series. I loved that one.

NotYourAverageJoe19

I know. I saw your post about it and it sounded good.

FaeAtHeart

> And is it?

NotYourAverageJoe19

Impossible to put down. Just like you said.

I don't trust that Troy guy.

FaeAtHeart

> I'm not saying anything.

FOUL TERRITORY

NotYourAverageJoe19
> She's going to pick the wrong guy isn't she?

FaeAtHeart
> Is there another choice?

NotYourAverageJoe19
> Yeah, Vincent, the quiet guy from her village. He's been hanging in the background waiting for his chance to make a move.

FaeAtHeart
> He's so mean to her though. They are like fire and ice.

> What's wrong with Troy?

NotYourAverageJoe19
> He has an agenda and it isn't helping Aster. He's using her and her power to get control.

FaeAtHeart
> And Vincent? What does he want?

NotYourAverageJoe19
> He wants to make her his priority. He would watch the world burn if it meant she was safe.

FaeAtHeart
> You don't think Troy feels the same? He's a nice guy.

GINGER WALLS

NotYourAverageJoe19

> He's nice because he wants something. If we could read from his point of view, I bet it would all be lies.

> Who do you think Aster should pick?

FaeAtHeart

> Herself.

NotYourAverageJoe19

> You answered that fast. Is this something you had to do?

FaeAtHeart

> It's something I should have done.

NotYourAverageJoe19

> Why didn't you?

FaeAtHeart

> Because the quiet boys from the village might look unassuming on the surface but they have some magic of their own.

6

KOA

My phone buzzes as I walk out of the house to my car. I take a quick glance at the screen and stop short when I see it's a text from Sydney. It catches me off guard. After her abrupt exit from dinner, I assumed it would be a few days before she would reach out to me.

SYDNEY:

> So you can spot me at the bar tonight. I hope you and Nash approve.

Always the little brat testing my restraint.

The text is followed up by an image that has me frozen in place and cursing under my breath. It's a bathroom selfie of her at Ray's—she's wearing a pair of dark wash jeans that hug the flare of her hips and the curve of her ass, and her light pink Ray's shirt has been cut and distressed exposing her midriff.

She lives in flowy tops and loose fitting pants, and she loves pairing overalls and jumpsuits with tank tops and cropped tees. Sydney in a pair of tight pants is a rare sighting on any given day of the week around campus. When she's at Ray's? She wears her clothes like a second skin.

I don't bother texting her back. I put my phone on the charger in my car and start the engine. Responding to her texts never does me any good. She'd never believe me if I told her that I don't enjoy fighting with her.

When she walks away from me angry? I hate it.

I'm not sure why she started sending me photos of herself. It isn't just because Nash wanted me to keep tabs on her. She has her own agenda. Texting me photos isn't anything new. The bratty comments, however, is something she's added over the last year or two.

Being younger has never stopped him from being protective over his big sister. He takes it to extreme levels commenting on everything her clothes to who she should be spending her time with.

Have I made comments to Sydney about what she wears? Yes. It's not something I'm proud of. I know I've overreacted in the past. Last Halloween comes to mind.

God she looked incredible in the floral corset dress she had on. I knew exactly who she was—the lost fairy queen from the book series she read over the summer and never stopped talking about in the forums. I was probably the only one who recognized her. Not that I could have said anything about it.

She hates it when I speak up about what she should or shouldn't be wearing. If you want to set Sydney off, tell her to change clothes.

The thing is, if I don't get mad and demand she wear something else, I'll slip up and tell her how fucking gorgeous she is. It isn't fair to her and I know she doesn't deserve it.

It's not her fault that it's my coping mechanism and default mode with her now.

How would she react if she knew how bad I still want her? Would she be willing to give me a chance after everything? I'm nervous about what Nash would say too. He's adamant about his ban on his sister. I don't want to lose his friendship but there isn't a day that passes when I don't think of what it would be like to truly be hers.

It's gotten even worse seeing all of my friends pair off with their girlfriends. I'm happy for them but damn I want that with Sydney too.

The parking lot is full when I pull up to Ray's. For being hidden off the highway, they get a steady stream of customers. I like to think it's the cheap beer that lures them here but I know better than that.

It's the entertainment. Every hour the bartenders take over the dance floor and put on a show. Some even dance on top of the bar.

Walking past the dance floor full of couples spinning around to a classic country song, I find a seat at one of my favorite tables. It's far enough in the back I can easily blend in with the crowd but close enough I have a decent view of the bar.

The waitress, Margo, brings me a beer without being prompted. She gives me a knowing smile. After my tenth visit, she put together why I sat here for hours nursing a beer until it was half empty. She said her boyfriend did the same thing when she first started working at Ray's.

GINGER WALLS

I didn't correct her that I wasn't Sydney's boyfriend. I wasn't much of her anything anymore. It guts me to even think about how much our relationship has changed. It went from fucking to perfect to absolute disaster in a blink of an eye.

I am trying to be better. Baseball keeps me away some nights. Something I'm sure Sydney is happy about. I also don't stay her entire shift anymore. I usually show up the last hour or so to make sure she gets home okay.

It may seem like I'm possessive, or borderline psychotic. I like to think I'm being a good friend. That I'm looking out for her safety. I don't talk to her or bother her while she's working. It's like I'm not even here.

Sydney's smile widens as she places a mixed drink in front of a customer. Her hair is down and secured on one side with one of her handmade clips, and tight ringlets of black curls cover her forehead and bounce slightly when she laughs.

I used to be the one making her laugh.

I pick up my phone and check the time. One more hour, give or take, and I'll be back home talking to her online. When I lift my gaze to search for her behind the bar, I catch her watching me. She quickly looks away and busies herself clearing glasses off the bar.

When Margo comes by to check on me, I go ahead and pay my tab. I'm done drinking for the night. I usually don't even finish the one I order. I only get something to blend in, which clearly I'm failing at with the way Sydney keeps glancing over at me.

She's writing something on a piece of paper and talking to one of her fellow bartenders. Any minute the music will turn to a familiar one that will have everyone up on their feet.

I've learned there is only a few routines that Sydney participates in. Any time I hear one of the songs, it puts me on edge. It has nothing to do with the men who watch her and everything to do with the images I have burned into my brain.

She moves around the bar along with Lauren and another bartender clearing glasses and plates out of the way in preparation for what's about to come.

The guy in the DJ booth—if you can call it that since it's essentially a table on a small raised platform that mimics a stage—signals to the girls he's about to switch to their song.

On the third eight count they walk up steps that are built into the bar in sync with each other. They are clapping their hands, stomping their boots, and dropping down to a low squat to tease the customers lucky enough to have front row seats.

Colorful lights flash across the room catching every now and then on Sydney, highlighting various parts of her silhouette. I would never admit this but as much as I hate her working here, I'm glad she said yes to doing it.

Dancing on top of the bar—working here at Ray's—offers her the opportunity to be carefree and happy which is something she hasn't been for a long time. On the surface, maybe. But deep down? No.

She can try and tell me differently but I would never believe her. That is a story I would never buy.

GINGER WALLS

The song ends and the girls work their way back down the stairs to start serving drinks again. Before Syd gets too far, a hand shoots out and grabs the back of her calf.

I stand so fast I have to catch my chair to keep it from toppling over. Her eyes connect with mine over the guy's head. She shakes her head slightly telling me to stand down.

Her mouth curves in a salacious smile and her eyes narrow slightly. One could assume this is Syd being sultry, but I know better. This is her getting angry. I've been fooled by this look myself.

She dips low, balancing on the balls of her feet. Then palms his forearm with both hands. Her grip tightens which again could be mistaken for her reciprocating the advance of this guy.

Twisting her hands in opposite directions, she sneers at the guy. I can't hear her but reading her perfectly shaped lips she tells him to let go. He doesn't hesitate after the way she almost peeled the skin off his arm.

I've been on the receiving end of one of Sydney's forearm twists before and they hurt like a bitch. I would do whatever she wanted if it would get her to stop her torture.

After Syd hops off the bar, she grabs the piece of paper she was writing on earlier and flashes it in front of Lauren. She nods in acknowledgment as Sydney passes her, walking toward the dark hallway to the left of the bar.

Mr. Grabby Hands doesn't take his eyes off Sydney and a few seconds later he's following her step for step. This hallway leads to the break room and two storage rooms. He has no reason to be over on this side of the building.

I know every face that walks in this place. He's been here a few times and is well aware the bathrooms are on the other side of the bar. He's chasing after Sydney, and he's delusional if he thinks he will have another shot at putting his hands on her. He's lucky he got away with it the first time.

I quicken my steps, bumping into people as I go. Suddenly being on the other side of the bar doesn't seem like such a good idea. I'm too far away from her. Sydney unlocks a door in the hall and flips the light switch on. He waits for her to walk inside before entering the storage closet after her.

The vein in my forehead pulses and my fists clench at my sides. I don't like getting in fights. It's not a good look especially if I want to be a professional athlete. At the moment, I don't care about the public eye. I care about Sydney. I promised her years ago I wouldn't get into any more fights. Not over her.

Promises are meant to be broken. If this guy has his hands on her uninvited...I can't even finish the thought.

Sydney's squeal in surprise has me moving my feet faster. "What are you doing here?" she asks.

"I came to apologize," he says. I call bullshit but wait outside the door just in case it's true. I don't want to charge in there making a scene and get Syd angry at me when I didn't need to. The only reason she hasn't sent me packing every night is because I keep to myself while I'm here.

"Go ahead," she quips.

"I'm sorry. I thought I felt a connection between us."

"Apology accepted. You need to leave now. I have work to do."

"Awww. Don't be like that, sugar," he drawls. Glass clinks from somewhere inside the room.

"I really think you should leave."

"Nah, I don't think so," he sneers, then the door starts to close. I rush to the entry and jam my size fourteen in the gap before I get locked out. I push the door open, startling this asshole who can't take a hint.

Sydney's eyes widen at my sudden appearance. He has her backed against a wall to wall shelving unit full of liquor bottles. With every step I take in her direction, her breathing steadies and her body loosens. *That's right. I'm here now. Nothing will happen to you.*

"The girls said you were back here," I say, announcing my arrival. I maneuver around the guy, checking his shoulder as I pass. "Sorry man," I snarl in his direction. "Hi, baby." The term endearment slips past my lips with ease. Sydney inhales a sharp breath and her lips part.

"Hi," she whispers. Her eyes lift and she glances over my shoulder. I don't like the fear I see in them.

Standing in front of her, I put one hand on her hip and pull her flush against my body. I wrap my other hand around the back of her neck and dig my fingers into her hair. "Don't look at him. Look at me."

My thumb skims her bare skin above the waistband of her jeans, causing her to shiver. She's still so soft and warm.

Just the way I remember. The guy behind me growls. I don't like having my back to him but there is no way I'm switching positions with Syd.

"We were having a conversation here," the guy has the nerve to say.

I glare at him over my shoulder. "And now your conversation is over. Take a walk." I nod toward the open door.

"Are you with this guy?" He points a finger in my direction but his eyes are focused on my girl. I would love to snap that finger in half for pointing it at her. Or maybe poke out his eyeballs for the way they leer in her direction.

Her gaze drops to the floor. I angle her head to where she is looking back at me and see vulnerability trapped in her dark eyes. It's an emotion I'm not used to seeing. "Yes," I answer for her. "I'm hers." Truer words have never left my mouth.

Her eyes flutter closed for a moment and she exhales a slow breath. "You both need to leave." She fights my hold but it only makes me tighten my grip on her side.

The guy behind me chuckles. The noise is irritating and makes my jaw tick. Punching the grin off his face flashes through my mind but that would mean letting go of Sydney.

"Looks like you aren't welcome here, *pal*." He crosses his arms over his chest.

I don't reward him with a response. Instead, I focus on my girl. "Do you want me to leave?" I ask, pulling her closer until there's barely any space left between us. Her hands instinctively find my chest to push me away if I had to guess.

Yet, those slender fingers of hers dig into my pecs welcoming my touch.

Running my nose up her cheek, I whisper once I get to her ear, "Please don't hate me even more than you already do after this."

I don't give her the opportunity to ask the question that has her eyebrows squished together and her eyes narrowed. My mouth hovers for a moment before I lean forward and erase the last centimeter of space between us.

Pressing my lips against hers for a moment, I test the water. It's been too long since I felt her mouth against mine and I hate that the asshole behind me is ruining the moment. I can feel his eyes on me, drilling screws into my skull. He isn't happy I'm the one kissing her. If I had to bet, Sydney feels the same.

The guy snarls again. He can't take a hint. He isn't going to leave unless I make this believable. Tilting her head back, I apply more pressure to her pillowy lips before pulling gently on her bottom one. A quiet whimper escapes her and that fuels me further.

I move my mouth over hers mapping out every contour as one of her hands slides to the back of my neck. Her body skims mine and it takes all my control to not push her up against the shelf. I'm sure she can feel how hard she's making me.

There's a small part of me that's glad she knows how bad I want her. That all it takes is her being in my vicinity and I'm thinking about her in ways I have no right to be. This kiss is simple, chaste almost, but it has a trigger effect. Reminding me of the last time I held her close. The last time she let me kiss her.

The door slams behind us and that breaks the momentary hold I have on her. She pulls away, a little stunned, then pushes me off of her. This time I let her go.

Her eyes flit around my face and then the room as she fights a war in her mind. Her tongue flicks out and glides over her lower lip. *I wonder if she can still taste me.*

"I had him under control. You didn't need to do that. You took it too far," she says with a bite in her tone. She turns, giving me her back, picks up a liquor bottle with a trembling hand, and places it in a crate.

"I'm sorry you feel that way but I'm not sorry I kissed you."

Her body tenses before she lets out a breath. "You need to leave."

"Sydney..." Her name is a plea and filled with a raw emotion I'm not used to exposing.

"Just go," she murmurs.

"Okay," I say, sighing. "I'll be waiting in my car to follow you home."

She laughs derisively and mumbles something to herself. I am only able to catch the word *unbelievable*.

I crowd behind her leaving just enough distance to slide a piece of paper between us. "Believe it. There isn't anything I wouldn't do to make sure you're safe," I say.

I pull her hair to the side and expose the expanse of her neck. She shivers as I run my thumb over the scar on the back of her shoulder. My lips connect with her skin without considering the consequences.

Before she can yell at me like I'm sure she's itching to do, I back away, and leave the small storage room. I walk every inch of Ray's looking for the guy who followed Sydney and do the same in the parking lot.

I catch him getting inside his white beater of a car. Once his taillights disappear into the void, I get in my car and wait.

FICTION FORUM

FaeAtHeart
I had such a long night at work. I don't think I can talk to one person.

Not even my roommate.

NotYourAverageJoe19
But you want to talk to me?

FaeAtHeart
I...yes.

NotYourAverageJoe19
Is everything good at work?

FaeAtHeart
It's fine. There was an incident with a regular.

NotYourAverageJoe19
A regular?

FaeAtHeart
I bartend at a local place where I go to school.

GINGER WALLS

> How was your day?
>
> Do anything fun?

NotYourAverageJoe19

> It was one of the best days I've had in awhile.
>
> Just school and grabbed a drink at a bar I go to a lot. I guess that makes me a regular?

FaeAtHeart

> Yes. It would.
>
> Where do you go to school?
>
> If you don't want to say, I understand. Can you at least confirm you're not underage?

NotYourAverageJoe19

> I just said I was at a bar drinking.

FaeAtHeart

> I've had a fake ID since I was seventeen. That statement means nothing.

NotYourAverageJoe19

> Trouble.

FaeAtHeart

> Me or you?

NotYourAverageJoe19

> You.

FOUL TERRITORY

FaeAtHeart
You're probably right.

NotYourAverageJoe19
I'm in college. What about you?

FaeAtHeart
I'm in college too. A senior.

NotYourAverageJoe19
Same. Senior.

FaeAtHeart
I probably should have asked you all of this weeks ago.

It didn't seem important then.

NotYourAverageJoe19
But it does now?

FaeAtHeart
Yes.

NotYourAverageJoe19
Why?

FaeAtHeart
I don't know. I like talking to you. It makes me want to know who you really are.

NotYourAverageJoe19
Not sure you can handle who I really am.

GINGER WALLS

FaeAtHeart
What does that mean?

NotYourAverageJoe19
I'm intense.

FaeAtHeart
What if I like that in a guy?

NotYourAverageJoe19
What else do you like in a guy?

FaeAtHeart
He must love books.

NotYourAverageJoe19
Obviously.

FaeAtHeart
Supportive of my creative endeavors.

NotYourAverageJoe19
We'll circle back to this later. I'm curious what that entails.

FaeAtHeart
It's not anything sexual if that's what you're thinking.

NotYourAverageJoe19
I wasn't but now I am. What else?

FOUL TERRITORY

FaeAtHeart
Someone who takes care of themselves.

NotYourAverageJoe19
Is this your way of saying you want someone with a fit body?

FaeAtHeart
No. I enjoy physical activities.

NotYourAverageJoe19
So do I.

FaeAtHeart
OMG. Stop. THAT is not what I'm talking about.

I like athletics.

NotYourAverageJoe19
Oh yeah? Like what?

FaeAtHeart
Maybe I should clarify.

I like watching my man being athletic.

NotYourAverageJoe19
You have a man?

FaeAtHeart
No. Oh lord. Is it hot in here?

GINGER WALLS

NotYourAverageJoe19

I don't know. I'm not in the same room as you.

Wish I was though.

FaeAtHeart

Are you flirting with me?

NotYourAverageJoe19

If I was, would that be a problem?

FaeAtHeart

No. I like it.

I bet you flirt with all the girls at your school.

NotYourAverageJoe19

Not really. That's not my style.

FaeAtHeart

What is your style?

NotYourAverageJoe19

Single minded. Once I like someone it's game over.

FaeAtHeart

Is there someone who has your mind occupied?

NotYourAverageJoe19

Yes.

FOUL TERRITORY

FaeAtHeart: Oh. Well, she's a lucky lady.

NotYourAverageJoe19: Nah. I'm the lucky one.

FaeAtHeart: She doesn't mind you talking to strangers on the internet?

NotYourAverageJoe19: I don't think she minds since the "stranger" is the same person who occupies my mind.

Are you still there?

FaeAtHeart: Yes.

Yes. I'm here.

What does this mean?

NotYourAverageJoe19: I don't understand your question.

FaeAtHeart: What are we doing here?

GINGER WALLS

> I don't even know where you live.

> I can't like someone when I don't know their name, what they look like, where they live. This is important information.

NotYourAverageJoe19

You like me?

FaeAtHeart

> Of course that's what you comment on.

> You're not terrible to talk to.

NotYourAverageJoe19

That's a start. I'll win you over.

We are getting to know each other. That's what we're doing.

And if it makes you feel better, I'll tell you where I live.

FaeAtHeart

> It would.

NotYourAverageJoe19

Alabama.

FaeAtHeart

> You're not just saying that? You didn't look at my profile first?

FOUL TERRITORY

NotYourAverageJoe19

No, I'm not just saying that. You don't have your location listed on your profile. I already checked. I have no reason to lie to you.

Now tell me where you live so I can keep getting to know you.

FaeAtHeart

Alabama.

NotYourAverageJoe19

Good.

Nice coincidence.

FaeAtHeart

I'd say more like it's convenient.

NotYourAverageJoe19

Oh yeah? Why's that?

FaeAtHeart

We might want to meet in person one day. It's much easier to do that living in the same state than if you were in Michigan or somewhere across the country.

I mean if that's something you might want to do.

Is it something you might want to do?

GINGER WALLS

NotYourAverageJoe19
> Yes. But not yet.

FaeAtHeart
> Of course. I understand. You don't really know me. It would be weird.

NotYourAverageJoe19
> It has nothing to do with you.

> I want to make sure you like me enough you won't go running when you see me.

FaeAtHeart
> I don't think that will be a problem.

NotYourAverageJoe19
> I've changed my answer.

FaeAtHeart
> About?

NotYourAverageJoe19
> I'm the one who's in trouble here.

FaeAtHeart
> I think we both are.

> I should probably go to bed. I have an early class tomorrow.

NotYourAverageJoe19
> Can I talk to you again soon?

FOUL TERRITORY

FaeAtHeart

Yes.

Goodnight, Joe.

NotYourAverageJoe19

Goodnight, trouble.

7

SYDNEY

Someone should bottle up the scent of book pages and sell it as cologne or perfume. Candles are great, but as a cologne on a good looking guy...it's like a pheromone to me.

My fingers glide over the spines of the newest book releases in the fantasy section. I'm hiding out at the bookstore in town. Koa summoned me earlier to start planning Nash's birthday party but I refuse to reply to him. I didn't want his help with the party before and I definitely don't want it now.

He kissed me.

The kiss was soft, sweet, and nothing like what I expected. I've kissed Koa before. It was a mess of tongues, teeth, and lips. Neither one of us knew what we were doing back then.

The whole event has played on repeat in my head the last few days. I'm used to men pushing it with their words when I'm at work. They attempt to flirt after a few rounds but no one has ever physically touched me or followed me into a stock room before.

That customer scared me more than I was letting on. The liquor closet was secluded. Sure the girls knew where I was but they wouldn't have any reason to check on me. They definitely wouldn't have heard me scream if he was able to advance on me. And he would have if Koa didn't follow us.

My skin still tingles from where he touched me. He erased all my fear in seconds and replaced it with desire. I bang my head against the top row of books. I'm not supposed to be feeling this way about him anymore.

He moved in on me so easily as if it was something he does on a regular basis—saving damsels. He seemed unaffected by our close proximity, meanwhile I had to claw at his chest to keep myself from sinking into the floor.

I expected him to grab the guy by the collar and walk him out the door. The last guy who touched me without permission came to school the next day with a busted lip and a black eye.

No, instead he acted like my boyfriend. He kissed me and he called me baby. Maybe I'm the one who should have put up a fight. Am I even capable of doing that? I've never had to try before. He's never put me in a position where I'm forced to choose between pushing him away or pulling him closer. *You definitely didn't push him away.*

My hand clamps down on the bookshelf in front of me. One kiss and my heart was ready to start planning a wedding. Then I looked over Koa's shoulder and remembered it was all an act. That everything he did and said was to get that guy to leave.

"How many books do you have at home that you haven't read, give or take twenty?" Koa removes the book I've been cradling from my arms and looks over the title. Then flips open the front cover as if he's actually interested in what the book is about.

It's the second book in a duet. And no, I haven't read the first one yet but they are going to look so pretty on my shelf together.

He closes the book and hands it back to me.

"Less than you think," I reply, especially if he's giving me twenty. The corner of his mouth ticks. I wait for him to tell me that I shouldn't be wasting my money on more books but it never comes.

"We need to talk," he says.

"We have nothing to talk about." I walk past him toward the romance section. I'm not going to let his presence ruin my shopping trip. If he thinks I want to talk about what happened or him kissing me, he's crazy.

I want to forget about it and move on. Talking about it will put me at risk. I'm not a good liar. I won't be able to hide the fact that he still has a hold on me.

"We do."

Biting down on my back molars, I expel a breath through my nose. Blinded by my frustration I almost bump into an older couple passing us. Koa presses against my elbow moving me out of the way in time.

"Excuse me," I say to them, then jerk out of his reach. "Don't touch me. You've done enough of that already, don't you think?" I grit out behind a clenched jaw. He chuckles darkly. I don't know what he thinks is so funny.

"No, I don't think I have," he says with conviction. "I'm here because we need to talk about Nash's party. His birthday is only a few weeks away."

Ignoring him, because what the hell? *'No, I don't think I have.'* Is he saying he wants to touch me more? I can't overthink that statement at the moment.

I walk a little faster until I reach a bookshelf with familiar titles. The sight of them alone makes me feel calmer and more at ease. Letting my guard down completely isn't something I can do. He has fooled me into thinking he cared before, but I won't let it happen again.

He is here for Nash at the moment. Not me. I need to remember that.

"Why don't you plan it by yourself? You know him best after all. You don't need me." I tilt my head towards him. "You never did."

His face falls showing a moment of what? Regret? If it was, it's gone in a flash. I scan the books on the shelf looking for one I don't already own. Koa clasps his hand over mine, stopping my movement.

"I need you." His thumb runs circles over my skin. The gesture is soft, barely there, but I notice every little touch from him. They all get cataloged and locked away for safekeeping despite my better judgment. "I don't plan parties."

Pulling away from him, I take a step out of his reach. The thought makes me laugh. *Have I ever been out of his reach?* "Interesting, considering you were so eager to volunteer. I doubt Nash expects much anyway. Drinks, some food, music." I shrug. "Oh look at that. We just planned a party. Goodbye."

"It's his twenty-first. We need balloons and decorations," he says, his gaze focused on my profile. I continue to scan book titles and admire their pretty spines and artwork in an attempt to forget he's even here. It isn't as easy to do as one would think.

"Sounds like you know how to plan parties to me. You have it all figured out and under control." I smirk at him. I slide a book off the shelf and examine the front and back—the cover has a cool font and pretty colors. *Don't mind if I do.*

"You promised Nash."

"I don't recall promising anything. Even if I did, I think I'm owed one or two of my own promises to break," I snap.

Koa lets out a frustrated breath, and then takes my book selections out of my arms. "Are you getting anymore?" He gestures toward the rows of bookshelves we're standing in between.

I shake my head but he dips his chin giving me a knowing look. I glance around until I see another book that's been on my list for awhile. He tracks where my eyes are zoned in on and picks up the book in question. I nod confirming my selection.

"Where are you going?" I ask when he starts walking away.

"To buy your books. Then I'm going to get you one of those sugar filled iced coffee drinks you like and we're going to sit down and plan this party."

"Give me those." I reach for the books but he holds them over his head. "You are not buying my books." I go to grab them again but he strong arms me this time, holding me back.

I cross my arms over my chest as we wait in line. He is so frustrating. Who does he think is? Barging into my life and buying me books. Showing up where I work and kissing me. I've tried my best to keep a safe distance between us but suddenly he's everywhere.

I should not be thinking about Koa's kisses whenever I have one—maybe two—other options in my life. Really good options actually. I still haven't confirmed if Joe online is the same Joe on campus but I will. And if they are the same person, then that's a great option.

I don't understand why Joe hasn't told me already. I have my first name displayed on my profile. He could ask and confirm it's me but he hasn't. He said he wants me to like him first. Little does he know, I already do.

Which should make being around Koa easier, but it doesn't. Every time I'm near him it undoes any progress I've started to make with getting over him. It's why I try to avoid him when I can and that only extends so far considering our friend group is so tightly woven.

It's not that I don't want to be around him. It's that I can't. I'm in self preservation mode. Then there are times I look at his face and see the boy I fell in love with. I step back in time and ask him to have lunch or hang out, and I completely forget how much he hurt me.

One more semester. If all goes right, that's all I need to get through and then he'll be off playing baseball and I'll be in a new city starting over.

I've been lost in my thoughts for so long I didn't notice Koa's already tapped his credit card and is being handed a bag full of his purchases. He takes it from the clerk with a thank you and then ushers me toward the cafe located on the right side of the store.

"I can carry them," I say, reaching my hand toward him. He glances at my palm before grunting.

"And let you slip out the door? I don't think so. These are collateral. You can have them once we're done."

What am I doing? Why am I still here? I didn't pay for anything. I can buy them myself later. In fact, I can order them now, and they will be delivered to my dorm tomorrow.

"Are you coming?" he asks, realizing I've stopped following him.

"No, I don't think I am." I turn on my heel and start walking toward the door. I pull in a deep breath of fresh air as soon as I'm outside. This is what I needed. I can think clearly out here.

"Do you really hate me that much?" he asks. We're separated by a few square blocks of concrete on the sidewalk. He clutches the handle on the shopping bag in one hand and his other is balled in a fist.

"I don't hate you." I mentally pat myself on the back for saying that without hesitation or emotion. He doesn't get to know my true feelings for him.

"You can't even be around me for more than five minutes anymore without running away." He takes a step closer and I retreat one. That makes him grin as if I'm proving his point.

"I was at your house for dinner just last week," I remind him.

"And you left as soon as you could." He steps closer.

"I had to work as you know." A flash of him kissing me pops into my head and I feel warmth spread through my cheeks.

"What are you thinking about?"

"How much I want you to leave me alone."

"I'll let you have that lie." He smirks. "I can't leave you alone." His tone of voice is too sincere for my liking. The old me would read into his words and believe that maybe there is more to what he's saying. He's got me backed against the brick wall of the bookstore but at least he's left some space between us this time.

"Well, I can't keep doing this with you." *I can't do anything with you.* Koa's brown eyes stare into mine.

"If this is about the other night, I'm sorry. It was a mistake to kiss you like that."

I drop my head and stare at the concrete. I need a moment to compose myself before I go postal on Koa. "A mistake. That isn't the first time you've said this to me. You should really get some new material." I wish I could control my emotions but I'm afraid some of my anger slipped through my defenses.

He takes a small step toward me and tips my chin. "Sydney," he says, and his tone is apologetic. "I said it was a mistake to kiss you like that. I'm still not sorry for kissing you.

It was the only thing I could think of at the moment. That guy wasn't taking a hint."

"It's fine. I'm over it." I unzip my bag and fish out my keys.

"I don't want you to be over it. I want..." his voice trails off.

"To be honest, I don't really care what you want seeing as you've never once cared about what I wanted." I poke a finger at my chest.

"That isn't true and you know it."

"Do I? Your words and actions say otherwise. All you do is show up where you aren't needed." I step into his personal space this time.

"You needed me the other night. Who knows what that guy would have done if I wasn't there." He practically growls the words. A family of four walk past us reminding me that we are in public.

"Can we not do this right now? I don't want to hear what you think about me working at Ray's. You've voiced your hatred for the place enough over the last few months. I've heard you loud and clear."

"Yet, you chose to ignore me."

"That's because you aren't the boss of me." I meet his glare. My phone buzzes against my hip in my bag. A much needed interruption.

Checking my notifications, I see a new email from the cosmetics company I reached out to about starting my makeup and skin care brand. I can't stop the smile on my face. They're willing to answer any questions I have and mentor me. This is a great first step.

"Good news?" Koa asks.

"Yes," I reply, closing out my email. I'll write them back when I get home and can put together a clear thought.

"That's not much of an answer."

"That's the only answer you are going to get." I drop my phone in my bag and walk back toward the bookstore.

"Where are you going?"

I turn to face him and continue taking slow steps backwards. "You promised me a coffee and we have a party to plan."

It's possible I might regret this decision later. I'll blame my lack of judgment on the email I just received and not the fact there might be a small part of the old me that wants to spend more time with him.

8

KOA

Sydney walks back toward the bookstore with her ponytail of curls bouncing with every step. She has on one of her signature pair of jeans that is painted in a multitude of colors and a loose fitting floral top that skims her midriff.

At first glance you would think the patterns and colors clash, but she makes it work. She's never been afraid to be seen or stand out.

"Why don't you find us a table? I'll order our drinks." I pass her the shopping bag with her books inside.

"You trust me with these?" she asks, taking the bag with careful hands. I don't know if it's because she's trying to avoid touching me or because she's protecting her books.

"I do. Go ahead. I'm sure you're dying to crack them open and look at the pages." I place my hands on her shoulders and spin her around. "I'll be there in a few minutes."

She takes one last glance at me over her shoulder before she finds a table in the middle of the cafe. She excitedly pulls out one of the books from her bag and admires the cover. Her fingers trace over the illustrations while she smiles like a kid in a candy store.

I had a feeling I would find her here. After I texted her several times with no response, I figured she was hiding out at one of her favorite places. I keep messing up with her. The only thing I know how to do is make her angry or guilt her into spending time with me.

I move up a spot in line and place our order. I hope she still likes the sweet caramel drink she used to get. It's been a long time since I've had the privilege to buy her an iced coffee.

Sydney snaps a selfie with one of her books and taps away on her phone. Once she's done, she goes right back to reading. Her lips twitch trying to hold back her reaction to the words she's reading on the page. She's always been a pro at keeping a poker face when it comes to reading.

You would never be able to tell if she was reading about someone falling in love or someone getting chased by a serial killer. Shit, in some of her books it's probably one in the same.

Her face might be hard to read when it's stuck in a book, but when she's looking at me? She doesn't hide a thing. Sometimes I wish she did. She may blush thinking about our kiss but that doesn't negate how upset she is with me or how much I've hurt her. My only hope is somewhere underneath all that pain there's still a part of her that remembers what we used to be.

My phone buzzes in my hand, lighting up with a notification from the *Fiction Forum*. Keeping one eye on Sydney, I pull open the app. It's a private message from *FaeAtHeart*.

Clicking on the message, my pulse quickens. She's cropped the image where most of her face is hidden. All I can see is her chin and a portion of her mouth that is in a full smile. The book is the main focus.

FaeAtHeart

> Look what I have. I can finally start reading the series now that the duet is complete.

NotYourAverageJoe19

> You bought it. Book ban over I see.

I glance at Sydney as she reads my message. Her eyes catch mine momentarily before going back to her phone. I turn toward the baristas and pretend I'm waiting for our coffees instead of her reply.

FaeAtHeart

> Technically my book ban is still intact. A friend bought it for me.

A friend? She's obviously just saying that. As much as I want it to be true, Sydney Pierce stopped considering me as a friend a long time ago. She tolerates my presence at best and puts on a good act in front of everyone to keep the peace.

NotYourAverageJoe19

> Nice friend. It's pretty well known the friends who buy you books are the best ones. A total keeper.

I hit send and put my phone on do not disturb. The last thing I need is my phone going off in front of her after she sends a message to "Joe" and she figures out not only does he live in Alabama but he also goes to the same school.

Oh and fun fact, he's also the same guy who's been in love with you since the ninth grade and the guy you can't stand to spend more than five minutes with.

The barista calls my name and hands over my coffees with a flirty smile. As I walk away, I notice there is a phone number written on one of the cups. That's bold considering I'm here with Sydney.

Taking the seat beside her instead of across from her like I'm sure she hoped, I slide the cup with the phone number in Sydney's direction.

"I think this one is yours," she says, eyeing the number.

"They're the same drink. You can have that one."

Sydney lifts her gaze over my shoulder. "She's staring at you."

"And? I'm here with you." I grab her chair and pull her closer to me. "Let her watch." I run my finger over the barrette she has in her hair. "This is new."

"I made it the other day." She grabs my hand and holds it under the table. "This isn't going to be a thing," she says, dropping my hand in my lap.

"What isn't?" I ask, leaning back in my chair and taking a sip of my coffee. She got me hooked on these frappuccino drinks freshman year.

"Us pretending to be a couple to ward off unwanted attention. You can deal with your groupies on your own. I don't want anything to do with that."

"You act like I have girls following me around all the time." Sure there are random groups of girls hanging out at our games and practices. I can't control that. There are also over thirty guys on the team. They aren't coming just to see me.

"I wouldn't know. I don't pay attention to who's showing up at your games and practices."

"We have something in common. I don't pay attention to them either." *I'm too busy paying attention to you.* My eyes hold hers for a beat before she looks away.

"Great. Can we get started with this?" She taps around on her phone until a blank note appears. "We should keep the food simple and order pizza. Maybe some chips. A cake of course. Can you get the decorations?" Her eyes meet mine and she rolls them in frustration. "Fine. I'll get them."

"I didn't say anything."

"You didn't have to." She adds streamers, balloons, and a sign on her list.

"Why don't we both go get them?"

She regards me for a moment before going back to her phone. "I don't think so. We can do the planning part together but after that it's better if we split up."

I scoff. "That isn't true. We've always been better together," I murmur.

Her jaw ticks as she bites down on her lower lip. "Should we have a theme?" she asks, ignoring my remark even though it clearly bothers her.

"Like what? You, Charlie, and Wyatt are the only ones who like costumes."

"We could do a luau or sports themed or maybe a masquerade," she says, deleting her original decorating ideas and typing up new ones. Then she takes a quick sip of her coffee.

"But then you wouldn't be able to see my face," I joke.

"All the more reason to do one," she grumbles. "Let's do a luau. Nash will like that. He can get lei'd all night by girls in bikinis. It will make all the other guys happy too. Can you handle the guest list if I make invitations?"

"Yeah, I can do that. I'll invite a few guys from the football team, his friends from class, maybe some of our neighbors."

"Not too many. Hart will never forgive you. Don't forget about Enzo and Marco. We need to do this on a night they're free too."

I pull out my phone and send them both a quick text. They may go to a different college but we all went to high school together. They're an important part of our friend group. They're family, with some of us more so than others.

"I'll let you know what they say," I tell her, but my mind keeps drifting back to the dress code for the party. "What are you going to wear? Nash won't be able to relax and have fun if all his friends are checking you out and hitting on you." The lie is one I've perfected over the years.

The truth is I'm going to be the one struggling to keep myself in check around her if she's wearing nothing more than a bathing suit. I have a hard enough time being around her when she's wearing everyday clothes.

Like right her blouse dips low on her back. I'm tempted to drape my arm over the back of her chair and trace my thumb over the scar she has on her shoulder—she got it when she fell out of the tree in her backyard.

She lets out a slow breath. Her eyes narrow on me. "That sounds like a Nash problem to me. What did he ask you to do exactly when we left for college?" She puts her elbows on the table and leans toward me. "He obviously put you on some kind of big brother mission. Whatever it was, you can stop now."

I'm not sure how to answer her. The truth is he asked me to keep an eye on her. Make sure she's happy, making friends, and adjusting. I'm the one who chose to make all of her business my business.

I'm the one who couldn't stop watching her once she got settled in her new life on campus. I'm the one who can't let her go.

"He asked me to keep an eye on you when he isn't able to." I shrug to play down the whole thing.

She chuckles coldly. "Right. You know what. Why don't you pick out my outfit? That way it will be something you both approve of."

"Sydney," I say with a sigh.

"I'm serious. Add it to your list. You can rummage through my closet and find me something *appropriate* to wear to the party."

The idea of watching Sydney trying on outfits has my jeans feeling like they're suddenly a size too small. I squirm in my seat hoping that will offer me a little bit of relief.

"Fine," I reluctantly agree.

"Great. So you'll do invites and coordinate outfits. I'll handle the food, drinks, and decorations. Anything else?"

"No, I think that about covers everything. I can help with decorations."

"Don't worry about it. I'll get Charlie or Wren to help me. You're already busy enough with games, practice, and following me around everywhere. I would hate to burden you more," she snarks.

"Helping you with Nash's party isn't a burden."

"Of course. You would do anything for your best friend." She begins to gather up her things and stands from the table.

"Wait a minute. What does that mean?" I ask, taking a step toward her, blocking her departure.

"Don't worry about it. In fact, don't worry about me either," she says with a fierceness in her eyes. "I don't want you hanging around everywhere I am anymore."

All I can do is stare back at her and wonder what I can possibly do to fix this. Her deep sigh seeps under my skin. I'll be carrying it with me as a reminder of how bad I've managed to screw everything up between us.

"Can we just get through this and go our separate ways?" she asks.

"I don't want to do that."

"Maybe it's time you start bossing around someone new. Here." She pushes her coffee cup into my chest. "Start with her. She looks like she might like it."

Sydney walks toward the exit but I'm right on her heels. I stop by the trash can and make a show of draining the coffee and tossing it in the trash.

It doesn't take me long to spot Syd in the parking lot. I slide in between cars and manage to reach her as she opens her door. I drop my forearm on the roof of her car and keep the door open with the other, essentially caging her in.

The air thickens between us as we both stare at each other waiting for the other one to say something. I know I need to speak first.

"You used to like me bossing you around," I say, leaning closer to her beautiful face.

"Once. A long time ago. It won't happen again."

"Why's that?" I ask, not thinking straight. Being this close to her has me opening my mouth and saying all the wrong things.

She rears her head back. "You can't be serious right now." Her body tremors as she takes a steadying breath. "I guess you forgot. Let me remind you. It's because," she says, pushing me on my chest. I give her the space she's requesting. "I was never enough." Her car door slams shut punctuating her statement.

I was never enough.

Her parting words play on repeat as I stand in the parking lot watching her drive away. Is this what she's thought all these years? That she wasn't enough? That couldn't be further from the truth.

An oversized SUV honks a horn forcing me to move so they can have her vacated spot. Walking back to my car, I know things have to change. I can't let her go another day thinking she wasn't enough.

FICTION FORUM

NotYourAverageJoe19

How was the rest of your day?

Did you start reading your new books?

FaeAtHeart

It was good. Great actually.

NotYourAverageJoe19

Oh yeah? All because your friend bought you books?

FaeAtHeart

No. I got some good news I've been waiting for.

NotYourAverageJoe19

That's great.

FaeAtHeart

All of my friends have been busy making plans for after graduation. It's nice to know I have something to look forward to.

GINGER WALLS

NotYourAverageJoe19

What are you going to be doing?

FaeAtHeart

Did I tell you about my dream?

NotYourAverageJoe19

Maybe. Tell me again.

FaeAtHeart

Okay. Well, I want to start my own makeup company. Everything from lotions and cleansers to eyeshadows and lipsticks.

NotYourAverageJoe19

That sounds like something you would love doing.

FaeAtHeart

It does?

NotYourAverageJoe19

So the good news is about that?

FaeAtHeart

Yeah, there's a company I reached out to with the same values as me. They are open to answering a few questions and mentoring me.

NotYourAverageJoe19

That's great. Congratulations.

FOUL TERRITORY

FaeAtHeart
> Thanks. Do you have plans for after you graduate?

NotYourAverageJoe19
> I think so. There are a few places interested in hiring me.

FaeAtHeart
> Will you be moving out of Alabama?

NotYourAverageJoe19
> It seems most likely.

FaeAtHeart
> Do you have a preference on where you end up living?

NotYourAverageJoe19
> No. There's only one factor that has an impact on my decision.

9

SYDNEY

"Are you nervous?" Joe asks as we wait for the clerk to collect the bowling shoes we requested.

Glancing over at the lanes full of bowlers and hearing the clinking and banging noise of bowling balls hitting the pins, my palms begin to sweat. "I am. The last time I went bowling the ball bounced over into the next lane."

His eyebrows furrow together. "Bowling balls don't really bounce."

"Mine did. One of my many talents," I joke, making him grin.

"What other talents do you have?" he asks. After he pays for our shoes, I take my pair off the counter. They should really make these cuter. Maybe brighter colors. The dark red and blue is going to clash with my outfit.

We walk toward a rack of bowling balls. At least I can pick one of these that will match. Not that I'm vain about it. I just appreciate color coordination.

"I'm pretty crafty," I reply hoping he will remember the comment I made in one of our chats awhile back.

"Is that so?" His eyes travel from my shoes to the top of my head. I'm wearing another set of hair clips I made and matching earrings. My thrifted jeans have colorful hand embroidered flowers on the back pockets. It was another project I had to try after watching a video online. They turned out pretty good for my first try.

"I did this," I say, turning and showing him the pockets of jeans. I wince, realizing I'm telling him to essentially check out my ass.

"You did a good job." He flicks his tongue over his bottom lip.

These jeans make ass look almost as good as my leggings do. *Or maybe I just have a nice ass.* I never really thought of that before.

"Do you know what size you need?" he asks, nodding toward the bowling balls in the rack.

"Hmm...I think maybe this one." I point at the only hot pink one left.

"Solid choice. Follow me. We're at the far lane," he says after picking out his own ball.

Even with its close location to campus, the bowling alley is a lot busier than I expected it to be. "Are there always this many people here?" I ask, as we weave our way through a crowd of people by the snack bar.

"Not all the time. But on the nights we all come out and play it can get crowded. Once a month we have a mini bowling tournament. It's supposed to be for fun but we're a competitive group."

I shuffle the bowling ball until I have it cradled securely in my arms. "Who's we?" I ask, but the words die on my lips when I see my brother and his friends at the lane next to ours.

"A bunch of us from the athletic department." He drops his ball in the return and reaches out for mine. "Is this okay?"

"Yeah of course." I smile assuringly. Who doesn't want to spend their first date with their little brother as the third wheel? It's not like this hasn't been happening my entire life.

I find an empty chair and switch out my shoes.

"Hi, I'm Sydney," I tell the girl sitting beside me.

"Julia. You're here with Joe?"

"Yeah. What about you?"

"I work with these guys."

"Lucky," I remark, glancing around. I recognize several football players sitting with Nash along with a few of his friends on the soccer team. Behind me I'm almost certain are players of both basketball teams.

"It does make the day go by faster. It also makes every one of these guys off limits." She laughs when I pout. "Don't be too sad for me. I'm biding my time. In a few months, I'll graduate and they'll be free game," she says with a wink.

"You would like my friend Charlie. The two of you would have fun trading dating tips and secrets."

"She sounds like my kind of girl."

I chat with Julia while Joe greets all of his friends and helps set up the game. There are six of us in this lane. Nash and his three friends are using the lane on our right.

"Hey Jules," Joe says, taking a seat beside me. She gives him a brief wave. "You're bowling fourth. Should I warn everyone about your arm?" he whispers to me.

"Very funny." I slap his leg. He takes the opportunity to hold my hand and balance it on his knee. It's a little awkward but the gesture is nice. *I think.*

Nash steps up to the ball return in his lane. He's laughing with his friend Gage when he notices me sitting here. His smile dims when he sees me holding hands with Joe. I knew he didn't really want me to go out with him. I'm not going to let Nash ruin my date or my mission.

I don't know how I'm going to be able to find out if Joe is *my Joe* online while we're bowling but I've got to try. He didn't take my bait with the creativity thing. I'll need to try a different angle.

"This isn't what you expected for our first date is it?" he asks.

"It's fine. Fun I mean. It's fine and fun." I smile awkwardly. "I admit I wasn't expecting a group thing but this is cool. Julia is nice and we can talk and get to know each other in between turns."

"We can definitely do that," he says, giving my hand a quick squeeze before letting it go. "My turn."

"Good luck."

Joe jokes around with a few of his friends on his walk up to the lane. With perfect form, he easily knocks down nine pins on his first try. He tosses a confident smile in my direction.

I sit on the edge of my seat as he stares down his last pin. He sends the bowling ball pummeling down the lane. I think for sure he's going to miss the pin, but at the last minute the ball curls and knocks it down.

I jump from my chair clapping and let out a little scream. "How did you do that?" I ask after he's finished being congratulated by all of his friends.

"Lots of practice. It's your turn, babe. Are you ready?"

My insides jolt at the word babe. He says the term so casually it holds no meaning. It doesn't make me feel special but more like another '*babe*' on his roster.

When Koa called me baby my heart rate increased, my knees went weak, and damn if it didn't turn me on. My body didn't get the memo that it was all fake.

"Ready as I'll ever be." I retrieve my ball and get a feel for it in my hands. Swinging my arm back and forth a few times until someone stops me. Looking over my shoulder I see Joe with a playful smile on his lips.

"You almost took me out," he teases.

"Sorry." I wince.

"Do you want help?" he asks.

I stare down the lane for a moment. "I think I got it. You just throw the ball down there. I can handle that."

"Good luck, babe." He squeezes my shoulder while I try not to visibly cringe. *Is it rude to ask him to stop calling me that?*

I line myself up in the center of the lane, shuffle my feet to the line, wind my arm back, and let the ball go. It lands with a hard bounce and slowly rolls down the lane. It has just enough momentum to get to the pins before falling into the gutter. *Damn*.

"You got this," Joe shouts from his seat. He takes a slow sip of his beer.

"Didn't expect to see you here tonight," Nash says from his lane.

"I didn't either." I sigh.

"He must not know you very well if he took you bowling," Nash snickers, picking up his bowling ball. I yank mine off the return and cradle it with two hands. It's not heavy. I've carried books bigger than this before. It's just awkward. I'm not trying to break my toe.

"I know you aren't educated in the aspect of dating, seeing as you've never had a girlfriend. Usually on dates that's when you get to know each other. Furthermore, a lot of people like to surprise the other person on their first date with something fun to do."

"As long as you're having fun. Why don't you try to knock down a pin this time?" he jokes as I set myself up at the line. Maybe if I start here I can throw it harder. "Oh and Sydney," he says. I glance at my brother over my shoulder. "Stay in your lane."

Nash can be such a jerk sometimes. It was at Koa's fourteenth birthday party when my ball went bouncing across the lane like a rock skipping over lake water.

When you're trying to get the cute boy to notice you, that is not the way to do it. I was so embarrassed. Koa was the only one not laughing. He was mad. I guess I ruined his party and he probably didn't want me there in the first place. I was the only girl thanks to big sister benefits. A nice little pity invite.

I throw this ten pound ball as hard as I can, picturing Nash's head as the pins. I don't even care if I knock anything down. That felt good. I walk away before the ball even makes it down the lane.

There is a bunch of clattering behind me. Joe's eyes go wide. "Holy shit, babe! You knocked them all down." He lifts me up and spins me around just in time to see the pins being swept off the lane.

"I did it! Oh my god!"

"You did." Our eyes lock for a moment and his green eyes search mine. He leans forward slightly. He isn't going to kiss me for the first time here? In the middle of a bowling alley? In front of my brother?

"Alright, break it up," Julia says, moving us out of the way. "Let me get in here and show you how it's really done." Julia pats my arm and gives me a nod. Did she notice the panic in my eyes?

"Show us what those magic hands of yours can do Jules," Gage says, biting down on his lower lip.

Joe ushers me to a table just outside the bowling area. "I ordered you a beer and some food. I wasn't sure what you liked so I got a little bit of everything."

"This is great. Thanks." I gladly take a sip of the beer. I'm not much of a beer drinker but at this point, I'm not going to be choosy. I need something to calm my nerves.

"We have a few minutes before it's our turn again. What do you want to talk about?" he asks, grabbing a slice of pizza for himself.

"Oh um." I take a plate and add a slice of pizza and a few fries. "When did you start bowling?"

"My granddad was part of a league. I spent the summers with him when I was younger. I guess all his lessons stuck with me."

"That's sweet. I got my infatuation with crafting and making things from my grandmother. She was really big into decoupage."

"Decoupage?" he questions. "I've never heard of it before."

"It's when—" I start to say but someone else begins to talk over me.

"You take pieces of paper and glue them on to different objects to decorate them or create art," Koa says.

The sound of his voice coils around my heart and squeezes in an attempt to bring it back to life. Suddenly it feels wrong to be sitting here next to Joe with his arm draped over the back of my chair.

"When did you become so well versed with arts and crafts?" Joe jokes with him. Koa doesn't seem amused.

"Never. I'm well versed in her." He nods in my direction. His admission shocks me. It's unexpected. Why is he pretending he knows me so well when we barely have conversations anymore? I have more conversations with myself than I do Koa. What is he trying to prove?

"Oh, right, you and her brother are friends." Joe's thumb grazes against my shoulder. I fidget in my seat. Koa stares at Joe's hand like the protector and watch dog he has always been. He looks like he is ready to tear his entire arm off.

"We are," he replies.

"Maybe you should go say hi," I suggest. Koa ignores me and pulls out a seat across from me.

"I'm good here." He reaches across the table and lifts my beer to his mouth. I gasp. "You don't like beer," he says with a shrug.

"You should have said something. What do you like?" Joe stands.

"I like beer just fine," I assure him. Koa huffs a quick laugh. "It's your turn next anyway. Don't worry about it." I take my beer back from Koa and drink the rest of it. "See? It's delicious." Or is it better knowing Koa's lips were pressed against this glass before mine?

"After my turn, I'll get you something else, babe." He squeezes the top of my shoulder before leaving to take his turn.

"What are you doing here?" I ask Koa once Joe is out of earshot.

"Well, *babe*, last I checked this was a public bowling alley."

"I thought we agreed to plan Nash's party and stay away from each other." I glance over at Joe. He's getting ready to throw his second ball.

"I don't remember agreeing to anything," he replies.

My teeth grind as I stand from my seat. Why is he here? Why is he purposely making this harder for me? I can't focus on forming a relationship with someone new when he's here reminding me of everything from my past. *Our past*.

I feel Koa's eyes on me the entire walk to the lane. I hastily grab my ball but take my time setting up my shot. I feel more confident than I did the first time. *I can do this*.

This time I picture Koa's face on all the pins. Unfortunately the ball slips out of my fingers before I'm ready and bounces straight into the gutter. A few people laugh, bringing me right back to Koa's birthday party years ago.

I'm once again trying to impress a boy that will never see me. Except he does now. Koa watches me with concern. Like I'm this fragile thing that will break at any moment.

With my sights set on the front door, I walk past the ball return.

"Where are you going?" Joe stops me before I can get too far. "Ignore them. You get another chance. It's all for fun anyway. No need to get so worked up."

"I know. I just need a minute," I say through clenched teeth, willing myself not to cry. It's too much. I already feel silly for having this freak out moment over the situation. Joe reminding me that it's for fun isn't helping me feel better.

"What about your turn?"

"Just throw it in the gutter. That's probably where it would go anyway. I'll be right back."

Ignoring the worry etched on Nash's face, I push my way past oversized athletes and other bowlers having a night of fun, avoiding eye contact with everyone until I reach the front doors.

I breathe in the cool night air. It feels good on my warm skin. All the attention was making me feel flush. I lean against the brick facade. How long can I stay out here until it's beyond awkward?

My body straightens when Koa pushes through the front door with my shoes in hand. I want to be mad but I'm actually grateful. I'm definitely done bowling for the night.

"I told them you weren't feeling well and I was taking you home. I'll text Nash to take your bowling shoes inside once we've left."

"I'm on a date. I can't just leave. It's rude."

"I let him know," he says evenly. The slight tick in his jaw makes me believe there is something he isn't telling me.

"He didn't want to say goodbye?" I ask. He doesn't say anything as he stares at me. "What did he say?"

"He said '*okay*.'"

"That's it?" I can't hide my disappointment. The Joe online wouldn't have let me walk out on our date. And if I insisted, he would be out here with me. I should go back inside and finish my inquisition. I need to know if it's him or not. *You already know it's not him.*

He confirms with a slow nod. "He's not good enough for you."

"You don't know anything about him and you definitely don't know what type of man would be good for me." I snatch my shoes out of his hand. I slide my left foot out of the rented shoe and shimmy it back into mine.

I hop on one foot as I attempt to balance and tie my sneaker. Koa grabs the back of my heel and places my foot on his thigh. "I know that if I were him I would have followed you," he says as he ties the laces.

His hands should be too big for this task but he does it with ease. He switches my feet and it knocks me off balance forcing me to grab his shoulders. His hands freeze in the middle of making a double loop. Maybe I should remove my hands. It's clear he doesn't want me touching him.

"I would have made sure you were okay. I wouldn't have let another man do it. That's for damn sure." He tugs hard on my laces, tightening them on the top of my feet.

"You're such a prince. I'm sure that's exactly what you would do for your date." I push off his shoulders. I'm feeling more confident with both of my feet back on solid ground.

"I'm here for you now, aren't I?"

"We both know why you're here."

A smug smile distorts his full lips. "And why's that?" He crosses his arms over his muscular chest waiting for me to answer the obvious.

"Nash. He was worried and sent you out here."

Koa grunts a derisive laugh. This seems to be the only way he knows how to laugh anymore. At least around me.

"I'm not your brother's lap dog. I don't heel to his commands. He didn't ask me to do anything. I saw the panic in your eyes. I made the call to find you." He tips my chin with his hand to get me to look at him. "I'm here because I wanted to make sure you were okay. I'm here for you because I want to be. Not because anyone asked me to."

His eyes soften around the edges. A silent plea for me to believe him. I have no reason not to, other than it contradicts every conclusion I've come to as to why he chooses to do certain things for me.

Any other time we're in this same situation I was told he was sent by Nash. Excuse me for being a little skeptical.

"Thank you for bringing me my shoes. As you can see I'm fine." A breeze wraps around us, blowing some of my hair over my face. I try to shake it back but it doesn't work.

He lifts his hand, his fingers grazing the side of my face as pushes my hair aside. I hate myself for closing my eyes and enjoying his touch. I add it to the list of memories that will continue to haunt me at night.

"Good. I'm going home. Do you want a ride or are you going back inside?" he asks. I should finish my date and see if there is anything salvageable. I'm afraid I already know the answer.

Joe is just another man who will never measure up.

"Take me home."

Koa opens the passenger door to his Camaro and waits until I'm safely inside before walking around the front of the car. For a brief moment I think about what it would be like if this was our date and he was really taking me home.

My heart races and butterflies go wild in my belly, but then I remember that isn't my reality and it never will be.

FICTION FORUM

FaeAtHeart
Do you have any siblings?

NotYourAverageJoe19
Yes.

FaeAtHeart
Do they ever get in your business and try to ruin your life?

NotYourAverageJoe19
Not as much as they used to. They're older and have lives of their own. I'm just the fun uncle to their kids.

I'm guessing you don't have the same type of relationship with your sibling?

FaeAtHeart
No, I don't. My brother is a gold medalist at inserting himself in my life.

It's not just him. He's enlisted his friends too.

GINGER WALLS

NotYourAverageJoe19
> I'm sure they all mean well.

FaeAtHeart
> Maybe.
>
> Can I ask you something?

NotYourAverageJoe19
> You can ask me anything.

FaeAtHeart
> I don't know what's happening between you and me. Maybe nothing. Maybe it's something. I don't want to hurt you by what I'm about to say.

NotYourAverageJoe19
> It's okay. I'm tougher than you think. You'd be surprised what I've been through emotionally over the last few years.

FaeAtHeart
> I had a date tonight.

NotYourAverageJoe19
> Ouch. You went on a date without me?

FaeAtHeart
> It was terrible. I would have preferred to go on a date with you. But you aren't here. Or are you?

NotYourAverageJoe19
> I could be. I might be closer than you think.

FOUL TERRITORY

FaeAtHeart
> Don't tease me.

NotYourAverageJoe19
> Tell me about your date. What does that have to do with your brother?

FaeAtHeart
> Do you really want to know?

NotYourAverageJoe19
> Yes. Just don't get mad if I get jealous over this guy being able to take you out and I can't.

FaeAtHeart
> I'll keep that in mind.
>
> Are you comfortable?

NotYourAverageJoe19
> Yeah. I'm good.

FaeAtHeart
> I'm probably going to embarrass myself by telling you this but you need to know the whole story to understand why the date was doomed from the start.
>
> When I was a teenager I really liked this boy. He was one of my closest friends at one point.

GINGER WALLS

> Then he became friends with my brother and it felt like a lot of what we had went away. The two of them became inseparable.

> They were best friends.

NotYourAverageJoe19

> You weren't friends with the other boy anymore?

FaeAtHeart

> I was but it was never the same. Sometimes it felt like I was kept around by default because of his new friendship with my brother instead of the friendship I thought we had. Anyway, I was invited to his birthday party.

NotYourAverageJoe19

> I bet he liked you too. He was probably too shy to admit it. Or maybe he was afraid.

FaeAtHeart

> You don't have to make me feel better. It was obvious he didn't.

NotYourAverageJoe19

> How?

FaeAtHeart

> The only way to describe it is that he was cold to me. We were friends first. Really good friends.

> As our personal interest evolved, so did his interest in me. It was clear something had shifted

FOUL TERRITORY

> between us. He didn't hide his feelings about me very well.

NotYourAverageJoe19

> When I was a teenager I didn't know how to express my feelings. Maybe that was his problem too. He liked you but didn't know how to tell you.

> He might have been in a tough spot since he was also your brother's friend.

FaeAtHeart

> We aren't defending him. He was my friend first. He knew I struggled making friends and he proved to be like everyone else.

> Using me to get what they wanted.

> It wasn't until I met my roommate in college when I felt like I finally had someone on my side again.

NotYourAverageJoe19

> I'm sorry.

FaeAtHeart

> You have nothing to be sorry about.

> Anyway, at his birthday party I wanted to impress him but instead I made a fool out of myself. The same thing happened tonight.

GINGER WALLS

NotYourAverageJoe19

You wanted to impress your date?

FaeAtHeart

No. I wanted to impress him. My crush from when I was a kid. He showed up. I wanted…

I wanted him to see that I'm doing fine without him.

NotYourAverageJoe19

Are you doing fine without him?

FaeAtHeart

Most days.

10

SYDNEY

"What's all of this?" Lauren asks, lifting up one of the dresses I've pulled from my closet.

"I'm picking out my outfit for Nash's party." I flip through my closet until I see something that remotely says Hawaiian or tropical. My options are limited since most of my clothes are back at home.

"We still have two weeks. What's the rush?" She sits on my bed crossing her legs.

"Koa's coming over to help me decide my final look. This was the only day he was free." He gruffly reminded me last night when he dropped me off after my date that his schedule is packed with games as they get closer to the playoffs and if I was serious about having him help me it needed to happen today.

"Why is Koa picking out your outfit? Doesn't seem like something either one of you would volunteer for."

"I wouldn't but he pissed me off. He made a comment about how the outfit I wear to Nash's party shouldn't be distracting."

She gasps. "And he's still breathing?"

"For now." I drop the hot pink bodycon dress on my bed and walk over to my dresser. I dig through the second drawer until I find my bathing suit. "I'm secretly hoping this will give him a heart attack." I hold out two different bikinis.

I bought them for spring break but I haven't had the guts to wear them yet. I'm ashamed to admit that Koa's reaction to me wearing them crossed my mind at least once when I picked them out.

The idea of strutting around Nash's birthday party in a bikini holds zero appeal. Trying them on in a private show for Koa? There's something taboo about the idea. I'm off limits, out of bounds. He shouldn't be alone with me like this. Yet we keep toeing the line between what's expected of us and this foul territory where there are no limitations.

"He's going to lose his mind," Lauren says, holding back her laughter. "You're evil for torturing him like this."

I'm not convinced I'm torturing him in the way she thinks I am. I wish I had that kind of control over Koa. "He deserves it. I'm mad. I'm tired of him telling me what to do."

"Yet, you invite him over here to do exactly that."

"No, I invited him over here to prove a point. It doesn't matter what I wear, he'll find something to say about it," I correct her.

"If you model that for him," she points to the bathing suits, "he will definitely have something to say. I doubt all of the words will be coherent, but there will be words. Are you prepared for his reaction?"

"I'll tell him to get over it like I usually do."

"That's not the reaction I'm talking about. I mean the flip you on to the bed or push you up against a wall type of reaction."

"That would never happen." Do I want that? Yes. No. I meant to say no. *The answer is no.* Oh who am I kidding? A part of me does but I know how it will end. I'll be left alone once again wondering why I trusted him with my heart. "Even if I manage to turn him on a little, he would never act on it." The only emotion I've been able to pull out of Koa is anger.

"If you say so," she singsongs. "Is that him? They had an extended practice this morning. He should still be there," she says, after someone knocks a few times on our door.

I glance at the clock on my nightstand. "I know. He should be at least another ten or twenty minutes."

"Maybe it's Charlie. I'll go check. You can keep prepping for your little show," she teases and hops off the bed.

"It's not a show. It's a punishment." Even though I doubt Koa will get turned on, the painstakingly long process of trying all the clothes on will annoy him. That brings me an immense amount of joy.

"It's for you," Lauren says, ducking her head in my room.

I look over her shoulder and my eyes widen. "What is he doing here?" Out of all people, Joe is standing awkwardly in between our kitchen and living room holding a brown paper bag in his hand.

"He didn't say," she whispers before disappearing. "She'll be right out," she tells him before entering her bedroom.

GINGER WALLS

I do a quick mirror check. My lack of makeup is a concern, but at least my bangs cover my newest blemish. I'm still wearing my pajama shorts and tank top. I grab the first sweatshirt I see that's oversized enough to cover me up and throw it on over my head.

I'm a little apprehensive as I walk out of my room and close the door. For some reason, I don't want him to be able to see my personal space. It's weird enough he's here at the dorm.

Joe straightens his posture as I enter the room. His eyes trail over my bare feet and legs, finally landing on my face.

"Hey," I say, walking in his direction. I fumble with the cuffs of the sleeves as they hang over my hands.

"Hi. I'm sorry to show up like this."

"It's fine. I'm a little surprised. After last night, I thought…" I shake my head deciding not to finish the thought.

"Last night I messed up. I wasn't thinking. Koa said he would check on you and take you home and I accepted it. I should have been the one doing that. I'm a day late but I'm checking on you now. I've brought breakfast and an apology."

"Tell me what you have in there and I might consider forgiving you."

"I got Nash to help me. He said you really loved the chopped smoked salmon bagel from The Round Table," he says, lifting the brown bag.

I stack our mail and a few books I've left covering the small breakfast bar in our kitchen and push the clutter to the side. "Have a seat." I gesture toward one of the bar stools.

He digs two bagel sandwiches out of the bag while I get us both a glass of water.

"Your brother knows you well," he says, watching me savor the first bite of the delicious bagel.

"He does. But you didn't come over here to talk about my brother."

"I didn't. I handled everything wrong last night. I'm really sorry. When Nash explained why you were so upset, I realized I should have done more. You were joking about the incident from your childhood. If I had known how hurt it made you, I would have told them to cut it out."

"I appreciate it. To be honest, I didn't expect to panic like that either. It kind of came out of nowhere." I probably wouldn't have if Koa wasn't there. He is the catalyst for most of my emotions.

"Are you doing okay now?" He wipes the corner of his mouth with a napkin and crumples it in his hand.

"I am much better. I don't think I'll be going bowling for a while, but I'm good. I'm sorry for leaving the way I did. I was embarrassed."

"I understand but your gutter ball was long forgotten when Trevor got a little overzealous and threw the ball so hard he slipped and fell flat on his back."

"He didn't?" I gasp.

"Oh he did. I think Julia has it on video. I'll ask her to send it to you."

"Poor guy. But also, please do," I say, making him laugh. When I take a bite of my bagel, too much tears off forcing me to lean forward to avoid a mess. I attempt to gracefully chew the oversized bite.

"I will." He glances at me. "You have…" He points to my face. I wipe at the cream cheese or whatever it is on my face with my finger. "Let me," he offers when I miss it.

His thumb tenderly grazes the corner of my mouth. My eyes stay locked on him and the way he stares at my lips. He lifts his eyes to mine before dropping back to my mouth.

"What did I tell you about locking the door?" Koa scolds, barging into the dorm without knocking and startling me.

"Got it," Joe says, ignoring Koa's presence.

"What's going on here?" Koa asks, his eyes bouncing between me and Joe.

"I brought Sydney breakfast. What are you doing here?" Joe counters. "I didn't realize you two were the type of friends who had an open door policy." His tone is laced with irritation.

"We aren't," I say.

"I don't know about that. Not too long ago you let yourself in my house and were waiting for me to get home," Koa says.

"That is not what I was doing and you know it," I seethe. Koa smirks and that angers me further. "Besides the fact that he lives with my brother, my roommate is dating Hart," I explain to Joe. "I was there with Lauren helping her make dinner."

"You helped? If that's the case, why didn't the house catch fire? She struggles making toast. Good thing you decided to order in this morning." Koa reaches across the counter and tears a piece of my bagel in half and stuffs it in his mouth. "This is good," he says, licking his thumb.

"Room. Now," I demand. I am beyond livid with him. He's trying to make me look bad. I wish I knew why. "I'll be in there when I'm done." I glare at him.

I expect him to be mad that I've sent him away. Instead, he smiles and slips off his shoes. "I'll go make myself comfortable. Enjoy the rest of your breakfast."

A growl works itself up in my throat but I swallow it back down. He makes me want to scream.

"Maybe I should go." Joe begins to pack up the rest of his breakfast. He releases a frustrated breath. "Is there something going on with you and Mahina? I like you, Sydney, but I don't play games."

"I don't either. There isn't anything. He's only here to help me plan Nash's birthday party."

"Oh. I didn't know he was having a party." He stands from his seat. I take the trash from him and toss it in the kitchen trash can.

"It's kind of last minute. You'll come, right?" I don't know if I'm inviting him for me or because I know Nash would have put him on the list anyway. "It's going to be a luau theme. I can text you all the details."

"Wyatt is going to enjoy dressing up."

I walk him toward the door. "I'm sure he already has a coconut bra and grass skirt somewhere ready for the occasion."

He chuckles. "Probably. Yeah, I'll be there. What are the odds you'll be wearing a coconut bra?" he jokes.

"Slim to none I'm afraid."

"Whatever you wear, you'll look beautiful."

"That's sweet. Thank you. And thanks for breakfast, too, even though Koa ruined it."

"That's my fault. I should have called first."

"Well, it was a nice surprise." I open the front door.

Joe moves to step outside but stops and kisses my cheek first. "I'll text you later."

"Sounds good." I close the door and lock it this time. Leaning against the front door, I take a moment to get my head on straight before I deal with Koa.

Joe is a nice guy. Koa shouldn't have made it look like something is going on between the two of us when he's made it clear he's not interested. I push off the door, determined to put Koa in his place.

"You have some nerve," I say as I open my bedroom door. Those are the only words I'm able to speak before I lose my ability to think straight.

Koa has pushed all my clothes to one side of my full size bed and stretched his mammoth body out on the other side. He has one hand tucked under his head and the other rests on his lower abs where his shirt has risen up exposing enough skin to have me salivating like a Saint Bernard.

Damn him for being so attractive. He's only gotten better looking over the years. His once round face has become more square and defined. His bronze skin gets covered in more ink every year which highlights his defined muscles.

It's just rude. All of him is just fucking rude.

"Why are you trying to ruin my relationship with Joe?"

"You need to water your plants," he says, ignoring my question. I glance at my bookshelf and assess the health of my plants. I hate that he's right. The one he bought me is on the brink of death. How ironic?

"I asked you a question. Why are you sabotaging my dates all of a sudden? Last night and now this morning."

"I didn't do anything. I came over at our agreed upon time. You should be saying sorry to me. You double booked yourself. That wasn't very thoughtful," he says with an undertone of sadness. I can tell he's faking by the way the muscles in his jaw ticks.

"That isn't what happened. He just showed up. He wanted to apologize for last night."

"That's the least he should have done," he mumbles with his eyes still closed.

"Can we get this over with please? I'm sure we both have better things to do. You clearly need a nap." I reach over his legs and grab a small sample of the clothes I've pulled out of my closet. I tap the top of his thigh. "Scoot over. What?" I ask when I notice him staring at me.

He sits and swings his legs to the floor. "This is what you wore in front of him," he says, lifting the hem of my sweatshirt and exposing my sleep shorts.

I swat his hand away. "You know I did. What do you think of this dress?" I ask, holding up a flowy halter top dress.

"You look like you aren't wearing any shorts underneath the sweatshirt."

"Why does that matter?" I walk across the room and hang the dress back up in my closet. "I know I'm covered up. It's no different than wearing a dress. What I wear is really no one else's business."

I hold up another dress. It's even shorter than the last one. Koa shakes his head and I put it to the side.

"It matters because it gives people ideas. It makes them wonder if you're wearing shorts, underwear, or nothing," he says, staring at my bare legs.

"That sounds like a personal problem."

"It definitely is," he mutters.

Is he suggesting it's a personal problem for him? Or is he agreeing with me that it's a problem for whoever is looking?

I pull my arms through the sleeves of my sweatshirt and lift it over my head. "There. Now you won't have to wonder what I'm wearing."

His gaze roams over my bare arms, shoulders, and chest, leaving a trail of heat behind. My breathing deepens causing my breasts to rise and fall, attracting even more of his attention. My nipples pebble as the atmosphere in the room shifts.

Koa curses and scrubs a hand over his face. "This isn't any better. Can you put something else on?" His eyes meet mine. "Please."

Letting out a sigh, I search through the clothes some more. "I'll try on one of these. I can't promise you'll like them either."

"Can't get worse."

"No? Not even this?" I hold up one of the bikinis I haven't had the nerve to wear.

"Cute."

Cute isn't exactly the response I was hoping for. I don't expect Koa to suddenly have a change of heart about me, but a small sign that the fierce attraction I felt for him years ago was never one-sided would be nice. I feel like he was able to get over me in one night. He got what he wanted and he was done.

Turning to my mirror, I tie the bikini top around my neck over my tank top, keeping a watchful eye on Koa in the reflection. His nostrils flare and his fingers dig into his knees. I hold up the bikini bottoms and twist side to side.

"You're right. This would be really cute. I could get a *cute* little sarong to wrap around my waist." I remove the bikini top and clutch the suit in one hand. "Thanks for your help. This was easier than I thought it was going to be."

"Wear that to the party at your own risk," he says, clenching his jaw.

"Don't mind if I do. It's not like I'd be the only person dressed like this anyway. People need to learn how to control themselves."

Koa reacts so fast I don't even realize he's grabbed me and I've moved until I'm standing in between his legs. His large hands smother my hips as he gives them a gentle squeeze. "I have spent years being in control. I could teach a master class on it. Especially when it comes to being in the same room as you."

He leans closer to my face, stealing my breath. My clit starts to tingle and pulse as he draws me into his web. I'm pretty sure it's sending Morse code to my brain. *S.O.S. Mayday. Mayday. Abort. Abort.*

"Don't push me Sydney. I'm not sure you can handle the consequences."

"What are the consequences?" My question is barely a whisper. It floats through the short distance between us.

His face remains emotionless but his body hums with power. I've seen Koa like this once before. It ended with him gifting me my first man made orgasm and the best sexual experience I've ever had still to this day.

"Something that you won't be able to stop once it gets started."

Why is he speaking to me in riddles? What does that mean?

He begins to stand, pushing me out of his way as he goes. The air once again shifts in the room. Suddenly it's a lot cooler than before.

He sifts through the pile of clothes on the bed, until he finds the piece of clothing he's looking for. Folding it neatly, he passes it to me. "Wear this one. You always smile more when you have it on." He pauses. His lips twitch as if there's more he wants to say.

"I'll keep that under consideration. Let me know the headcount when you have it. I need to know how much food to order."

He nods and then silently walks out the door.

My fingers trace over the bright floral pattern on my favorite dress. I don't put a ton of thought into the clothes I buy. If the clothes are designed with bright colors or patterns and made with comfortable fabric, I usually buy them.

This dress is like a cape of confidence. It's the one that makes me feel most like myself when I wear it. It speaks to my hippie soul I don't let a lot of people see.

But he still does.

FICTION FORM

NotYourAverageJoe19

I'm tired.

FaeAtHeart

Stay up too late last night?

NotYourAverageJoe19

Not physically tired.

Emotionally.

FaeAtHeart

Do you want to talk about it? I'm a pretty good listener.

NotYourAverageJoe19

I've gotten really good at hiding my feelings but it's exhausting.

Feeling one way but forcing myself to act another in order to keep everyone happy.

GINGER WALLS

> **FaeAtHeart**
> You don't sound very happy right now.

NotYourAverageJoe19
> I'm not.

> **FaeAtHeart**
> Then stop.

NotYourAverageJoe19
> If I do, there will be backlash.

> **FaeAtHeart**
> Fuck the backlash. You aren't doing anyone any favors by not being honest.

NotYourAverageJoe19
> What if I hurt the people I love because of my honesty?

> **FaeAtHeart**
> If they love you, they would want you to be happy too.
>
> Are you sure everyone is happy? Maybe they're good at hiding their feelings too. It's possible they're just pretending to be happy. You should tell them how you really feel.

NotYourAverageJoe19
> You make it sound like it's an easy thing to do.

FOUL TERRITORY

> FaeAtHeart
> It isn't, but you can do it.
>
> Practice on me. Tell me how you feel…when you get a message from me.

NotYourAverageJoe19
> Do you remember when Aster wrote the first letter to Vincent?

> FaeAtHeart
> The one that made him realize she was his fated mate?

NotYourAverageJoe19
> Yeah. It feels like that.

11

KOA

"How's the planning going for Nash's party? Are you and Syd playing nice?" Hart asks as we run laps around the field before practice starts.

"We're making it work." If you could call her giving me orders via text, and icing me out from the rest of her life making things work. She's been colder than usual lately. It makes me think the moment in her bedroom got to her as much as it did me. I was very close to showing her what would happen if I lost control.

The fact she is opening up to a stranger on the internet more than me is showing me just how much work I have ahead of me if I want to get her back. And I do want her back.

"The party is this weekend."

"I'm aware." The last week flew by with all our away games and classes. I hardly had any time to construct a plan to get back in her good graces. It didn't stop the memory of her in her tiny sleep shorts and tank top from playing on an endless loop in my mind.

I can still feel the softness of her hips in my hands and her warm vanilla scent still lingers in the air reminding me what it felt like to be close to her, even if it was only for a moment.

I admire her in the stands as we make the final stretch down the third base line on our last lap. She has her hair braided and twisted on the top of her head and a handmade headband keeping her bangs off of her face. She's wearing another pair of loose patterned pants and a cropped shirt.

She is temptation personified.

"I'm surprised Syd showed up today," I say, lifting the front of my workout tank and wiping the sweat off my face and head as we walk into the dugout.

"Lauren made her come. She said something about us not having very many practices left and coming to them is not the same without her. They also need to work out the details about the food for the party."

It makes sense that it took Lauren strong-arming her to get her to show up. She's been coming to our practices less and less since the new semester started.

She claims her classes and the extra hours spent in the lab are taking up more of her time but I know she's been avoiding me as much as possible. I hate it, but I'm not mad at her for it. It's my fault.

I tend to run cold or colder with her. When you love someone you can't be with, it's hard to know how to react around them. When we're together my natural instinct is to touch her. I want to hold her hand, kiss her forehead, wrap my arms around her waist, and breathe her in until she is my only source of oxygen.

But I can't because I promised her brother I wouldn't. At thirteen, I didn't think anything of it. It was a decision that allowed me to stay friends with both of the Pierce siblings.

It worked for awhile but as we got older and baseball took over more of my life, I could feel Sydney slipping further away. She retreated more to herself, focusing on getting her scholarship to Newhouse.

And me...I waited as long as I could until I couldn't take it anymore. I didn't go to her graduation night with the intention of having sex. I wanted to talk to her. I barely had the chance to say two words to her the whole night.

She looked like a dream laid out on her bed. All I could think about was making her mine permanently. Instead I held her for as long as I could before everything went to shit in the morning.

I take a long sip of my water and grab all of my catching gear before heading back out on the field for drills. Hart hops over the barricade into the stands to talk to Lauren while I head to the sideline to stretch.

Taking a seat in the grass, I lean back on my hands and bend my knees at a ninety degree angle. Moving my knees from left to right, I warm up the joints in my hips. Then I stretch out over one knee and repeat the process on the other side.

Every time I come out of my stretching position, I catch Sydney watching me. Her tongue flicks out between her lips and her eyes glaze over in a sultry stare.

I hold back my smirk. I guess it's good she at least likes what she sees even if she doesn't like me. I have to take the wins when I can from her.

I might as well give her a little show if she wants to watch. I face the infield and give Sydney and everyone else in the stands my back. Bending over I touch my toes, then drop into a squat. I press my elbows into my inner thighs and stretch until it burns. Then I grab the sides of my cleats and straighten my legs. I repeat this for a few sets of a ten until it feels like my limbs are loose.

I glance over my shoulder, pretending to look at something in the dugout, and make sure I still have Sydney's attention. She has her phone out, typing away, but I wouldn't be surprised if it's alphabet soup on her notes app because her eyes are glued to my ass.

Good. Getting down on my knees, I slide from knee to knee mimicking the same motions I would catching pitches on either side of the plate. I spread my knees apart and alternate stretching out my legs with each pass. I'm close enough to the ground I'm practically humping the grass.

What I wouldn't give to have Sydney underneath me instead. Now is not the time to be thinking about sinking my cock into her. I don't need the guys to notice and talk shit about warmups making me hard.

"You ready?" Wyatt asks. He readjusts his hat and pulls at the black hairband he's wearing on his wrist. "Or do you need some more alone time with the grass?"

"I'm good. Are you warmed up?" I pick up my chest protector, throw it over my head and clip it on.

"Yeah. I threw the ball around for a bit with Miller."

"Good. We need to win out the rest of the season if we're going to make it to the playoffs."

"I know," he says, annoyed with my reminder. Ever since Wyatt came back from spring break he hasn't been in the game like he was before. He still gives his best and plays to win, but his heart isn't in it.

It's almost like he's playing for us and not himself anymore.

"Enzo's been talking more shit. He said they're going to take us out in our last set of games." Enzo plays for Alabama State along with his little brother, Marco. Their dad is a professor here at Newhouse and they decided to attend one of our rival schools to put some distance between them and their dad.

"They could do it." Wyatt throws the ball into his glove as we walk toward the pitching mound.

"We aren't going to let them." I want another championship. I love my friends but I'm not willing to hand them the win. They will have to fight us for it.

"No we aren't," he agrees with a curt nod.

I put my helmet on and pull the mask down over my face. I take my place behind the plate and it feels like coming home. This is where I feel the most comfortable.

I was six years old when I put catching gear on for the first time. My dad wanted me to play in the outfield or first base like he did in high school.

But I loved the idea of being behind the plate. I liked having my eyes on the entire field. A lot of people think the pitcher is the one who controls the game, but I have to disagree.

I see what's happening behind the pitcher's back. Like when a runner is going to steal a base. I hear what a batter mutters when he swings and misses. I can figure out what pitch will send his confidence reeling and have him striking or fouling out.

Behind the mask, I don't have to hide my emotions. No one can see what I'm feeling based on the look on my face. Like right now, looking up at Sydney, I can smile at her and enjoy the way her hair blows in the breeze.

She has no idea how many of my smiles she owns.

Hart steps into the batter's box and I focus back on my job. I give Wyatt the signal for a fastball right down the center. He shakes it off. I knew he would. Hart would smash it easily out of the park.

"Is he going to give me something I can hit?" Hart asks.

"Probably not." I signal for a slider and Wyatt nods in agreement. Hart manages to get a small piece of it and fouls it off down the line. "Nice try," I say, grabbing a new ball and throwing it to Wyatt.

I signal for the slider again. I want to see if we can get him to swing a second time. Wyatt throws and Hart doesn't move a muscle as the ball lands in my glove.

"I'm not going to fall for that bullshit twice. Tell him to give me something high and fast. I want to see if I can hit the ball down right field."

"Alright." Wyatt doesn't like the call but he throws it anyway. Hart swings hard and the ball flies down the first base line into the corner. It would easily be a double if not a triple.

"Again," he demands. Rolling my eyes, I grab another ball and throw it back to Wyatt. I signal for the same pitch and he shakes me off. I try the signal again and he smirks back at me.

"You saw that right?" I ask Hart.

"Yeah. I'm ready for it."

Wyatt releases a nasty curveball but Hart tracks it efficiently and swings with everything he has. I laugh as Wyatt spins and watches the ball sail out of the stadium.

"Pleasure doing business with you," Hart jokes.

"You got lucky with that one. I practically gave it to you," Wyatt shouts as Hart heads out to the field to trade places with Scott, our backup shortstop.

"Do you want to give it to me again?" Hart pushes back, pointing towards me at home plate.

"Nah, I'd rather wrap this practice up and give something to Birdie." Wyatt turns his attention back to me. Thomas—Wyatt's least favorite teammate—is up at bat. Thomas said something about Wyatt's girlfriend before they got together and he still hasn't let it go.

Wyatt's first pitch is just outside and Thomas reaches for it. I shake my head. He should know better. "You're getting too cocky. You can't hit every ball. Wait for your pitch," I advise him.

"Every pitch is my pitch," he says, before swinging and missing again.

"Is that so? You can't touch his slider and you know it. No one can. That's why he's the best pitcher in our division."

"Then tell him to throw me something I can hit." He digs his cleats into the dirt and tightens his grip on his bat.

"I'd rather not," I say, as I slide on one knee to catch another ball low and on the outside from Wyatt.

"This is bullshit. I'm going to the cages." Thomas storms off the field. Wyatt gives him a goodbye salute and waits for his next victim.

"When are you going to let that shit with Thomas go? It's not good for team morale," I say to Wyatt once we're back in the locker room. After another hour of running drills, I am more than ready to get out of here.

"If he had said something about your girl, it doesn't matter if it was something insignificant, you wouldn't let it go either."

"Sydney would never wear another man's jersey to one of my games in the first place," I say.

Wyatt raises an eyebrow. "Interesting. Very interesting."

"What?" I ask. Hart joins, tossing his bag over his shoulder.

"You said Sydney," Hart states.

"And?"

"Wyatt said *your girl*. He didn't specify who. You did though," Hart explains, smirking.

"It doesn't mean anything," I mutter back, stepping into my locker more so to hide my face than to get my stuff together.

Fuck, I can't believe I let that slip. I know my actions speak louder than my words most days. It's been fairly easy to mask my true intentions behind my actions the last few years but it's starting to become a chore.

I wasn't kidding when I told Sydney I was emotionally exhausted from all of this pretending. Every day it becomes harder to fight against exposing every raw emotion Sydney draws out of me.

"Sure it doesn't," Wyatt jokes, laughing with Hart.

"You weren't even with Wren when she wore his jersey." It's a weak comeback but I've got to try something to get the heat off of me.

"We were together in my heart," he says, dramatically placing a hand over his chest.

"Didn't she still hate you?" Hart asks.

"Birdie never really hated me. It was all an act," he claims, waving a dismissive hand toward Hart.

"Oh yeah? Why don't we go ask her then? I'd love to get her side of the story," I say, lifting my pack onto my shoulder and heading toward the door.

Walking between me and Hart, Wyatt pulls out his phone and starts typing frantically.

"Are you warning her?" Hart asks.

"What? No. I wouldn't do that," Wyatt says, typing another message.

"It's okay. We all know the truth even if you deny it," I say, slapping him on the back.

"We know your truth too." Hart nods toward Sydney and Lauren who are waiting by Lauren's car and talking to Joe.

Protesting will only confirm he's right. Silence is sometimes my best friend. It isn't what I prefer but it's been the only option to keep myself out of trouble.

Right now I would like to tell Joe to hit the pavement and stop trying to make a move on my girl. I may not be obvious to everyone now but she's mine. There isn't another man who will be able to make her happy except for me. I know that for a fact. I just need her to give me an opportunity to show her.

She may be smiling right now at whatever dumbass thing he's saying to her but it's not real. This girl hasn't truly smiled since I dimmed it in the hallway outside her bedroom door. I said something I didn't mean, and before I could correct her she was already walking away and removing me from her life as much as she could.

Wyatt says his goodbye and gets into his truck while Hart pulls Lauren to the side, leaving me awkwardly standing in front of Sydney and Joe.

I'm not thrilled about seeing them together for a third time. Although this is a much easier pill to swallow than seeing him getting cozy with her back at her dorm.

The image of her wearing one of my old sweatshirts still pops up when I close my eyes. She's like one of those optical illusions. The longer I stare at her, she's all I see no matter where I look.

I bet she doesn't even remember I let her borrow that sweatshirt when she was over watching football with us. The temperature dropped unexpectedly and she was shivering on the couch while she was reading.

We didn't have blankets and shit so I offered her a sweatshirt. Seeing her curled up in my clothes is another memory I won't soon forget. Her nose would dip under the neck and I swear she was breathing in my scent.

If she didn't look so fucking good in it the other day, I would've asked for it back. I bet it smells like her now. I would love to take a hit of that every morning. Sydney sitting in her kitchen looking like mine is the only reason I didn't push harder for Joe to leave.

There's no way she is really interested in him. Please let him be another guy wasting his time.

"Syd, can I talk to you for a minute?" I ask. "About Nash's party," I add when I feel she is about to deny me and claim we have nothing to talk about like she usually does.

"We have plans," she replies, taking a step closer in his direction. Her arms are crossed over her chest defiantly.

"It will only take a minute. I won't ruin your *plans*."

Joe's eyes ping pong back and forth between us. "I'll wait for you by my car." He walks away, looking over his shoulder once. Hart and Lauren also say goodbye, leaving me alone with Syd.

"What is it that can't wait?"

"I wanted to make sure you had everything done on your end."

She scoffs and rolls her eyes. "You already know I do. The girls and I are coming over early to decorate and to get the food and drinks organized. If you and the guys can set up everything outside, that would be helpful."

"We can do that. Sounds like everything's coming together. Nash will be happy even if it isn't much of a surprise anymore."

Her back stiffens. "As long as Nash is happy. That's all that matters," she says coldly. "I need to go. I'll see you Saturday."

Sydney's statement doesn't work its way through my brain until she's halfway across the parking lot. She isn't talking about his party.

This is the culmination of all the times Nash's happiness has been prioritized over her own. It's been happening for years. I thought the choices I made were for everyone's best interest and I was the only one paying for it emotionally.

I need her to know she's always come first to me despite what she thinks. Maybe it is time to show her and fuck the consequences like she said. I just hope I'm not too late.

FICTION FORUM

NotYourAverageJoe19

Have you ever wanted to go back in time and do something different?

FaeAtHeart

More than once.

I never would have smiled in my second grade photo if I had known my mom was going to have it framed and put it on the wall for all to see.

NotYourAverageJoe19

Why not?

FaeAtHeart

I'm missing one tooth and the other one was holding on for dear life.

What about you?

NotYourAverageJoe19

Every day.

GINGER WALLS

I thought I was doing the right thing but I'm realizing now it was the wrong choice.

I've been hurting someone I really care about and I'm afraid it's too late to make it up to them.

FaeAtHeart

It's never too late to tell someone you're sorry.

NotYourAverageJoe19

Do you really believe that?

FaeAtHeart

I suppose there could be some betrayals that are unforgivable.

NotYourAverageJoe19

That's what I'm worried about. I don't want to be the villain anymore.

FaeAtHeart

But if your heart was in the right place then I think you should be fine.

You're too sweet to be the villain.

NotYourAverageJoe19

You think I'm sweet?

FaeAtHeart

Very.

FOUL TERRITORY

NotYourAverageJoe19

I never wanted to be the villain in her story.

FaeAtHeart

Her?

12

SYDNEY

Guests for Nash's party should start arriving in the next hour or so. Walking around the main floor of the townhouse, I do one last check to make sure everything is ready.

We spent most of the afternoon putting up decorations and hanging lights both inside and outside on the deck and fence line. It looks like a tropical paradise with palm trees and flowers in every direction.

Not that a bunch of college kids will care about our efforts.

I open the sliding glass door that leads to the back yard and step out onto their small deck. Wyatt and Eli are working on the fire pit with Wren directing them. Gage and Koa are on the other side of the yard setting up the beer pong table and the cornhole boards.

I check the list on my phone one more time. The food and drinks are good. Hart is waiting inside for the pizza delivery. Everything is right on schedule.

"Is there anything else you need us to do?" Gage asks, making his way up the deck stairs with Koa following behind him.

"No. I think we've done all we can until people start showing up. Thanks for all your help." I give him a quick hug.

"Of course. I'm going to go to my place and shower," he says. "Tell Nash I'll be back later and text me if you need me to grab anything on my way over."

Koa leans against the deck railing, glaring at Gage's retreating back as he walks inside the house. If I didn't know better, I would think Koa was jealous.

I don't have time for another one of his little games. I still need to get myself ready for the party. Without sparing him another glance, I turn on my heel and head inside too. Lauren and I are getting ready together in Hart's room.

"I helped too. Don't I get a hug?" he asks, before my hand reaches the handle. "He only helped with the tables and the cornhole. I hung all the lights and helped Wyatt with the wood pile."

"Are we bartering for hugs now?" I ask, turning back toward him. He pushes off the railing.

"Barter. Steal. Beg. What would it take?" The intensity of his eyes steals my breath. I could easily give him the same friendly hug I gave Gage. Standing toe to toe with Koa, my body craves more. One hug wouldn't be enough.

"I would love to see you beg but I'd feel bad if you got a splinter in your knees." Leaning into his chest, I wrap my arms around his shoulders. "Thank you for your help. Nash is going to love it."

His arms go around my waist and up my back. He pulls me into a tight embrace. Instinct has me wanting to melt into him, but I stand my ground. "I did this for you. If I was just doing it for Nash, I would have bought him a gift card and called it a day," he says, his fingers digging deeper into the cotton material of my shirt.

I drop my hands and step out of his arms. "I need to get dressed." I don't know how to respond to his statement. While I'm sure what he's saying is true, I feel like a fool for believing it. Everything is always for Nash. *I think*.

"Are you wearing the dress I picked out for you?" His eyes slowly peruse over the length of my body as if he's picturing me wearing it.

"You'll have to wait and see." I smirk, backing away toward the sliding glass door. "I wouldn't bet on it," I say over my shoulder. Koa shakes his head, grinning, and follows me inside.

"Fifty pizzas Sydney?" Hart asks the second I step in the kitchen.

"We can order more if we run out," I reply. Lauren winces. "What?" I ask her.

"How many people are coming?" Hart speaks before Lauren can answer me. She continues to stack and organize the pizza boxes by topping.

"That would be his department." I toss a thumb in Koa's direction. "I just ordered the food according to the headcount."

Hart directs his attention to Koa relieving me from his icy stare.

"Why don't we go upstairs and get ready while the two of you work this out," Lauren says, giving Hart a kiss on the cheek. Koa looks at me and I shrug.

"She can't help you," Hart says. "How many people did you invite? I thought we were keeping it small."

"Not sure if you know this but Nash is the starting quarterback at Newhouse. He's one of the most popular students on campus. The fact that I've kept it to one hundred people is a miracle," Koa replies.

"Oh no," Lauren whispers to me. "This isn't going to end well."

"One hundred people!" Hart shouts.

"Go, go, go," Lauren shouts, as she urges me toward the stairs.

"They'll mainly be outside," is the last thing I hear Koa say before I race after Lauren to Hart's room.

She falls onto his bed in a fit of giggles. "Poor Koa," she says in between her laughter.

"He's a big boy. He can handle himself. You're going to have to keep Hart calm. Work your magic on him." I close the door and then go over to my bag stuffed full of everything I need to get ready for tonight.

"He'll be fine. He's not a fan of crowds as you know. If it becomes too much for him, he'll come up here."

"I'll try to keep most of the guests outside if I can." I lay my dress out over Hart's bed. Then pull my makeup and hair stuff out of my bag and take a seat in the chair at Hart's desk.

"He's going to flip when he sees you in this dress." She runs a hand over the silky floral fabric.

"He probably won't care."

"Which *he* are you talking about?" she asks.

"Which one are you?" I counter.

"So there is more than one guy you want to see you wearing this dress. Not that I needed you to admit it considering I saw it with my own eyes. I figured something was going on when Joe and Koa both showed up the other morning."

"There really isn't anything going on with either of them," I admit. "Joe and I went out to lunch the other day and there was nothing there. It felt like I was having lunch with my brother." I turn sideways in the chair. "He leaned in for a kiss and I gave him my cheek."

Lauren cringes. "Oh no. I'm sorry. Does this mean you're done talking to him online too?"

"I'm fairly confident they're not the same guy."

"How do you know for sure?"

"I don't. I'm going to ask him tonight. The questions Online Joe asks and the way he responds to my questions are different than Campus Joe. It feels like I've known him for years. Not weeks. I look forward to talking to him every night. I don't get that giddy feeling about Campus Joe."

Lauren pulls her dress out of Hart's closet and starts to change clothes. She's also wearing a floral dress like mine except where my dress has cutouts on the sides and ties in the front, hers is backless and ties around her neck.

Both dresses show off enough cleavage and skin making them rank somewhere between sexy and indecent. It's not usually how I like to dress but I would be lying if I wasn't trying to get a reaction out of Koa.

In chemistry, there are several types of chemical reactions. Typically our interactions result in decomposition. Me breaking down. Tonight I'm hoping for something more along the lines of combustion.

I want to see him burn.

"What happens next? Are you going to ask this mystery guy who he really is or stop talking to him because he isn't Joe Clark like you thought he was?" she asks, giving me her back so I can tie the tiny strings holding the top of her dress in place.

"I'm going to keep talking to him. I like him. Don't laugh, but I think I'm falling for him." I pull the left side of my hair back and secure a comb clip in it. I found a plain one and glued on a few flowers that matched my dress. I thought it would be a nice touch and keep some of my curls back so I can show off my earrings.

"You act like people don't fall in love online all the time these days. Would it be nice to have some sort of confirmation that you aren't being taken advantage of and this person isn't lying? Absolutely. But if your heart is telling you something is there, I think you need to go with it. You've always had good intuition."

"Not always," I grumble. If I did, I wouldn't have fallen in love with Koa. I stand and start taking off my clothes while Lauren takes my place at Hart's desk.

"I'm going to confirm that Joe is one hundred percent not the Joe online." I step into my dress and adjust the straps on my shoulders. "Then I'm going to figure out who this other Joe really is and where he lives in Alabama," I say, tying the front of my dress. I do a little test shake to make sure my boobs are secure.

"I might know someone who could trace their account and find out their IP address. We would know exactly where they are located and who's hiding behind a computer screen."

"Do I want to know who this hacker is?"

"Probably not." She smirks. "Have you messaged him at all today?"

I shake my head. "We haven't talked since last night." I doubt he sent me a private message today but I pick up my phone to check anyway. "Oh my God," I say, looking at my notifications.

"What?" Lauren asks and comes to stand beside me. "Did he write you?"

"No. I have an email from that company I was telling you about in North Carolina." I scan over the email. My excitement level is rising as the enormity of this moment begins to sink in. "Not only did they answer all my questions but they want me to come out there after graduation."

"They offered you a job?"

"Yes. A paid internship. I can learn everything I need to start my own beauty line from one of the best brands in the business."

"That's good, right?"

"I think so. They want to have a meeting next week."

"Can we jump on the bed and scream in excitement now?" she asks.

I grab her hand and haul her up onto Hart's bed. It's been months since we've had a reason to do our celebration ritual of jumping on the bed and screaming.

Not since we had our first thousand dollar night at Ray's and then again a few months later when Lauren lost her virginity. That was mainly me because I was so excited for Lauren and Hart to finally be together.

Suddenly, in the middle of our shouting, the door flies open, slamming against the wall. Nash, Hart, and a shirtless Koa come barreling into the room. I know this is his house but clothing should be a requirement not a suggestion.

"Is everything okay in here? We heard you screaming," Nash says, concern etching his brow.

"Why are you jumping on the bed?" Koa asks, through a clenched jaw. His stare is so severe I almost fall over. I have to lean on Lauren to keep my balance.

Lauren and I keep hopping around but save them from our screaming. "Celebrating," Lauren answers.

"The party is downstairs," Hart says.

"We aren't celebrating Nash." I stop jumping and hop off the bed. Lauren follows behind me.

"Hey," Nash exclaims, mocking offense.

"I heard back from Blooming Beauty Co.," I tell Nash.

"And..." he says, encouraging me to spill my news.

"They want me to come work for them. They said they loved all my ideas and can't wait to hear more. We're meeting next week. Well, we will be once I write them back, which I'll do before I go downstairs."

Nash pulls me into his arms. "I'm really proud of you. I'm going to miss you next year," he says, releasing me. "It's not going to be the same here without you."

"Nothing is official yet," I remind him.

"I don't know, that email looked pretty official to me," Lauren claims.

"Don't sell yourself short, Syd. You've worked your ass off for this. We'll have to celebrate both of us tonight. I'm going to go downstairs but I'm saving my first shot for you," Nash says, giving me one last hug. "You coming?" he asks Koa as he passes him.

"In a minute. I need to grab a shirt."

"We're going too. See you down there." Lauren grabs Hart's hand and leads him toward the door.

"Why don't we make them leave and we stay? It's my room," Hart says, as he walks into the hallway.

Koa hasn't said much since he stormed through the door. I'm not entirely sure why he's still here. I let out a sigh when he turns toward the door to leave. Except he doesn't walk out. He closes it instead.

"Where are you going?" he asks with his head resting against the wood door.

"What do you mean?"

He turns in my direction and laughs mockingly. "This job. Where is it?"

"North Carolina," I answer with direct eye contact. I won't be distracted by his tattooed chest. Every summer he adds more and more to the design. What started out as one word—*Trouble*—is now surrounded by several lines of an intricate, woven design. I've never stared at it long enough to figure out what it is but from a distance it makes him look hotter than I care to admit.

"You were going to move to another state without telling me? I'm trying not to be offended here, but it seems everyone knows about your life except for me. Why didn't you tell me?"

"That isn't the type of relationship we have anymore."

"Bullshit. I know things aren't what they used to be but we still tell each other things like this," he says.

"Like you told me about the teams that want to draft you? I only heard about that because I was in the same room when you told Nash," I snap back at him.

He sighs. "I fucking hate that you're right."

"Even if we did, I still wouldn't have said anything."

"Why?"

"Because I don't want to hear you tell me it's a bad idea to move away from home by myself."

"I wouldn't have done that," he says, taking a cautious step toward me.

"But that's what you do. You can't help yourself. You always have something negative to say about my life choices and it isn't your place. You want to keep an eye out for me—protect me—when we go out in a group? Fine. But I have to draw the line somewhere."

"What if I want to erase the line completely? What if I want to go back to what we were before?" he asks, moving closer.

Before we slept together. Before he said we were a mistake.

"I can't do that," I say, shaking my head. He makes it sound so easy like turning on a light.

"And I can't keep living like this with you. Everyone was in here celebrating something important to you and I didn't know anything about it. I don't want to keep being iced out of your life."

"That isn't your decision to make. I decide who gets to be involved in my life." I push my fingers into my chest. "The moment you said I was a mistake..." I take a moment to calm my nerves. "That we were a mistake, you made that decision a lot easier for me. Isn't this what you wanted? Nash's sister to leave you alone—to stop bothering you with her books and fantasies?" I ask. "Well, you got it. You should be more grateful."

"Grateful? I lost you. That word cost me you. Why would I be happy about that?" he asks. "I've been living in hell and hating every minute of it. The words didn't come out right. This was never what I wanted." He says the last part almost to himself. I'm not sure what to think of this whole conversation.

What did he mean to say? I'm afraid to ask.

"You can't say things like that. You can't snap your fingers and reverse everything that's happened over the years. This is who we are now. Don't come any closer," I say, holding up a hand when he takes a step in my direction.

"Why not?" he asks, smirking.

"Because I need space." I'm already feeling the *Koa Affect*. Simply being in the same room with the guy has my pulse racing and my limbs weak. I don't need him touching me and breaking through my defenses. It's best to keep a shirtless Koa at least a foot or two away.

"I'm tired of having space between us. That's what we've been doing for years. I want you close," he says, moving toward me.

"Where is this coming from? Did you just wake up this morning and decide you wanted me?" I cross my arms over my chest as if it will give me an extra layer of protection over my heart.

"I've woken up every morning for the past decade wanting you in one way or another. This isn't a new revelation. It's something I've known since the first summer we met." He moves closer and grazes his fingers down the length of my arm.

"When we were kids I wanted to read books, ride bikes, and climb trees with you. In high school, I wanted you to wear my jersey and be my girl, and in college I've wanted you in every way imaginable."

"This doesn't make any sense," I whisper.

"Maybe not to you but it doesn't make it any less true. I want to give us a second chance." The sincerity in his eyes is almost too much to take. I have to look away.

"It's too late," I state, tossing him a quick glance. I expect to see a hint of disappointment in his eyes but instead they're filled with humor. "I don't want to be with you. We had our chance, if you can call it that. We've moved on."

He chuckles darkly. "Moved on? Is that what we're both doing?"

"No. That's what I've done. Now if you'll excuse me." I attempt to slip past him but he stops me with a hand on my waist.

"Why are you lying to me? To yourself?"

"I'm not. I've moved on. There's someone else."

"You can't be serious. Why him?"

I'm not sure how he knows about the guy I'm talking to online. Maybe Lauren said something to Hart and he mentioned it to Koa? It doesn't really matter how he found out. I'm telling him now anyway.

"Because he is nice. He listens to me. He doesn't tell me what to do and boss me around all the time. For example, when he sees me in this dress, he won't ask me to change." I make a mental note to snap a picture before I go downstairs and send it to Online Joe. Maybe I need to take the first step in revealing more about myself to get him to do the same.

"Do you want to know what I think about the way you look in this dress?" he asks. I shake my head. I'm scared. I feel confident and I don't want him to ruin it.

"It doesn't matter." I try to leave again but his grip only tightens. "Koa, let me go." He drops his hand and I miss his touch already. *Stupid hormones.*

"It does to me. Everything about you matters to me," he says, leaning so close his face is a breath away. "You look beautiful. You always do. But this..." his finger slips underneath the thin strap on my shoulder. He drags his finger down my chest and stops just below the bow holding my boobs in place. "This is going to plague me. I won't be able to stop thinking about how sexy you look right now."

"Why are you telling me this now when everything in my life is going good? Don't you want me to be happy?"

"That's how we got here. I wanted everyone to be happy, but you're not. I'm not either." He tips my chin to get my full attention. I swat his hand away when he doesn't let go. "I've seen you happy and this isn't it. Let me make you happy again."

"You don't have the ability to do that anymore. All you do is make me feel like crap for the decisions I make. I want to be with someone who makes me feel good about myself. That isn't you."

"Let me prove it to you. Let me be that man for you."

I step out of his reach even though my body aches to move closer. "I already told you. It's too late. You had your chance to be that man and you tried to break me instead."

Walking away from Koa should make me feel good. I'm leaving on my terms. It's my choice but why does it feel like the wrong one?

FICTION FORUM

FaeAtHeart
How did your apology go?

NotYourAverageJoe19
Not as well as I had hoped.

FaeAtHeart
What did she say when you said you were sorry?

NotYourAverageJoe19
You know. Now that I think about it, I never actually said the words.

FaeAtHeart
You need to do that immediately.

Who is she?

NotYourAverageJoe19
An old friend.

FaeAtHeart
I had a run in with one of those tonight.

GINGER WALLS

NotYourAverageJoe19

> Oh yeah? What happened?

FaeAtHeart

> He basically said he wanted to erase past mistakes. Pretend like nothing happened.

NotYourAverageJoe19

> Is that such a bad thing?

FaeAtHeart

> It's an impossible thing. I can't forget that easily.

NotYourAverageJoe19

> Maybe you shouldn't forget everything. If you were friends, it couldn't have all been bad.

FaeAtHeart

> No it wasn't. We had a lot of good times too.

NotYourAverageJoe19

> Hold on to those memories.

> Everyone deserves a second chance.

FaeAtHeart

> I don't know. I'll think about it.

> I have to go. It's my brother's 21st birthday and he wants to do a shot with me.

NotYourAverageJoe19

> You're at a party and you're talking to me?

FOUL TERRITORY

> FaeAtHeart
> What can I say? I like talking to you.

13

KOA

"Nash, time for another shot," Gage shouts from beside me on the deck. Nash has spent most of the night sitting by the fire like a king on his throne.

I've been perched outside on the deck doing my best to keep an eye on everyone partying in the backyard. I'm not worried about the noise since most of our neighbors are here. I am concerned about pissing off Hart even more than he already is.

"Are you going to have one?" a girl asks from beside me. I glance up from my phone to see Julia, one of the Newhouse student athletic trainers.

"No. I'm good."

"Oh come on, Koa. You need to have at least one shot with the birthday boy." Gage slaps my shoulder.

"Leave him alone. He did one earlier. That's probably all we'll get out of him," Nash says. "He seems to be occupied anyway." He nods toward my phone before entering the house.

GINGER WALLS

"Whoever you're messaging must be important," Julia says, pushing her chest out a little further. Trainers aren't allowed to date athletes but that hasn't stopped them from trying.

Julia has always been a flirt. I think she does it so openly because she can get away with it. She knows it can't go anywhere. I assumed it was innocent, but sometimes I wonder if she's actually interested.

"She is," I reply. Julia gives me a quick nod then joins Nash and Gage inside.

I read Sydney's latest message before pocketing my phone. I can't believe I finally admitted wanting her back.

I couldn't have stopped the words from coming out even if I'd tried. Seeing her excited over something I knew nothing about hurt. I used to be the first person she told this kind of stuff to. I'm the one she called first when she got into Newhouse. I'm the first person she called when she got her driver's license. It was always me first. Now I'm not even the last to know. I wouldn't have found out at all if I didn't walk in on it.

Admitting I wanted her was easy. There isn't a day that passes where the thought doesn't gnaw at me. I didn't expect her to jump into my arms at the declaration, but the last thing I imagined she would say is that it was too late.

I keep telling myself there isn't anything happening between her and Joe. Yet, there was something in the way she talked about this guy that felt different. For the first time, I might have real competition.

With the way they've been acting tonight, it's hard to believe she's really with him though. I've barely seen them together for more than ten minutes. If she were mine, I wouldn't give her an inch of space. Fuck she looks good in that dress she's wearing.

Joe's spent most of the party outside while she's been sitting in the living room with Wren. The only time I saw them together was when they were dancing. I was three seconds from ripping his hands off of her.

I'm normally pretty good about staying in control when Sydney is dating someone. I know they are meaningless relationships and these guys are placeholders. Someone to pass the time with.

At least, that's what I thought.

Sydney and Joe enter the kitchen together laughing. She bumps her shoulder against his. Maybe I'll have one of those shots after all.

The kitchen is standing room only as everyone wants a front row seat to watch Nash toss back another round. He's going to be hurting tomorrow. We never drink this much.

Wyatt fills small plastic cups full of whatever concoction Lauren and Sydney made earlier. They thought it would be better to have shooters premixed instead of straight liquor being consumed. Going by the looks of most of the inebriated people in the room, I would say they were right.

A few guys from the football team head back outside leaving a space for me to slide in beside Enzo, who's standing around the table watching everyone drink and chat with Nash.

The room erupts in cheers as Charlie, Nash, Wyatt, Sydney, and Wren all take their turn throwing back the pink concoction. Wyatt winces and Wren rolls her eyes.

"Would you prefer apple juice instead?" Wren teases him.

"It's not my favorite juice but at least it wouldn't eat away at my insides like that shit." He points to the pitcher in the middle of the table.

"Oh come on, man. Hart's mom makes drinks stronger than this," Nash remarks.

"Where have you been hiding?" Enzo asks me. I'm glad it worked out for him and his brother, Marco, to make it out tonight. It's rare our schedules line up to where we all have the same days off.

"I haven't been hiding. I've been keeping tabs on everyone outside."

"I'm surprised you haven't been keeping an eye on someone in particular tonight." He lifts a chin toward Sydney and Joe on the other side of the table.

"Maybe I didn't feel like playing bodyguard tonight."

"Are you feeling okay? There hasn't been a day in the ten years I've known you when you weren't looking out for that girl. And I know it has nothing to do with the boyfriend. They have never stopped you before."

"He isn't her boyfriend." They may have gone out on a few dates but Sydney has never had a boyfriend.

"If you say so. They look like they have something going on."

"Are you trying to piss me off?" I narrow my eyes in his direction.

"I need to do something to keep myself entertained," he replies, chuckling.

"That's what the girls on the dance floor are for." Hart punches him on the back. "Hey," he says, turning to me. "Lauren and I are going to bed. What do you want me to do with Sydney's stuff?"

"Why are you asking me?"

"I'll leave it in the bathroom then," he says, and starts to leave.

I grab the top of his shoulder. "Put it in my room." I doubt she'll stay in the room with me but at least holding her things hostage will give me another opportunity to speak with her.

He nods then makes his way back over to Lauren, pulling her away from her conversation with Sydney and leading her upstairs.

"How long did it take you before you were okay with your sister dating your best friend?" I ask Enzo as he watches Lauren and Hart leave the party with a trace of a smile on his face.

"I think deep down I was always going to be okay with their relationship. I just had to wrap my head around the idea of her being with anyone in general. Especially someone I've known my whole life. He's my best friend for a reason. He's a good guy. I trust him with my life and with my sister. There isn't anyone who would love her harder than him."

This is the same logic I thought Nash would apply to me and Sydney but he never has. I've received nothing but threats and warnings. He should know I would never hurt Sydney. *Not again.*

I never would have hurt her in the first place if it wasn't for Nash. I put distance between the two of us for him. I've been paying the price ever since. If I had it my way, I would have been her boyfriend the moment I figured out I liked girls. And not just any girls, but the moment I knew I liked her.

I'll never forget the moment it happened either. I took a baseball to the head for it. She was in the stands watching me and Nash play our first game of the fall season.

The team was out on the field warming up. I took my eye off the pitcher for a second and locked eyes with Sydney. She had her hair in braids back then and wore a bright pink sundress. It wasn't the first time I noticed her curves, but her dress didn't hide anything.

It was her smile that made me forget where I was. She smiled at me like I hung the moon. Like I was the only guy she sees. I was busy trying to figure out how I was going to keep my promise to Nash when a baseball almost knocked me unconscious.

"How do you think Nash would react if one of his friends finally said fuck it and started pursuing Sydney?"

He shifts in place. His eyes dart around the room from Nash to Sydney and back to me. "Any of his friends or you?"

"Does it make a difference?"

"Yes. It does."

I shouldn't be surprised by his answer but a new layer of irritation begins to fester under the surface.

"Hey, you two!" Nash shouts from his side of the table. "Stop looking so serious. This is supposed to be a party." He holds up his drink in our direction.

"I don't think they know how to loosen up and have a good time," Sydney taunts us from across the table.

"Is that so? What should we be doing? We're drinking, socializing. I even played one of your outdoor games," Enzo replies.

"Dancing. What's a party without dancing?" Her lips twist into an evil smirk.

"Enzo doesn't dance," Marco says from where he's standing by Nash.

"Everyone dances," she says, keeping her eyes on us.

"Not me. That's where I draw the line." Enzo takes a long pull from his beer.

"Koa?" she asks, raising an eyebrow. "What about you? I don't think I've ever seen you dance once in all the years I've known you."

I drain the rest of my beer and silently leave the circle we've formed around the dining table. I toss my empty bottle in the trash can while keeping my eyes on Sydney.

"I guess that's a no for Mahina too," Joe quips before taking a sip of his drink.

I ignore everyone as I round the table. Including the death stare from Nash. Sydney yelps when I grab her hand and pull her into my chest.

"Maybe you never saw me dance because the person I wanted to dance with wasn't available," I whisper close to her ear. "Dance with me now." I walk away, leaving the decision in her hands.

Standing in the middle of the crowded living room, I wait for her to make her choice. Is she going to break through the invisible barriers we've put on our relationship or is she going to let me walk away?

She leans into Joe and his arm goes around her waist. My hand clenches into a fist. Whatever she says has him smiling which pisses me off even more. Almost as if she's doing this to drive home the point I don't dance, not that she really wants to dance with me. She has no desire to be close to me while I'm dying to have her in my arms.

The skirt of her dress skates over her upper thighs with every step she takes in my direction. She looks flawless from the tip of her hot pink painted toes to the flower clips in her hair.

"Show me what you got," she says, with her hip cocked to the side. The song playing over the bluetooth speaker has a faster tempo than I prefer. I'm not much of a slow dance guy, but I'm definitely not a throw your hands up in the air and jump around kind of guy.

Fuck the tempo, I probably couldn't dance on beat anyway. I slink an arm around Sydney's back, pulling her against my chest. I place another hand on the curve of her hip and start rocking side to side.

"Is this what you call dancing?" she asks, breathlessly.

One at a time, I drape her arms over my shoulders. "You can call it whatever you want as long as it keeps you in my arms."

"Why do you keep saying these things to me? You need to stop." Her eyes shimmer with an emotion I can't pinpoint before it flickers out.

"Why should I stop? Because you like it?" I spin us around until we're hidden deeper in the living room. I drop my forehead to hers. "It feels right, doesn't it? Like everything is falling into place." My hands wander over her hips and up her torso, gliding over the silk of her dress and teasing her bare skin through the cutouts in the material.

"All I feel is you stepping on my feet," she says, deflecting. I laugh, knowing that is not all she feels with us being this close together. "I need to get back to my date."

Inhaling a deep breath, I stare at my defiant little trouble maker. I loosen my hold on her. Skimming my knuckles down her arm, I enjoy the way her skin pebbles. Once I reach her hand, I grab hold of it and start walking back toward the stairs.

"What are you doing?" She tries pulling her hand loose but it's pointless.

"I need to talk to you privately." I turn around, smiling at the fact she's stopped fighting me. I'll take this temporary reprieve as a small victory.

I catch Nash's eye across the room. The tight grip he has on the table and the flare of his nostrils tells me all I need to know.

I'll ask him for his forgiveness tomorrow. Tonight I need Sydney to understand I'm serious about giving us another shot.

"You have five minutes. I don't want people assuming we are up here having sex," she says, with her arms crossed over chest as I close my bedroom door.

"Relax. Everyone knows you hate me. That's how you feel about me, right? You can't stand to be in the same room with me?" I throw my arms out to the side. "How do you feel about me now that we're alone?" I move toward her. "Do you still hate me?"

"I never said I hated you. You're the one who keeps saying that. Not me."

"No?" I question. "It feels like it most days."

"Are we caring about each other's feelings now? Why should I care about how you feel when you don't seem to give my feelings a second thought?"

"You're right. I'm sorry, Sydney." I cup her cheek in my palm. "What will it take for you to give me a chance to prove to you that I care about your feelings? I didn't know how much I hurt you over the years. I'm not just talking about graduation."

She pulls my hand away from her face. "I'm not sure where you get your information from but you didn't hurt me over the years. I don't want to talk about that night or the next day. It's done. We're done."

"Don't be like that. I know you've felt like second best to Nash more than once. You've said it yourself. That doesn't sit well with me. You have always been my first concern."

"That's a lie," she scoffs. "You and Nash have been inseparable for the past decade. An impenetrable force. I've been an outlier to your little duo and you know it."

"That's how it looks, but it isn't how it feels to me. I want to show you but I can't do that if you don't give me a chance. Let me prove that you have always been my girl. I need you to see that we're meant to be together."

I stare into her deep brown eyes, watching as they slowly gloss over and pray that my pleading isn't falling on deaf ears.

"You're wrong. We aren't meant to be. All we do is hurt each other." Her eyes flutter closed and a single tear drips down her cheek. I brush it away with my thumb and pull her closer. "I don't want a man who only wants to control me and tell me what I should be doing."

"That's not all that I am and you know it."

"You could have fooled me."

"Let me show you then. I'm just asking for a chance, Sydney," I say, meeting her eyes.

"I'm afraid it would be another *mistake*," she says, pulling away from me. The word cuts like a knife. I've never realized how hurtful a single word could be until it's used on you.

"I'm going to prove you wrong," I say, as she opens the door. "I know you said it's too late for us, but you're wrong."

With a slight shake of her head, she slips out the door. I know she's wrong. We don't have an expiration date. I won't stop until she understands that she's it for me. Even if it means pissing off my best friend in the process.

FICTION FORUM

FaeAtHeart
Have you ever hated someone?

NotYourAverageJoe19
Yes but looking back I'm not sure he deserved it.

FaeAtHeart
What did he do?

NotYourAverageJoe19
He was a bully. Teased other kids relentlessly. He was a terror but his mom was really sick and he took that anger out on everyone.

FaeAtHeart
So sad.

NotYourAverageJoe19
Why do you ask?

FaeAtHeart
I got accused of hating someone the other day.

GINGER WALLS

NotYourAverageJoe19
And do you?

FaeAtHeart
No. Not even a little.

NotYourAverageJoe19
Why do they think you hate them then?

FaeAtHeart
Because the person hurt me. They broke my heart.

NotYourAverageJoe19
Seems like it's a good reason not to like them anymore.

FaeAtHeart
I've tried not to. But the memories.

He gave me too many good memories.

NotYourAverageJoe19
The kind that keep you up at night?

FaeAtHeart
Yes! Do you have them too?

NotYourAverageJoe19
I do but I don't mind. I like remembering all the good stuff.

FOUL TERRITORY

FaeAtHeart

I don't. The good memories hurt the most. It would be easier if there weren't so many of them.

NotYourAverageJoe19

I keep hoping one day I won't be living off of the old memories but making new ones.

14

SYDNEY

It's been a few days since Nash's party and Koa's confession. Is that what it was? A declaration? An apology? I don't know how to define what's happening between us. All I know is that I haven't been able to stop thinking about it.

What if it's true? What if we tried? What if I let my heart win?

I thought maybe hiding out in the chemistry lab and diving into one of my research projects would keep my mind occupied. Instead, I keep drifting back to everything he said. Everything he was asking of me.

Instinct had me wanting to run into his open arms. The boy I've loved my entire life wants to be with me. *He likes me.* It felt like a fever dream. Then my battered and bruised heart reminded me of what happened the last time Koa Mahina led me to believe there was something starting between us.

I can't do it again. Not when there's a possibility to have a healthy relationship with someone else. Our story is over. He can say whatever he wants, but I won't let it happen.

I'm going to focus on my new life in North Carolina and leave everything in the past where it belongs. Nothing good will come from a relationship with Koa. All that ever got me was a broken heart.

Thankfully he's been out of town for games and I haven't had to see him. He's sent me a few text messages, but nothing about our conversation in his room. They were random updates about his day. The same type of texts he would send me when he was on the road in high school.

How can he go back to what we were so easily? He was the one who said we couldn't be together. As soon as I heard the word, I froze. I panicked. My heart dropped to my stomach. The only thing I could do was agree with him. So I did and retreated to my bedroom. I avoided him as much as I could that summer.

I look into the microscope and make a few notes on my laptop. This is one of many research assignments I have to wrap up before graduation. I love being in the lab but I'm looking forward to the days when I'm working on my own formulas instead of projects my professor assigned to me.

"I thought I'd find you here. You've been avoiding me." Nash leans his elbows on the long lab table.

"I've been busy. There's a difference." I glance around the room and note several people have stopped what they're doing to check out my brother.

"So, the fact that I haven't talked to my sister in four days has nothing to do with Koa taking you up to his room? Or that when you came back downstairs you immediately called for a campus rideshare and left?"

"Nope." I ignore my brother and continue to log the chemical reactions from my sample on my laptop.

"Do you want to tell me what happened upstairs with Koa?"

"Not particularly. I don't see how it's information you need to know. I'm surprised you haven't already gotten the gossip you're looking for from your best friend." I raise an eyebrow.

"Not yet. He'll come to me when he's ready."

"How nice of you to give him space and wait for him to come to you. Too bad I don't get the same courtesy," I grumble.

"You're my sister. I want to make sure you're okay and I don't have to kick my best friend's ass for hurting you."

"Don't bloody your knuckles on my behalf."

"So, there's nothing that I need to worry about?" he asks.

I lean back in my seat and scrutinize my brother. "Why are you pushing this? I said everything is fine. Can you drop it? I don't want to talk to you about Koa."

"What happened with Joe? I saw Eva hanging all over him after you left."

"You're relentless." I release a sigh. "We decided to be friends. He's free to have whoever he chooses hang on him. We were casual anyway."

Turns out my suspicion about Joe and Online Joe being two different people was correct. When I asked him what he thought of the Fiction Forum, he said he hadn't had a chance to join yet.

That one action, or lack of one, told me all I needed to know. If he couldn't take a minute to check out one of my favorite things, then he wasn't really interested in me.

I don't want to fall in love so badly I'm willing to settle. I want a man who puts me first. I'm done feeling like second best or an afterthought.

"That seems to be your favorite kind of relationship," he snarks.

"You're one to talk. I don't think you've ever had a serious girlfriend."

"That's not my focus."

"You sound like a real asshole right now. It isn't my focus either. I have dreams and goals outside of having a boyfriend too," I say waving a hand around the lab.

He nods thoughtfully. "You're right. I'm sorry. You're going to change the lives of a lot of people."

"Thank you. I can't wait until you need a woman's help and she humbles the hell out of you."

He laughs. "I've been humbled all year but if a woman still needs to take me down a notch, I'll embrace it."

He watches me for a few minutes and I expertly ignore him. It is a skill I've sharpened over years being his big sister. He can't stand the silence. Nash has always been the one to break first.

"Koa didn't get that memo. About you and Joe," he adds, noting my confusion. "Hart told me Koa laid into Joe when they were loading up the bus to leave for their away games. Koa overheard him talking about Eva with another trainer.

Then Koa went off telling him how he is being disrespectful to you. I wonder why he did that."

"If I had to guess it's because he's become your perfectly trained soldier. Built by your design to defend me and keep the bad guys away."

He scoffs. "That's an interesting take. I think somewhere over the years your interpretation of our friendship with Koa has become clouded."

"What are you talking about? I know exactly where I stand in our trio. I'm the second rate Pierce sibling."

Nash laughs. "Do you really believe that? Do you know how many times he ditched me to spend time with you instead? You can't sit here and tell me there's nothing going on between the two of you."

Koa ditched Nash to hang out with me? I file through the memories and I do recall a few times he would watch a movie with me while Nash would be outside doing something with Hart or the other guys. Was he really picking me?

"There isn't. You have nothing to worry about." I glare at my brother. Why is he bringing all of this up? What is his agenda? He should know there isn't anything going on between us because it was his ban, his rules, and Koa's loyalty to him that got us here.

"Would you want there to be?" he questions cautiously.

"Why are you asking me about Koa? It seems very...random."

He throws his head back laughing. "Does it really?"

"Yes. Completely out of the blue. We had one conversation at your party and all of a sudden you think we should be in a relationship. It would make more sense if you asked me if I still wanted to marry Joshua Jackson."

"I don't see how. The likelihood of you marrying a celebrity would be slim."

"Exactly!" I throw my hands up in the air. I wince when I earn a few glares from a few people in the room. "But also more likely than something happening between me and your best friend."

He stands up straight, tilts his head to the side, and considers me for a moment. "Okay," he says, then slaps the top of the table.

"Okay? That's all you have to say after the incessant badgering. You're ending the conversation here?"

"We can continue the conversation if you want. I have a lot of thoughts about you and Koa I would love to get off my chest. Things I have been holding back for years."

"This has been you holding back? You have never held your tongue about your friends being interested in me. I can't imagine what else you could possibly have to say."

I do my best to keep my face neutral but inside I'm sweating. Does Nash know Koa and I had sex graduation night? It was the beginning and the end of us. I don't like thinking about that night too long.

It's one of my good memories that makes me miss what we could have been but it's also tainted with the reminder that the next morning Koa woke thinking being with me was a mistake.

"I see and know more than you think I do," he states.

"Whatever, oh wise one. I don't want to talk about this with you anymore," I grumble.

"He comes home later today. Maybe you should come over and have a conversation with him." He walks around to my side of the table. "It's okay if you like him. I'm not going to be mad if that's what you're worried about."

"I'm not going to be mad," I mumble his words back to myself because surely I heard him wrong. "For years you have warned him off of me. And now, you're okay with it? I have never needed your permission or approval to be with Koa."

"No you don't."

"Are you fucking kidding me right now?" I whisper-shout. How can he agree with me after years of keeping us apart?

"No, I'm not. You don't need my permission but he still doesn't deserve you. Not yet at least."

"It doesn't matter," I say, dismissing him. I meant what I said when I told Koa it was too late for us. "I'm not interested in starting up anything with him. Your BFF status can stay intact. You can continue to keep him to yourself."

He leans closer to me. "It was never about that. Maybe in the beginning, but things changed. Your relationship with Koa changed. Just talk to him." He kisses my forehead before saying goodbye.

I'm left even more confused. Maybe my brother isn't as selfish as I thought he was all this time. It doesn't make sense that he would spend so much energy warning all of his friends away just to tell me he would be okay with Koa and I being together.

The last time I was in Koa's room I didn't get a good look around. It was hard for me to focus on anything but him and my brewing frustration.

I've avoided going upstairs when I visit Nash. There's no reason to come up into Koa's personal space. It's too dangerous like standing too close to the fire. I need to distance myself from him. Otherwise, I'm constantly reminded of what will never be mine.

Koa's room is relatively clean and organized. This doesn't surprise me. His dad was in the military and taught all of his kids the importance of daily disciplines.

Walking around his room, memories begin to float to the surface. There is something about the familiar scent lingering in the air that brings me back to the beginning of high school.

His cologne sits on the top of his dresser along with a picture of our neighborhood crew at our graduation party. I ignore the photo and pick up his cologne and inhale a deep breath.

Smells like my first kiss and the only man I've ever loved.

Koa appears in the open doorway, making me jump. I fumble the cologne bottle as I hastily try to get it back where it belongs. "I can't believe you still wear the same stuff from high school," I snark, hoping to throw him off the fact I love the way he always smells like a giant ocean I want to dive into.

"You don't like it?" he asks, genuinely concerned.

"It's alright." I shrug.

"Hale gave me a bottle for my birthday," he says, closing the door and walking deeper into his room. Hale is his older brother. "He said it would make me irresistible." The side of his mouth tips up in a smile. "It didn't work. Did it?" he asks, sitting on the edge of his bed.

"I don't think I'm the right person to answer that question."

"You're the only person I want answering that question," he says, making my breath hitch. I'm not used to his bluntness. His honesty. "Why are you here?"

Admitting I'm here to talk about us doesn't seem like a good idea anymore. I need more time to think about everything. Out of the corner of my eye, I see my bag. The one I left here from the night of Nash's party. *Perfect.*

"I'm here to get my bag." I walk over to my made up excuse. "How did it end up in your room?"

He shrugs. "Hart must have thrown it in here whenever Lauren and him went to bed. I was going to bring it to you tomorrow."

"I saved you the trouble. I'll get out of your hair. I'm sure you want to relax after your games. Congratulations, by the way." They were able to win all three games and still have a chance to make the playoffs.

Koa stares at the bag in my hand as I fiddle with the strap, wrapping it and unwrapping it around my fingers.

"Why are you really here?" he asks again, bypassing my diversion tactics altogether.

"I don't know." My head falls forward and my shoulders slump.

"Will you sit down?" He scoots over and gives me enough room to sit and still leave some much needed space between us. I decide to sit facing him. If we are going to have this conversation, I'm going to do it head on.

I stare silently at his comforter while he stares at me. I guess I'm going to have to start. I might as well admit what is holding me back. "I'm scared," I whisper.

He readjusts his position on the bed, inching himself closer to me. "I'm scared too." He places a hand over mine and removes the strap of my bag from my grasp. It was a nice distraction. "I'm scared you're going to walk away. I'm scared you're going to move to another state and that's going to be the end of us."

"That was my plan. Leave after graduation and never look back."

"You said it was your plan. What's your plan now?"

"It's still my plan. I'm leaving after graduation," I answer. He rolls his lips and nods slowly. "This, you and me, isn't healthy. Whatever it is that makes us this way..." I sigh. "You need to let me go. Every time you interfere in my life I have to start the process of getting over you all over again. You said things at Nash's party that undid any progress I made."

"Then don't get over me. I'm not sure how I'm going to be able to walk away from us—from you—if you do. I won't stop trying until you let me in and give us a second chance."

I scoff. "You keep asking for a second chance. When did you give us a first chance? You ran before we even got started," I say, pointing a finger in his direction. "We were *never* together. You took my heart, crushed it, and then left me to put myself back together again."

"I'm sorry. I made a bad decision. I should have gone back to Nash and told him to fuck off. I should have told him how I really feel about you. How I've always felt about you. I didn't fight hard enough back then but I'm fighting now."

"I can't keep doing this," I say, wiping a lone tear from my cheek.

"Doing what?"

"Hoping and praying. Hoping I'm not going to wake up in the morning like I did before and everything you said will be null and void. Praying you don't change your mind. Take your pick. I have a million reasons why we should give up and move on."

"And I have one that says we shouldn't. My world has revolved around you since the moment you entered it," he claims, and moves to the floor, getting on his knees. He puts a hand on either one of my thighs and twists my body so I'm facing him.

"There is no more hoping. No more praying." He squeezes my hip. "There is only me proving to you that I am yours. That I have always been yours."

"But you haven't. You treat me—my heart—like a toy and you don't even realize you're doing it. I'm like a damn yoyo to you. You throw me out and pull me back in. It's time to cut the string."

"How am I supposed to do that?" he asks.

"It wasn't hard the first time. I'm sure you can figure it out again."

"You think that's what I've done?" He jerks forward. I'm forced to push my knees apart and let him get closer to me. "You think I let you go? Baby, I'm holding on to you as tight as I can. It may feel different to you because I've had to do it from a distance. But there is no part of me that has let you go. If anything, I feel like I'm holding on for dear life. I'm desperately trying to keep any part of you near me.

"Maybe you're the one who keeps pulling away. Maybe instead of cutting the string, I need to put a giant knot in it so you can't get away from me anymore," he says, gripping my hips tighter.

"What if that's not what I want?"

"What do you want? Whatever it is, I'll give it to you."

"I want the broken pieces of my heart to stop stabbing me in the lungs so I can breathe without feeling any pain. I want to be able to look at your face and not remember what it feels like when your lips are pressed against mine. I want to be able to look at my brother and not blame him for stealing my best friend away from me. You were mine first," I shout. "Mine. And you left me...you left me." I swallow back tears but I'm afraid it's too late as they begin to trickle down my cheeks.

"Baby," he whispers, pulling me into his arms. I should fight him but I'm too tired. "I'm so sorry. I'm going to make this right."

"I already told you. It's too late." Just saying the words has my mouth drying out as if my body is preserving all the water for the future tears I'll cry when I'm back home alone. "I told you there's someone else."

He pulls away slightly. I already miss being cocooned in his arms and having my cheek pressed against his chest.

"You can't be serious right now. You're going to pick Joe over me? Over everything we have? He was making out with another girl as soon as you left the party. I know you. That's not the kind of guy you're looking for."

"*We* have nothing but memories." I slide off the bed and walk across the room. I can't think with him so close to me. "You're right. Joe isn't the guy for me."

"At least we can agree on something," he says, standing. I liked him better on his knees.

"He isn't who I'm talking about."

"You're dating someone else?" The muscles in his jaw flutter and his eyes narrow on me.

"I was never dating Joe. We were getting to know each other. I didn't even kiss the guy."

Koa rubs his hands aggressively through his short hair and over his face. "Who is he?"

"I'm not telling you. It doesn't matter who I'm seeing. Just know it isn't you." I lift my chin. I can only imagine what he would say if I told him I was falling for someone I've met online. I can hear the lecture now.

"You're right. It doesn't matter who this other guy is," he says, taking a step in my direction. "There have always been other guys. I've watched them all come and go over the years and never once did I worry because I know, Sydney." He cups the side of my face.

I do my best to avoid eye contact but he keeps up with me easily so I give up and glare at him. "I know you're mine. It has always been you for me. I'm done sitting on the sidelines, baby. You're more than a memory to me. I'm not going to stop until we get it right."

"How are we going to do that when I haven't agreed to any of this?"

"Day by day."

"You plan on wearing me down to get your way?"

He shakes his head. "No. You're right when you said we didn't even get started. This is where we begin. Right here. Please, will you go out on a date with me?"

"You can't erase the past. I can't forget…"

"I don't want you to. I want the opportunity to make new memories. Let me show you what I already know. And if you like this other guy more, I'll do what you want and let you go."

A wave of panic rushes through my blood lighting it on fire. I should question why my body has a visceral reaction to the idea of Koa letting me go for good. It feels so final. I'm not prepared for that.

"Fine. One date," I say, knowing that despite my hesitancy, this is what my heart craves.

Yet, there is part of me that doesn't want to give up on my mystery man online and the connection we made. He may not be able to give me what I want physically, but emotionally he's everything I've been needing.

How do I walk away from that?

FICTION FORUM

FaeAtHeart
> What are the chances we'll meet one day?

NotYourAverageJoe19
> I'd say there's a good chance.

FaeAtHeart
> When?

NotYourAverageJoe19
> I need more time.

FaeAtHeart
> I understand.
>
> Can I ask another question?

NotYourAverageJoe19
> Always.

FaeAtHeart
> What are we doing here?

GINGER WALLS

NotYourAverageJoe19

> What do you mean?

FaeAtHeart

> I think you know what I mean. Are we becoming friends? Or is this something more to you?

NotYourAverageJoe19

> You still occupy my mind every second of the day. That hasn't changed. I don't think it ever will.

> Does that answer your question?

FaeAtHeart

> It does. It also leaves me confused.

NotYourAverageJoe19

> Why?

FaeAtHeart

> I'll tell you when I meet you in person.

NotYourAverageJoe19

> Nothing but trouble.

FaeAtHeart

> You love it.

NotYourAverageJoe19

> I do. I really do.

15

KOA

I roll up the sleeves on my pale pink button down as I skip down the steps. Tonight I'm taking Sydney out on our first date, at least it is according to her. In my mind, we've been on hundreds of them.

Wyatt wolf whistles as I enter the living room. "Where are you off to dressed all fancy?" He has a large bowl of chips sitting on his lap and his phone occupies the couch cushion next to him.

I glance over at Nash. His stare is cold and his mouth is clamped shut.

"You got a hot date or something?" Wyatt asks, not reading the room.

"Who are you going out with?" Nash asks, standing from the couch.

"Oh shit," Wyatt says, popping a chip in his mouth and settling on the couch like he's watching the best movie he's ever seen.

"Can we talk in the kitchen?" I ask. Wyatt holds his bowl of chips against his chest and grabs his phone before standing. "Privately," I add, giving him a knowing look.

"That's not very nice." He slumps back down on the couch. "Whatever. It's fine. Nash's voice carries anyway. I can hear you just fine from out here."

I snort a laugh and roll my eyes. Nash wordlessly follows me into our kitchen. Staring down at the white countertop on the island, I brace myself for Nash's reaction to what I'm about to tell him.

He stands opposite me. His arms crossed over his chest waiting for me to say what I need to. It feels like I've entered confession.

"Who are you taking out on a date? I swear to God if you say—"

"I'm going to say her name. I asked Syd out a few days ago, and with a moderate amount of begging she said yes."

Nash smirks. Strange. Not the reaction I expected. He's too casual. Too relaxed. It makes me feel uneasy. Where is all that anger from a few moments ago? "And this is you asking for what? Permission? My approval?" He tilts his head.

"No, I'm not asking for anything. I'm telling you I'm taking her out. If you want to get mad, now is your chance. After today, I'm not talking about it with you again. I love you, man, but I love your sister more."

"About fucking time. I've been waiting for you to finally man the fuck up and admit you had feelings for her," he says, grinning back at me.

My grip tightens on the counter. "How long have you known I've had feelings for her? I've been careful. I've never said anything."

"You did. Every day, but not with words. I've known since the first time I told you she was off limits."

"You what?" I roar, rounding the side of the island and inching closer to Nash. "You knew I liked her and you still gave me the ultimatum of picking you or her?"

"I was a kid. I saw my friend getting closer to my sister and further away from me. I was a jealous little fuck."

"You're an asshole is what you are," I say.

"I agree!" Wyatt yells from the other room. "That wasn't cool, *Nashville*."

"I didn't know how serious it was back then. We were kids, man. You don't fall in love that young. I figured you would find someone else in high school and it wouldn't be an issue."

Has he met his sister? There is no one who could ever compare to her.

"Why didn't you lift the ban? Every chance you had you warned all of us off of her. You knew I wanted to be with her and you still kept us apart. Why? Just to be a dick?"

"Probably!" Wyatt yells.

"I warned *you* off of her. I needed to know for sure you were serious about her. That you truly deserved her. All those other guys, they don't mean shit," he says. I couldn't agree with him more. "You, however, are my best friend."

"One of your best friends," Wyatt corrects him.

"We should just let him come in here," I say.

"Thought you'd never ask," Wyatt says, walking into the kitchen and taking a seat at the table.

"Like I was saying. You are *one of* my best friends," Nash repeats, looking at Wyatt who gives his nod of approval. "The only way I would know if you were serious about Sydney is if you said screw it to whatever I want and be with her anyway."

"You owe her an apology." I'm so mad at him right now. He had no right to interfere in our relationship like this. I've carried so much guilt for wanting to be with her but knowing that meant betraying him.

However, it's the pain the whole situation has caused Sydney that really guts me. She deserved better from both of us. I'm angry at myself for letting Nash hold our friendship over my head for so long.

"You're right. I do. I'll talk to her, and apologize for my part in this mess. I don't think you heard every warning. When I asked you to look after her in high school, I didn't mean sneak around behind my back and sleep with her. Do I get to punch you in the face for that?" he jokes. I don't find any of this funny.

"You wouldn't be making jokes right now if you knew how angry I am. I should be the one getting free rein on your face for playing games."

"Don't put all the blame on me. I realized my mistake. I did what I could to push you together. I asked you to help with my birthday. I texted you when she was out with Joe. I invite her over here to hang out and make myself scarce. I don't really like studying that much. You never pushed back. Not once did you speak up and say you wanted to be with her."

"You don't have to remind me. I feel like shit about it. I thought I was doing the right thing by being friends with both of you. I will be spending the rest of my life making it up to her."

"I have to ask though, why now? What's changed?"

"She asked me the same thing. She thinks it's because she's moving away. Maybe it does have to do with that a little." I can't ignore the slither of fear that once she leaves for North Carolina I will lose her for good. "Truthfully? I miss her. She has always been this bright light. Without her, I've been miserable."

Talking to her almost every night in the private chats has built a bridge between what we used to be when we first became friends and what we are now but it isn't enough. I'm greedy for more of her.

"You really have been a miserable ass," Wyatt says.

Nash laughs quietly to himself. "Is that why you've been so grumpy all these years?"

"It's probably more because he hasn't been laid in years. That always puts me in a bad mood."

"It still does," I say. "You're impossible to deal with when we're on the road."

"Wait, back up," Nash says, forcing Wyatt to hold his snarky comeback. "When was the last time you slept with someone?"

"I don't see how this is any of your business," I mumble. I like to keep this part of my life private.

"Don't tell me you haven't been with anyone since Syd," Nash says, wide-eyed. My silence must be answer enough. "Holy shit. Does she know?"

I shake my head. "I'm not sure what she knows or what she thinks."

"I can tell you right now she assumes you're enjoying college life and all the perks of being a star athlete," Wyatt says.

"Well I'm not." I've never had the desire to be with anyone else. It would have been a waste of time. I understand her need to date other people. I'll never be mad at her about that.

I never felt the same. I knew after our first time together—maybe even before—that it would be her or no one at all.

"I'm sorry I kept you apart for so long. I was looking out for her. I didn't want to see her hurt. I needed to know you were serious about her."

"I said the same thing and we both ended up destroying her." I drop my head and sigh. "I don't like the way you went about it. You could have just asked me."

"What would you have said? Would you really have admitted to anything?"

"Probably not."

"I'm glad you told me now. I'm not sure how you're going to turn it all around for the two of you, but I'm rooting for you." Nash walks over and gives me a hug with a slap on my back.

"Thanks. I need to get going or I'll be late picking her up."

"Where are you taking her?"

"The park," I say, leaving Wyatt and Nash confused. The park isn't top tier dating material for most people.

But most people aren't Sydney. Unless she's had a complete personality transplant at some point in the last few years, she's going to love this place.

My palm sweats, weakening my grip on the steering wheel. I didn't think I would be this nervous for our date. It's Sydney. We've known each other for over a decade. I'm an idiot for assuming we could easily slide back into our old ways or be able to talk like we do when we're behind our computer screens.

"Where are we going now?" she asks, tapping her thumb on her thigh. Before that she was bouncing her knee up and down.

We stopped on our way out of town and picked up dinner to go at one of our favorite barbecue restaurants. Dinner at the Pierce home was a weekly thing. Once a month their parents let us pick out where we eat. When it was mine or Sydney's turn we always picked the local owned restaurant.

"It's a surprise." I grin at her.

"I hate surprises. You should know this," she says. Her little pout is cute.

"I know you always *say* you hate surprises but that's a lie. Otherwise you wouldn't get so upset when they get ruined."

"Can I get a hint?"

"No. Tell me about your day? What did you do?"

"I went to class. Spent some time in the chemistry lab. The usual boring stuff."

"Nothing you do is boring."

"That isn't true." She rolls her eyes.

"Try me." I shift gears and wait for her to give me what she thinks is an insignificant detail of her day. When she doesn't answer right away, I glance at her with my peripheral vision. I have to roll my lips to keep from smiling at the fact she has her eyes glued on my forearm.

"Baby," I say, dropping my hand to her thigh. "You were going to say something about your day."

Her eyes zone in on my hand resting on her leg. I remove it and hold onto the gear shift again. I shouldn't be touching her like that. Not yet, not until she's sure she wants this.

"It feels weird making small talk with you."

"Why? You act like we've never talked about small things before. Like not being able to find your matching purple socks," I say and she rolls her eyes playfully again. "I want to know everything about your life, big and small."

"It's scary that you remember my purple sock fiasco from months ago."

"Prepare yourself for the fright of your life with the amount of details I remember about you."

"Are you obsessed with me?" she asks, teasing me.

"Yes," I answer honestly.

Her eyes scrutinize me then she clears her throat. "Talking about missing socks still feels too simple. Even for someone with a fascination with me," she says, smirking. I love her teasing me. I will take this over her silent treatment. Maybe she's starting to warm up to me.

"You already know all of the basic stuff anyway."

"Twenty years from now I will still want you to tell me about your day. Even if we spent the entire day together. I want to hear about it from your perspective." I take my eyes off the road for a moment to look at her.

"That makes no sense if you were there too. Why would you want me to tell you everything you already know?"

"So you agree we'll be together in twenty years?" I ask, stopping at a red light. She wiggles in her seat.

"We should get through our date first." Her eyes hold mine captive and the atmosphere in the car becomes electric. My eyes drift to her lips. She put on a light layer of gloss or maybe lip balm that pulls my attention to the lush pink center of her bottom lip. I want to swipe my tongue over her lips and see if they taste as good as they look.

The car behind me honks ruining the moment and forcing me to focus on the road again. "We're almost there." The sun is starting to set behind us. We'll have just enough time to find a spot and get everything set up before we lose the natural light.

"How is everything going with your new job? Do you know when your first day is?" I ask to kill the silence. We haven't gotten to the point where the silence feels comfortable. At least not for me. I can't sit here quietly and not wonder what she's thinking. Everything about tonight has to be perfect. I can't afford to mess anything up.

"Oh, um. Immediately after graduation. I started looking at apartments today."

My grip on the steering wheel tightens. "Did you find anything good?" If she doesn't find anything, she can't move, right? She'll have to stay here in Alabama.

"Nothing promising. Not without a roommate. All the money I've been making at Ray's is going to come in handy for deposits."

"That's good. About having the money. I still don't like you working at Ray's."

"Why? I thought it was because of Nash but now..."

"I already told you I've never done anything for Nash. He asked all of the guys to keep an eye on you when we started high school and again when we came to Newhouse but just to make sure you weren't left to the wolves."

"That doesn't make any sense."

I turn down the street that leads to the park. "I said he asked, but that isn't why I did it. I was always going to look after you because you were mine to look after."

I put the car in park and undo my seatbelt. Turning toward her I say, "I don't like you working at Ray's because I don't think it's safe. I worry about you. If you want me to say I'm jealous, I can, but that's not why."

She unbuckles her seat belt and twists her body so she's facing me. Her pink blouse tightens against her chest, exposing her cleavage that's peeking through a floral tank top. It's hard to keep my eyes focused on her face and she knows it.

"You mean when I'm dancing with other men or they flirt with me that doesn't drive you crazy?" she asks with a smirk. "Just before spring break when the whole team came out to Ray's you about lost your mind when me and the girls did our routine on top of the bar for them."

"You're right, I did. It wasn't because they were touching you or looking at you like they wanted you." I run the back of my pointer finger down her bare arm. "It was because I couldn't do the same. I couldn't show you how much I wanted you. Me looking like I wanted to kill them was me trying to stay in control around you."

"Did this happen every time you looked angry around me?"

"More than likely this was the reason, yes," I admit. She nods, inhaling a deep breath while staring down at her hands. "Come on," I say, hopping out of the car. I walk around to her side and open the door. "We need to hurry before it gets dark."

I hand Sydney the food to carry while I grab my backpack and the blanket I brought from the backseat. With a hand on her back, I usher her down the path to the park entrance.

This park is a mix of walking trails, nature preserve, and botanical gardens. When I was trying to find something for us to do, I stumbled across this *Starlight in Spring Festival*.

Going by the look of awe on Sydney's face as a few fairies hand out maps of the park, I'm on the right track.

"Let's head out to the lawn and eat first. Then we can look around and explore everything," I say after taking a quick look at the map.

We walk down one of the pathways passing elves, a few more fairies, and other woodland creatures. Sydney squeals and grabs hold of my arm when we pass a row of small cottages. "I want to go in there," she says, craning her neck to keep looking at it.

"We will, but first we need to eat." I nod toward the open area in the middle of the gardens. She drops her hand from my arm but I snatch it back before she gets too far away.

She looks down at our hands laced together. I give her hand a gentle squeeze before focusing on finding us a place that is private but also where Sydney can enjoy the ambiance.

When I spot a row of willow trees, my heart pumps a little faster. I rub a hand over the tattoos on my chest. The trees are larger and more mature than the ones I have back home but they still manage to dredge up all the memories of us together.

"How did you find out about this? I've lived here my whole life and have never been here," Syd says, slowly spinning around, absorbing her surroundings.

Unfolding the blanket, I lift it a few times letting it slowly drift to the ground until I position it the way I want it halfway under the willow tree branches.

I hold open the branches like a curtain allowing her to step inside. "It took some research but once I found it my gut told me this would be a good idea. Is it okay?" Maybe I've made the wrong choice.

"You're kidding, right? This is incredible with everyone dressed up and the decorations. Every little detail is perfect. This is perfect," she says, settling herself on the blanket.

"I'm basing my choices on the Sydney that I think I know. You said you've changed a lot over the last few years."

"You know me better than I'm willing to admit." She pulls out the styrofoam containers from the bag and checks to see which one is hers. "Or maybe more than I'm willing to accept." She passes me my sandwich platter.

"You've always been a little stubborn. Among other things." I eat a large chunk of my sandwich and chew while I enjoy the blush on Syd's cheeks.

"What about you? How much have you changed since...before?"

"I don't think I've changed much at all."

She pops a kettle chip in her mouth and lets her eyes wander down my body. "I'd say you've changed a little bit."

Her perusal makes my cheeks warm. It isn't often she blatantly checks me out when she knows I'm looking. "I think I grew about four inches since high school," I say, then bite into my sandwich.

Sydney's eyes dart to my crotch where I have my container of food sitting on my lap. The piece of bread I'm chewing gets lodged in my throat. I cough a few times but it only makes it worse. She passes me an open water bottle and I take a long swallow.

Fuck. After the way she was just looking at me, all I can picture is her...no. I won't even go there. Not tonight. As much as I want her, she needs to understand I want more from her than that.

"Fucking trouble," I mumble to myself.

"Are you calling me trouble?" she asks, feigning innocence.

"Yes."

"It's not the first time someone's called me that," she says, and her eyes widen at her admission. She's talking about me—well online me—I'm the one who called her trouble.

"Do you know how many times I got grounded because of one of your wild ideas? Two whole weeks for sneaking down to that private lake," I say, to get her mind off of what we've talked about online. I'm not ready to fess up to that yet.

"Maybe you should have done a better job at not getting caught," she says, smugly. "You didn't have to go with me."

I scoff. "You say that like I had a choice."

"I never forced you."

Stuffing the last bite of my sandwich in my mouth, I wipe my hands with the courtesy wet napkin the restaurant provided. I place all my trash back in the bag and then lean back on my hands.

Sydney daintily picks at her nachos until she creates the perfect bite. Her hair is pulled back in a high ponytail and tied with a silk, pink bow that matches her blouse.

"You wouldn't have to force me. You still wouldn't. Tell me what we're doing next and I'll be ready to go." If I knew she was ready to hear it, I would tell her I'm not talking about tonight. I'm talking about forever. Is it North Carolina? Fine with me. My bags are already packed.

The sun is moments away from setting behind the trees. Reaching behind me, I grab my backpack. I dig around until I find the tiny battery operated lantern.

"You thought of everything," she says, closing up her container of food and placing it in the bag with mine.

"I didn't really know what to expect. I wanted to be prepared."

She tips her head back and looks up into the branches of the tree. "I love these trees. Sitting under the branches like this..." her voice trails off as if she's afraid to finish the thought and admit it reminds her of us.

"They remind me of the trees in my backyard." I maneuver myself so my back is leaning against the tree trunk. "We met under those trees all summer. Every day was a new adventure. One look at you in your favorite worn down overalls and I knew the answer would be yes. It didn't matter what you had schemed up. I was in," I share the memories that still haunt us both.

Her head drops into her hands and she groans. "Those overalls were so ugly."

"They were cute with all the patches you had sewn on them." I poke her arm.

"I had to do something. They kept getting holes in them."

"Because you were climbing trees and jumping off rocks all the time." A slow, cool breeze floats between the branches. They swing back and forth as if they are being manipulated by invisible fairies setting the mood.

"What else did you bring in your bag?" She nods to where it's sitting beside me.

"Come over here and I'll show you." I smirk. It's a cheap shot but I have to take my chances when I can if I want to get her close.

"You're not playing fair." Her arms cross over her chest, she squints one eye, and her lips purse.

Holding out my hand towards her I wait for her to make her decision. My palm grows clammy and my pulse quickens. I swallow as my eyes bounce from her hand to mine silently willing her to take hold of it.

When she does, my chest deflates, expelling a breath, and I guide her toward me until she is resting against my side. "I'm playing to win." My lips press against her forehead over her curtain of curly bangs.

Reaching into my backpack I pull out what I hope is my smoking gun. The proof that Sydney has been, and will always be the only woman for me.

16

SYDNEY

The sound of strangers strolling through the park silences the moment he places a copy of *The Princess Bride* in my lap. Not just any copy but one of the original covers from the seventies.

"My mom had it packed away. When I told her I wanted to read it, she went up into the attic and pulled it out for me. I know I shouldn't have written in it but I didn't want to forget." His eyes glaze over watching as I trace my finger over the cover.

My heart beats hard against my chest and my palms are slick with moisture. I have to wipe them off on the blanket before I open the cover. "What did you want to remember?"

"All your favorite parts," he whispers. I can't even bear to look at him. If I do, I know I'll kiss him. That might be the sweetest thing anyone has ever said to me.

Slowly opening the book, I turn the pages over until I reach the first chapter. With a blue ink pen he has crossed out the name Buttercup and written in mine right above it in scratchy handwriting.

Memories I wasn't prepared for hit me hard enough to knock the wind out of me and leave me struggling to catch my breath. Reading through Koa's footnotes I'm brought back to days I spent pretending to be a princess.

Not just any princess. *His princess.* In my mind and heart, I was always his even if he didn't feel the same way.

As if moving in slow motion, the tree line surrounding us lights up one at a time. The forest comes alive with millions of twinkling lights. Our willow tree begins to glow from the inside as well.

It feels magical and surreal. Sitting here in the dark, under an enchanted tree lit by what feels like millions of little sprites, with the prince I lost years ago.

"Will you read to me?" he asks, pulling me tighter against him. I inhale a deep breath, taking in his ocean scent. I'm on the edge of the cliff and I have to make a choice. Do I dive back in or do I take a step back?

His question is simple and should come with an easy yes or no. But, nothing about us is simple or easy anymore. Reading to Koa was never about the words on the page. It was having his full attention.

It was being the center of his world for a moment in time. It was having him look at me like I was the most incredible thing he's set his eyes on. He shifts behind me and places his hand on my thigh.

The same electrifying sensation I felt earlier in the car runs up and down the length of my leg. The fear of him walking away a second time weighs heavily on my heart. It's crushing and too influential. It has me saying no when I want to look in his eyes and say yes.

"Maybe we should walk around." I sit upright and hand him the book back. He doesn't reach for it. His brow furrows as he looks at my face and back down at the book.

Sighing, he says, "Take it. I want you to have it." He stands and starts busying himself with cleaning our small mess.

I put the book in my bag for safe keeping and exit the safe cocoon of the willow tree. "I'm sorry."

His eyes meet mine through the branches. The warm lighting from the trees illuminates his large silhouette and makes his face glow. "You have nothing to be sorry about. I'm pushing you too hard." He releases an irritated groan then steps through the branches and stands in front of me. "Don't let me push you away."

I bite down on my lip to keep myself from telling him that could never happen. As much as I say I'm moving and walking away for good, it's an empty threat. It's like me saying I'll only stay up and read one more chapter, but then the enemies turn to lovers. Next thing I know it's three in the morning and I have class in five hours.

"We can't recreate the past. We need to move forward. *I* have to move forward." I grab one side of the blanket as he grabs the other end.

We each hold an end and walk toward each other. "Then we move forward together." He bends and grabs the other side of the blanket and backs up.

We walk toward each other again. "What if I'm not ready?" I ask, unsure if I want to know his answer.

He takes the blanket and tucks it under his arm. With his other hand he cups my neck and grazes my cheek with his thumb. "Then we stand still and wait until you are. I'm not going anywhere."

My hand wraps around his wrist. His pulse beats steady beneath my fingertips. My heart is rioting but I'm not sure where I stand in this fight. Are we conceding? Or are we going to stand our ground? My gut is telling me to give him this.

"Okay," I agree, putting some distance between us. He nods, slings his backpack over his shoulder, and readjusts the blanket under his arm.

I'm not sure what I'm agreeing to. Is this our fresh start at a romantic relationship? Are we picking up where we left off? Or did I agree to see if we can have a friendship that someday leads to more?

Friends with Koa? We may have labeled our relationship that way, but we've always been more.

His hand slipping into mine is like putting on a favorite sweater. There's this unexplainable comfort from knowing he has a hold of me. That he's right there if I need him.

We stroll back the way we came. This time there is a lot more to see. Hidden beyond the pathways there are little creatures made of lights that scamper across the ground and up trees. It feels like we're walking through a Grimm's Brothers Fairy Tale.

"I wasn't trying to recreate the past," he says, stopping outside the row of makeshift cottages we passed earlier. He turns his head in every direction observing our surroundings. "I wanted one more adventure with you. With the girl who taught me about fairies and other realms when all I knew about was catching baseballs."

Affection shines in his eyes and it warms me to my core. This isn't the same man who has been growling and grunting at me for the last four years. This man is sweet and soft, but also strong.

I could tell him that I'm done for good or that I needed a year to see if I can make it on my own. He would still be standing steady waiting for me. How can he be sure about me now? He said we were a mistake. I heard it with my own two ears but what if that's not what he meant.

Shaking the thought out of my head. If he wanted me then, he would have said something. Right?

"Should we go in? Our adventure awaits," I say, ignoring my protruding thoughts. Because if what I'm thinking is correct, then the fallout of everything that happened is my fault, not his. And he's taken the blame without complaint this whole time.

"As you wish," he says, gesturing toward the door of the first cottage. I suck in a harsh breath and rein in the tears that want to form. *We are not doing that now.*

I've forgotten how much that little phrase made me smile. I went to bed at night pretending that those words held the same meaning as it did in the book but I knew better than to believe in that fairy tale.

It did become an inside joke between the two of us. It didn't matter who asked us to do something, we both would always answer *'as you wish.'* It drove Nash crazy. He didn't like being left out. It was one thing I shared with Koa that I got to keep to myself.

Inside the cottage, there are two tables filled with different paints and stencils for face painting. Children are lined up on either side of the tables while their parents attempt to turn them into unicorns, princesses, and kings.

Koa gets in line and I giggle. "You can't be serious."

"Why not? You can paint whatever you want on me."

I glide up to him in line. "That is a dangerous offer. Are you sure you trust me?"

Koa sits in the chair that a newly crowned princess just vacated. He drops all of his stuff at his feet and pushes it underneath the chair.

His knees spread apart inviting me closer. "My body is yours. Do your worst," he says, spreading his arms wide.

Heat rushes to the surface of my skin. Clearing my throat, I focus my attention on all the various colors of paint. It's much safer than looking at the guy with a pair of slanted brown eyes and cut jawline.

Oh God, I can't paint his face. My cheeks will flush. I'll start to sweat. No way will I survive the five minutes—minimum—needed to paint something decent on his face with him staring back at me.

I turn my head enough to gaze at him out of the corner of my eye. Of course he's already looking at me. He is always watching me. I was under the impression it was out of allegiance to my brother but now it seems it was to satisfy his own needs.

I would be lying if the thought of me satisfying his needs didn't make me feel a little wet and needy myself.

That thought puts wind in my sails and knocks me down a flight of stairs at the same time. I wasted years believing my attraction was one sided. He had to know how I felt about him? Why didn't he ever say anything?

I gather a few paints in various shades of blue, purple, and white. Then I turn back toward Koa. "Some of my favorite books are based on Greek mythology." I undo the top button of his shirt, revealing more of the white shirt he's wearing underneath. "Are you familiar with any of their stories?"

His eyes flit around the room, checking to see if anyone is paying attention to us.

"No one is watching," I whisper, stepping closer in between his legs, while continuing to unbutton his shirt.

"Yes." His voice is huskier than before. I pull on one of his sleeves and help him out of the right side of his shirt. I leave the sleeve dangling behind him as I push up the sleeve on his white T-shirt until it's rolled tight over his shoulder. His skin pebbles as I glide my hand over the cut lines of his biceps and over the line of tattoos he already has on his arm. They are the perfect canvas for what I want to draw.

"They believe the constellations immortalize their stories." Holding the pot of blue paint in one hand and a paintbrush in the other, I carefully start drawing on Koa's upper arm. "That the stars serve as a reminder of their legacy." I exchange the blue paint for white.

"Stars represent truth and destiny. They are constant and reliable." I continue to paint stars on his arm in an array of shapes and sizes. "You can even use stars for navigation to help guide you to where you need to be."

I blow gently on his arm encouraging the paint to dry faster. Koa's eyes shutter closed and he grabs my thigh for support. I write out a few words in between the clusters of stars.

"No matter what. Our story will be remembered in the stars." I barely get the words out before my emotions get the best of me. Giving him my back, I busy myself cleaning off the paint filled brushes with a baby wipe they have available.

"Sydney," he pleads, grabbing my elbow urging me to turn around. His face begins to blur as tears pool in my eyes. "No matter what," he says. The warmth and softness in his voice dull a few of the sharp edges of my heart.

"No matter what," I repeat.

He pulls his phone out of his pocket and passes it to me. "Can you take a picture for me?" he asks. I nod and snap a quick photo of his arm before handing his phone back. The corner of his mouth twitches, forming half a smile before he puts the phone away.

"Do you like it?" I can't help asking.

"I love it. Switch places with me." He grabs hold of my waist and helps spin me around. Once I'm settled, I wait patiently for Koa to get started. The way his eyes wander over my body feels like he is stripping me bare.

"What are you going to paint?"

"At first I was thinking about a crown." His pointer finger slips underneath my bangs and pushes them to the side. "But I don't want to get paint in your hair," he says, as my curls bounce back into place.

I had my hair in braids last semester. As soon as I took them out, I had an itch to cut bangs. It's usually something I would do and regret but I've loved the way they frame my face. I'm even more grateful knowing they are saving me from having Koa within kissing distance. If he were that close, nothing could stop me from staring at his plush lips. I shouldn't be thinking about his lips or kissing him. One of his kisses will only make me want more.

He pulls out another chair and sets it in front of me. Before he sits down he selects a pot of red paint. His finger glides down the side of my neck and over the top of my cleavage. I'm afraid to move, to breathe.

"How about a pretty little necklace?" he asks, placing his hand at the base of my neck. "Would you like that, baby?"

Instinctively I lift my chin and push my throat against the side of his thumb and pointer finger. "I think I might."

Koa's eyes darken and the muscles in his jaw flex as he grinds his teeth. His thumb brushes against the sensitive skin at the base of my throat. "Maybe next time. Can you hold out your hands for me?"

"Sure," I agree. I would say yes to anything he asked at this point. I'm so turned on. I'm not proud of how easily I'm falling back in line with him. A few sweet words and I'm ready to fall at his feet.

He tenderly takes my empty hands in his, flipping them where my palms are facing the ceiling. Silently he dips the brush in the paint and begins to spread paint on the inner part of my palm where my hands are touching.

My right hand flinches without warning. "Tickles," I say, when he pauses and looks at me with a raised eyebrow.

"I'm almost finished. I'm not much of an artist." He puckers his lips and a slow breath of air skates over my hands sending shivers down my spine. "Done." He leans back and discards the brush on the table with the others.

"It's a heart," I say, lining up my pinkies and cupping my hands. It's uneven and a little wonky but it's definitely a heart.

"It's *my* heart."

In the palm of my hands. The unsaid words hang in the air.

"You're going to make me fall in love with you again, aren't you?" I whisper.

"Again?" he asks with raised eyebrows and a hint of a smile.

"We should probably go look around before it gets too late." I stand abruptly.

He crowds me and blocks my escape. "I'm going to do whatever it takes to make you wonder why you ever stopped loving me in the first place." He steps aside letting me pass.

Inhaling deep breaths, I take a moment to collect myself. I'm afraid his plan is already beginning to work. I've been carrying around years of feeling betrayed and hurt. Why am I torturing myself? Is he really the only one at fault? Maybe some of the heat should fall on me. Regardless, it's becoming a burden and I'm tired.

"Are you ready?" he asks, coming up behind me. His palm presses against my lower back. For the first time in years, his touch feels comforting instead of commanding. In the past, I felt like he was leading me around like a child.

His eyes fill with concern as he waits for my response.

"Yes," I answer. Am I saying yes to him? To us? I don't know. I think I'm saying yes to trying. To figuring it out. To putting one foot in front of the other and seeing where that takes me.

Because as much as I've been trying to move forward, I've been stuck in one place. Maybe the only way to truly get over Koa is to date him.

We walk around the gardens, taking in the lights and the people. Everywhere you turn there is something hidden in the lush greenery. Little details straight from a fairy tale.

Conversation is minimal, and I don't know if it's because neither one of us knows what to say or if we're enjoying the ambiance. I'm walking beside someone I've known half my life but at times I feel like I barely know him at all anymore.

While we've spent time in each other's presence, we have never fully let our guard down around each other the past few years.

"Look!" I shout, pointing at a photo booth they have tucked in between oversized hydrangeas, making it appear like it belongs in the middle of a secret garden. "We have to do it."

"The pictures never turn out good. I never know when they are taking the photo," he grumbles.

"That's half the fun. Come on." I take hold of his bicep and drag him toward the booth.

"You said that the last time we did one of these," he says, dropping to the bench and placing our stuff on the floor in front of him. He leans forward and pulls out his wallet from his back pocket to pay for our impromptu photoshoot.

"I did?" I squeeze in next to him. We awkwardly shift our bodies trying to get comfortable. "These things aren't as big as they used to be," I say, laughing at my awkwardness.

"They're the same size. We've gotten older," he says, taking control and putting his arm around me. I'm forced to lean into him. "And yes, you did. At my fourteenth birthday party."

"I think I blocked most of that day out of my memory." After embarrassing myself with my bowling skills, I wanted to forget the whole day. "Look at the camera," I tell him.

The screen counts down and the camera flashes. "You didn't look. You don't have to smile but you have to at least look." I straighten my hair and position myself in a different angle for the next shot.

"I am looking. I've been looking for years," he murmurs. I slant my head enough to see his face. His eyes are soft and his mouth is curled in a boyish smile. "I almost kissed you that day."

"What?" I rear my head back. He catches it in his palm and slides his hand down to the nape of my neck. His fingers weave in between my hair. "Why would you want to do that? You didn't even want me there."

The flash of the camera goes off momentarily blinding me. "I don't know what gave you that idea. I wanted you there."

"But you were mad when I ruined your party."

"I was mad at all my so-called friends for laughing at you and making you upset." His hand grips me tighter, pulling me an inch closer to him.

"So when you said *'I guess you can come if you want'* while you and Nash were planning the party..."

Koa drops his head. "I never should have said that. I was trying hard to not be obvious in front of Nash. I went to bed praying every night that you would be there."

"I see."

"I don't think you do. Not yet, but I'm going to show you. I'm going to show you everything if you'll let me. Whoever this other guy is..."

"I'm not really thinking about him right now," I admit.

"That's good to hear." He smirks, dropping his hand to my leg. "We only have a few photos left. We better make them count."

"Are you going to smile this time?"

He shakes his head. "I'm going to kiss you this time." He leans closer. Any oxygen left in the tiny booth is gone now.

"You've kissed me before," I say, flicking my tongue over my lips.

"I've never kissed you the way I wanted to." His breath tickles my nose.

"And how's that?" I can barely form the words, it's so hard to breathe.

"Like you're mine." Koa slowly leans toward my face. Closing my eyes, my heart races waiting for him to make contact.

When his mouth presses into mine, I'm practically levitating out of my seat. This isn't like the kiss at Ray's. That was a performance. It was collateral damage to get that creep to back off and leave me alone.

This kiss is a claiming. There is power behind it. His fingers push further into my hair, controlling the way I'm positioned as he alternates nipping at my lips. I don't know which way is up or down anymore. All I know is I need to be closer to him.

It's hard to move in this small space but I manage to slip one arm behind his back and the other around his neck.

A moan slips out of me when my breasts press against his chest. He swipes his tongue across the seam of my mouth and I'm lost completely in the taste of him.

The camera flashes and I pull away smiling. He doesn't give me more than a millisecond to catch my breath before he's back on me again. Our tongues tangle and explore each other's mouths.

With every swipe of his tongue, he deepens the kiss. For years I've been holding on to old memories of what I *thought* it felt like to be kissed by Koa Mahina.

My memories have failed me because I don't remember his kisses feeling like this. This feels like he's rewriting every misstep, every angry look, or hurtful word with the swipe of his tongue against mine.

Maybe that's his super power. He has the ability to administer temporary amnesia with a single kiss. Slowly, I drag myself away from him. He groans, making me laugh.

"I wasn't finished with you," he says, pulling me closer and popping another kiss on my mouth.

Eyes squinted and brows furrowed, his gaze lingers on me. Examining the effect of our kiss. His mouth curves into a smug smile when his eyes land on my lips. He's pleased with how swollen they are I'm sure.

When we were kids, occasionally Koa and I could talk across a room with various eye movements or head shakes. It was a skill we developed after we got in trouble one too many times.

Every time our parents would interrogate us we would blink once for yes and blink twice for no, making sure our stories matched up. There were also winks, eye rubs, yawns, and ear tugs.

I want to give him the signal that everything is okay, but I'm not certain it is. I wring my hands in my lap. It's too quiet. There's nothing but the sound of us breathing, the occasional person walking by, and all the thoughts running through my head.

"Sydney," he says, breaking the silence.

"I wonder what the photos look like." Ignoring him, I stand and slice through the curtain. Why is it harder to breathe now that I'm away from him? Shouldn't it be the other way around? I inhale a few deep breaths of fresh air.

He says my name again.

"I hope there's at least one of you smiling." I fish our strip of photos out of the dispenser. Distancing myself further from Koa, I stroll down the path and examine the photos.

"Syd, stop." He grabs hold of my shoulder and spins me around. His hand cups my cheek. "We're done running, remember? We're either standing still or we're moving forward together. There's no more running."

Easy for you to say. You're not the one being called baby and having the person you've loved for most your life finally wanting you back.

I can easily see myself careening back into Koa's atmosphere if I allowed myself the freedom to do so. However, in the back of mind I keep thinking about my online mystery man. I can't deny the fluttery feelings I get when I'm talking to him.

Do I give Koa and I another try or do I take my chances on something new?

FICTION FORUM

NotYourAverageJoe19
> A good book keeping you up?

FaeAtHeart
> That would make things easier.

NotYourAverageJoe19
> That's the good thing about books. They allow you to escape from reality.

FaeAtHeart
> Is that what you've been trying to do lately when you read? Escape reality?

NotYourAverageJoe19
> No. I don't even want to waste time sleeping. I'm afraid I might miss something.

FaeAtHeart
> Life is that good, huh?

NotYourAverageJoe19
> When I'm talking to you it is.

GINGER WALLS

FaeAtHeart
> Who are you? Besides a smooth talker.

NotYourAverageJoe19
> I'm just a guy.

FaeAtHeart
> No. Who are you really? I need to know. I love chatting with you but I need more. I thought you were someone I knew in my real life.

NotYourAverageJoe19
> This is your real life. You do know me.

> Wait, who did you think I was?

FaeAtHeart
> You're going to laugh.

NotYourAverageJoe19
> Try me.

FaeAtHeart
> The night we started chatting online. Well, earlier that day I met a guy on campus and his name was Joe. I thought you were him.

NotYourAverageJoe19
> How do you know I'm not him?

FaeAtHeart
> Because he never made me feel the way you do with a single conversation.

FOUL TERRITORY

> **FaeAtHeart:** I've said too much.

NotYourAverageJoe19
> No. I'm glad you feel that way.

> **FaeAtHeart:** Now you understand my problem.

NotYourAverageJoe19
> Not really.

> **FaeAtHeart:** I don't know how to say this. I don't want you to be upset.

NotYourAverageJoe19
> It's fine. You can tell me anything.

> **FaeAtHeart:** I went out on a date the other night. A really good one. And now I don't know what to do.

NotYourAverageJoe19
> I'm the other guy.

> **FaeAtHeart:** Huh? Yes, I guess you could say that. Or maybe he is because I was talking to you first.

NotYourAverageJoe19
> Do you like this guy?

> **FaeAtHeart:** We have history.

GINGER WALLS

NotYourAverageJoe19

> That doesn't answer my question.

FaeAtHeart

> I do. I also like you.

NotYourAverageJoe19

> Is this same friend you were telling me about with the good memories that haunt you at night?

FaeAtHeart

> Yes. It's him. I'm sorry. I feel terrible not telling you that he was once more than a friend.

NotYourAverageJoe19

> Don't feel bad. I understand.

> And you still have feelings for him?

FaeAtHeart

> I'm still figuring all of that out because I also like you.

> I'm confused.

NotYourAverageJoe19

> Maybe I should step back until you figure things out with this guy.

> If a woman like you was willing to give me another chance, I would want a fair fight with no obstacles.

FOUL TERRITORY

FaeAtHeart
> I don't want to stop talking to you.
>
> You're the only one who will talk to me about books and not get bored. You really mean a lot to me too.

NotYourAverageJoe19
> This other guy doesn't like books? I thought that was a requirement.

FaeAtHeart
> He does but I haven't talked to him about stuff like that in a long time. A lot has changed since then.

NotYourAverageJoe19
> Did he give you that impression on your date?

FaeAtHeart
> No.

NotYourAverageJoe19
> Then try. Give him a chance to prove himself to you.

FaeAtHeart
> What about you?

NotYourAverageJoe19
> I'll be here.
>
> But don't think about me. Give this guy your all.

GINGER WALLS

> And if you end up with him, I'll be happy you're happy.

FaeAtHeart

> Okay. I'll message you soon.

17

SYDNEY

Laying flat on my stomach, I reach under my bed, shuffling around different boxes, until I find the ones I'm looking for. My craft supplies are a little bit of organized chaos.

I've resorted to sorting the various supplies in shoe boxes while at school. It forces me to keep each collection manageable. My crafting hoard at home is another story. I will need to slim that down before I move.

I stack the shoe boxes and carry them out to the dining table. I've been an emotional mess the past few days and in need of some creative therapy.

Between spending more time with Koa and losing my connection with *NotYourAverageJoe19*, my heart has been in a tailspin. I know he meant well by giving me space, but I do miss our chats a little.

I have taken his advice and slowly started talking to Koa about these things again. It was weird at first to text him a photo of the book I'm reading along with a silly anecdote. I was worried he would tease me or leave me on read.

He may have kept a book we read since we were teens but that doesn't mean he's reading now. I've never seen him with a book other than something for a class since he started playing baseball in high school. That's when the sport took over his life.

To my surprise, he texted me back almost immediately. We ended up texting back and forth all night. I don't want to say it felt like old times because I don't think it did. Talking with Koa now feels new and exciting.

I'm not sure what to expect from him next. He's still the shy boy who lived down the street but he also has an air of confidence to him. He speaks with such certainty.

Sighing, I grab the remote off the table and scroll through the list of rom-coms until I find one of my favorites and hit play. I slide over the box full of thread and jewelry making supplies.

Digging through the box, I find a few unfinished pairs of earrings. I should probably finish those, but I found a new tutorial I want to try. They will have to wait. I unearth my phone from the mess I've already managed to make to look up the video and notice a new text from Koa.

> **KOA**
> Have you read this one yet?

I bite my lip to keep from smiling. It doesn't stop my cheeks from heating up as I look at the screenshot.

> **ME**
> Not yet. I like the cover.

> **KOA**
> I thought it was cool too.

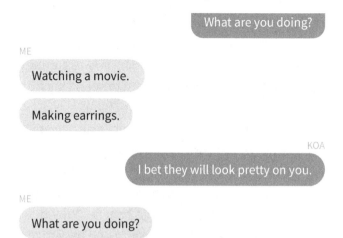

I barely get the text sent when someone knocks on the door. "I'm coming," I yell, as I pause my movie. I check the peephole and grin.

"I'm knocking on your door," Koa says, as I let him inside.

"I see that. Were you in the hall waiting for me to text you back?"

Koa strolls over to the dining table and looks over all the different colors of thread I've started working with. "No. I was waiting in my car. When I saw the bubbles, I came upstairs. Can I make something?"

I follow him over to the table. "You want to craft with me?"

"Yes." He kisses the top of my head and takes a seat. He snatches the remote off the table and starts the movie.

I eye him suspiciously as I sit down beside him. "Do you want to make a bracelet?" I pass him a shoebox full of beads.

"Why are you looking at me like that?" he asks, smirking at me.

"I'm just surprised you want to spend your free time making bracelets." I shrug and pick up the teal thread I was using.

Koa places the stretchy, white cording he was cutting down and twists his body toward me. "I want to spend my free time with you. I don't care what we do. Okay?"

I nod and go back to my earrings while also keeping one eye on Koa as he measures out the cording by wrapping it around his wrist.

"Let me help you," I say, when he starts to struggle knotting the end of the string with his large fingers. "Why don't you pick out what beads you want to use?" I nod toward the box.

He pulls out a bag full of colorful discs and puts them to the side. Then adds another bag of round beads to the pile. "You have letters," he says excitedly, making me giggle.

"Should I be worried?" I pass him back his string.

"No, but I might make your brother a bracelet with a choice word or two," he grumbles.

"Why is that?" I haven't talked to Nash since Koa and I went out on our date a few days ago.

"He knows about us."

"Oh, okay. Was he mad or something?" I chew on my bottom lip.

"No, he wasn't." He adds another bead to his bracelet. "I was though." He grips a bead so tight it pops out between his fingers. "He already knew how I felt about you when I told him about our date."

"That doesn't surprise me. He hinted at it a little after his birthday party. He asked what happened when we went upstairs. I told you people would get ideas," I say, joking with him.

He grins. "Good. Let them talk. But apparently he's known I've liked you since before we started high school."

My entire body freezes. I should be ecstatic that Koa just admitted he's liked me this entire time. However my ears are ringing with the knowledge Nash has also known.

"And he still warned you off of me?" My fists clamp so tight my fingernails dig into my palms.

Koa nods as his hands reach for mine and I loosen my fists. "I'm upset with him too."

I scoff. "And you want to make him a friendship bracelet? He's going to be wearing it to his funeral because I'm going to kill him," I say, letting go of Koa's hands and snatching my phone off the table. I'm going to give him a piece of my mind. I can't believe he did that.

"He had his reasons. It made sense in his head." Koa takes my phone and drops it back on the table. I purse my lips at him.

"Of course you would side with him." I stand from the table and walk toward the kitchen.

"I'm not taking his side." Koa stands and confronts me where I'm leaning against the kitchen counter. "I'm furious at him," he says, caging me in. "But I'm not going to let him get between us anymore."

He pushes my bangs off my brow and the air in the room shifts. I skim the hem of his shirt with my fingers. He hisses from the contact to his skin.

Our eyes meet and I drag my palms across his bare skin until I reach his back. I haven't touched him like this since the night we slept together. I don't know how it's possible but his muscles feel bigger, firmer.

"I don't want Nash to come between us anymore either." I press my body into his to demonstrate how close to him I want to be. "I don't want anyone to come between us," I say, tightening my grip on his back.

"What are you saying?"

"I'm saying I want to be with you. The other guy I was talking to," I say, biting on my lip. "I never met him. I just talked to him online. He's great but he's not you. And I want you." I glance up at him with a new sense of hope.

"Sydney," he says, hesitantly. "I don't know how to tell you this."

"Then don't. Not now." I push up on my toes and lean in, pressing my lips slowly to his. I pull away only to have his hand grip the nape of my neck and hold me in place. "See. This is a much better idea than talking." I smirk.

"It is, but I want you to be sure. There is no going back. I'm not letting you go again."

"I'm sure. I'm done fighting my heart. I was never going to get over you. I tried and maybe came close, but it wasn't meant to be."

"That's because *we* are meant to be. I've always known this. I'm glad you're finally catching up." He smirks, then captures my lips between his.

Koa's arms wrap tighter around me. I have to fight the urge to climb up his body. Especially when his left hand drifts down to my ass, giving it a squeeze. It's almost like he's inviting me to hitch my leg over his hip.

I roll my hips slightly and it puts just enough pressure against his erection to make me gasp. "Baby," he groans into my neck. "We need to stop."

"Why?" I ask, tipping my head back and savoring the way his mouth feels on my chest and neck.

"Because if we don't, I'm going to take you back to your room and I really want to finish my bracelet."

I pull away from him. "You would rather finish your bracelet than help me finish?" I flick my tongue over my lips and drape my arms over his shoulders.

"Trouble," he growls, turning me on even more. He kisses my lips then cups my pussy in his hand. He presses his thumb over the seam of my pants, pushing it against my clit. I whimper and dig my fingers into his hair.

Gripping the back of my thigh with his free hand, he lifts me off the ground. His show of strength is so hot. I try hiding it on my face but going by the way his lip twitches I'm not doing a good job.

He carries me into my room and lays me down on the bed. Hovering over me—his arms on either side of my head—his eyes drift over my body, stopping for a moment on my chest before retreating back to my face.

"What do you want, trouble? My fingers or my mouth?"

I raise an eyebrow. "Are those my only two options?"

"Today? Yes." He places a quick kiss on my lips. "You will have to wait another day for my cock."

"Pity." I pout, making him shake his head. "I want both."

Koa's eyes darken as he unbuttons my pants and slides them down my legs along with my underwear. He stands back, admiring me for a moment. My breathing increases with every second that passes.

"Spread your legs, baby. Let me see all of you." He swallows hard watching me lift my shirt over my head. Then leaning back on my elbows I slowly widen my legs.

He drops to his knees on the bed and crawls over my body. "You look fucking delicious. I'm going to enjoy tasting every fucking inch of you," he says, before kissing his way down my body.

"You don't come until I say." His commanding voice skates up my skin, making me shiver. I nod in agreement but once his thumb pushes against my clit I know it's a lie.

Keeping his hand in place, he kisses and licks his way up my legs like he has all the time in the day. I lift my hips and press my clit harder against his hand.

"Patience, baby," he says, when he finally reaches my pussy. He moves his hands under my ass cheeks and dips his nose into my center, inhaling a deep breath. He's making me so wet for him.

"I never got to taste you before. Not like this," he tells me before dragging his tongue through my slit. I buck off the bed when he sucks on my sensitive clit. He maneuvers one of his arms over my hips and pins me down.

My right hand slips through his hair while I strangle the comforter on my bed with my left. Tilting my head, I watch him lick, suck, and dip his tongue into my cunt. His feral eyes catch mine and it almost makes me come.

"Koa," I plead and attempt to move my body where I need him. "Please."

"Not yet," he growls. Then pushes a finger inside me. He slides it in easy enough but I feel so full. He adds a second finger, stretching and pumping inside me. "Are you ready, trouble? Do you want to come?"

"Yes," I moan.

"Come for me, baby." He puts his mouth back on my clit while working his fingers and I'm done.

I tighten my grip on the bedding as I ride out my orgasm. He moves out from between my legs but continues to move his fingers inside of me. "You look blissed out," he says, smirking.

"I am." My eyes flutter closed and I rake my teeth over my lips. He pulls his fingers out of me and kisses me on the lips. His erection presses into my thigh and my eyes widen.

"Don't even think about it. Today is about you. I'll go home later and fuck my fist with the taste of you on my tongue. That is enough for me. *For now.*"

"Do you do that a lot?" I ask, scooting off the bed and throwing my shirt over my head.

"More than I should admit." He stands and wraps his arms around me as I finish buttoning my pants. "You don't really want to know the answer to that question. Let's just say if I get carpal tunnel, it will be your fault."

We walk out of my room and I sit down at the table while he goes to the sink and washes his hand. "Why would that be my fault?" I ask.

He tilts his head and looks at me as if he's asking *'really?'* "Do I need to list off all the times you've turned me on so much over the years I resorted to jacking off into a sock or taking a cold shower?"

"We have time." I put my elbows on the table, rest my chin on my fists, and bat my eyelashes at him.

He laughs and picks up the bracelet he had started making earlier. "Fine. I'll confess everything. The first time was the summer before we started high school."

"Also known as the summer Sydney got boobs."

"One and the same," he grumbles, making me laugh.

I blush and smile with every story he tells me. I'm flattered, but also confused because I never would have guessed any of this was happening. He was always quiet and reserved. He acted like nothing ever bothered him.

Had I known I was getting under his skin, I would have tried a little harder to get on top of it too.

FICTION FORUM

FaeAtHeart

Hi. How have you been?

NotYourAverageJoe19

Good. Great actually. How about you?

FaeAtHeart

Same. Really good. I took your advice.

NotYourAverageJoe19

Oh yeah? How did it go?

FaeAtHeart:

Better than I expected.

Amazing actually.

NotYourAverageJoe19

I'm happy for you.

FaeAtHeart

I'm sorry. I feel like I've led you on.

GINGER WALLS

NotYourAverageJoe19

> Don't apologize. You did nothing wrong.

> I should be thanking you.

FaeAtHeart

> Thanking me? For what?

NotYourAverageJoe19

> You gave me hope. When I felt like I'd never get the chance, you kept the hope alive.

FaeAtHeart

> The chance at what?

NotYourAverageJoe19

> A chance with my dream girl.

18

KOA

Sydney nibbles on her bottom lip as she highlights sections of her text book. I've forgotten how cute she is when she studies. It's been awhile since I've sat across the table from her with books spread out in front of us.

Somehow she convinced me to study and work on my assignments at the library instead of alone with her at my house like I wanted to. I will have to think of another way to get her over there.

Maybe after she's caught up on her work she'll be willing to do something else for the rest of the day. After the last chat we had in the forum, I know I need to tell her it's me she's been talking to. I just need to do it the right way so she'll understand why and not hate me.

I read over the paper I've been editing for the last half hour. It's basically finished. I only have a few points I want to tighten up before I turn it in to my professor.

Sydney's foot bumps against my calf under the table. My eyes pop up to meet hers. A light blush covers her cheeks and I want to see how many other ways I can make her blush.

"I need to get another book." She stands and pushes in her chair. She weaves through the tables on the second floor of the library until she reaches the tall bookshelves in the very back of the room. She glances over her shoulder in my direction before disappearing between two bookshelves.

I lock both of our laptops and shut them down before finding Sydney. She is up to something. If she wants to play, I'm taking her home. This might be my chance to get her alone and confess everything.

"What are you doing back here, trouble?" I pull her towards me from behind with my hand on her throat and kiss her. She tilts her head and gives me access.

"I told you I needed a book." Her hand clutches the spine of the book she's holding while my hands roam over her hips and thighs.

I glance at the book in her hand and grin when I read the title. "When did you start studying law?"

She spins around and looks up at me through hooded eyes. "You never know when I might find myself in trouble and need a little legal help."

"Oh, I'm sure you'll find it," I tease her. "Let's get out of here." I take her hands in mine. She runs her thumb over the beads on the friendship bracelet I'm wearing on my wrist. I made a few during our craft session but the one that spells out *'trouble'* is my favorite.

"And do what?"

"I don't know. What would be your perfect day?" I ask. She drops her arms around my neck.

"Hmm...I have an idea but I'm not sure if you'll like it."

"Baby, I told you, I don't care what we do as long as we're spending time together." I pop a kiss on her lips.

"Alright. Give me thirty minutes and I'll meet you back at your place. I need to pick up some essentials."

"Can I get something?"

"How about some snacks?"

"I think I can handle that."

"Are you going to let go of me?"

"I don't think I will," I say, before leaning down and kissing her slowly so I can savor the taste of her. "Any chance more of that is on your list somewhere?"

"You'll have to wait and see." She bites down on her bottom lip and I groan quietly as I follow her back to the table to get our stuff.

As soon as I get back from the store with chips, chocolate, and the caramel popcorn she loves, I rush upstairs to straighten my room. She's been in here a few times recently but not like this.

It also isn't lost on me that she is the only girl to ever step foot in my room. I straighten a stack of books and ultimately decide to push them under the bed. I can't hide every trace of my obsession but those are books we talked about in our chats. I will bring them out later when I tell her about who I am online. Because I am telling her today.

"You're sorry? How could you? You had no right to interfere in my life like that!" Sydney's voice carries up the stairs. Damnit. I knew this fight was coming. I'm not prepared for it today.

I bolt down the hallway and take the stairs two at a time to play referee. Sydney has dropped her bags on the couch and is standing in front of Nash. He's holding his hands up pleading for her to hear him out.

"I was looking out for your best interest. I was protecting you."

"Protecting me?" She steps into his personal space. "You were looking out for yourself. You were being selfish. You didn't care about me."

"That's not true and you know it." His eyes soften as he attempts to reach out for her hand but she steps away.

"No. Don't touch me right now. You kept him away from me," she shouts and punches him in the chest. Pretty sure she hurt herself more than she did him.

"Syd." I hook an arm around her waist before she tries punching him again. Her body melts into mine. The water collecting in her eyes is enough to take me out. I glare back at Nash. He has the decency to bow his head.

"He kept us apart on purpose. We could have been together this whole time," she says, with a tremble to her lip.

"It wasn't just Nash. It was me too."

"You wouldn't have stayed away if it wasn't for him." She glares back at her brother.

"Oh, you think so?" I raise an eyebrow and smirk at her. "You think I was so hung up on you I would have come running the moment he took me out of my chains?" I brush her hair off her shoulders.

She moves closer, pressing her breasts against my torso. "Yes." Her voice is sweet, yet seductive, and has my body on high alert.

"You're not wrong. Let's go upstairs. I promised you a perfect day."

"Yeah, y'all can take that somewhere else." Nash waves us off, encouraging us to go to my room. Sydney growls and lunges at her brother. I grab her by the waist and her legs kick up in the air. I miss seeing this feisty side of her.

"Put me down." She pushes and pulls at my forearms.

"Are you going to behave?" I ask.

"Probably not," she says, making me chuckle.

"Try for me, trouble." I loosen my grip on her, letting her stand on her own two feet.

"I really am sorry, Syd. You know I love you and would never do anything to intentionally hurt you. I needed to know Koa was serious about you. That he deserved you."

"What about what I deserved? All I've ever heard about for years was what you and Koa wanted. What about me?" She slaps a hand against her chest. "I deserved a chance to make my own choices. You stole that from me."

"I thought I was doing the right thing," he says, placing his hands in his pockets.

My head swivels between my best friend and the woman I love. They're both hurting. This isn't going to be resolved today and I would rather her be in a better mood when I finally tell her what I need to.

"Why don't you go upstairs? I'll grab your stuff." I give her a quick kiss before she nods leaving us alone. Once she's out of view, I face Nash.

"You just kissed my sister in front of me," he comments dryly.

"Get used to it."

"Are you together now?"

"Yes," I say as confidently as I can, knowing full well she may never speak to me again once she finds out I'm the guy she's been talking to online.

"It's kind of bullshit that she's forgiven you so easily and won't even accept my apology."

"You think she's forgiven me? Not even close, man. Getting to where I am with Sydney was far from easy. It's work and I will gladly put in that work every day if that's what it takes to keep her."

"I'm glad to hear it. Just make sure I don't hear anything else." He shudders.

I grab her bags off the couch. "I suggest you invest in ear plugs," I say, as I make my way up the stairs. I've been waiting too long to be with Sydney. The last thing I'm going to do is ask her to be quiet.

"I'll have to go back down and get the snacks," I say, as I enter the room. "Are you okay?" I shut the door and place her things on my desk. "Baby?" I ask again since she's ignoring me.

She's sitting on the side of my bed with an open book in her lap. One of my books. It's one we read together a few years ago. Well, she doesn't know that we read it together but we did.

"Say something please," I plead, as I sit down beside her.

"Are they all like this?" she asks, flipping another page. Her finger traces over the highlighted passages and my notes in the margins.

"Almost all the books on that shelf." I nod toward the bookshelf over my bed. I keep all my favorites there. I like seeing them first thing when I walk into my room. "The stack on the other shelf are books I still need to read. I've gotten behind since the season started."

"How long have you been doing this?" She closes the book. Then stands on the bed to exchange it for another one. Her fingers slide over the titles until she finds the one she wants.

Sitting crossed-legged in the middle of my bed, she looks like every dream I've ever had come true. I have to blink my eyes a few times to make sure this is really happening.

I flip over on my stomach and lay down in front of her. Grazing my hands over her thighs, I expel a slow breath as her vanilla—and cinnamon maybe—scent envelops me.

"Since the first day," I confess.

"The first day?" she questions, her eyes meeting mine.

"The first day you came over and read to me while I practiced. You had all your smelly pens in different colors and highlighters."

"I forgot about those," she says with a quiet laugh.

"I didn't."

"I read this one in high school." She taps her finger in the center of the page.

"I know."

"You know?"

"You've read every book on that shelf," I tell her.

"That's not a coincidence, is it?"

I grin. "No it's not. Every time I'd see you with a book in your hand I made a point to buy it as soon as I had enough money."

"I didn't even know you liked reading this much." She flips another page, squinting to read my notes.

"I didn't, at least not at first. But you've made me enjoy reading over the years. I did, however, like you a lot. Still do if you haven't noticed." I give her thigh a gentle squeeze.

"I'm noticing." She closes the book and places it beside her on the bed. Her fingers glide over my face and into my hair. I lean into her touch and close my eyes. "I thought I was going to torture you with my perfect day, but I think you might actually enjoy it."

"I know I will because you're here." I grab her underneath her thighs and pull her until she is laying flat on her back. Her yelp quickly turns into giggles. I stretch my body over her and position myself between her legs. "Do you know how long I wanted to have you here with me in my room like this?"

"Going by our conversation the other day I'm going to guess ever since you were fifteen years old." She smirks.

"You're going to be teasing me about that forever, aren't you?"

"Probably. It's nice to know everything wasn't one sided," she confesses. It's hard to hold her gaze when there is pain etched in her eyes. Hurt and heartbreak that was caused by me.

"I'm so sorry. I'll never stop trying to make it up to you."

"I know. I don't want you to think I'm holding the past over your head. I could have said something too. I thought I was the only one suppressing their feelings. Even now it's hard for me to take the leap when no one caught me the last time I made the jump. I'm afraid I'll just keep falling."

I climb even further on top of her until our bodies are flush. I allow myself to sink into her. I want her to feel me. I need her to know that I'm here.

"There's nothing wrong with falling. I keep doing it over and over every day." Leaning forward I press my lips against hers.

Kissing her with our bodies pressed together like this is a memory I want to get tattooed on my body so I never forget the way she feels under me. One of her arms wraps around my back while the other hand pulls at the hair at the base of my neck.

Sliding my hand behind her, I turn her head to deepen the kiss. My erection presses against the seam of her jeans, making her moan against my lips.

She raises her hips, rolling her body against mine. "What are you doing to me?" I ask, laying kisses against her jawline until my nose hits the soft fabric that hangs off the hoop of her earrings.

I inhale her sweet vanilla scent and lick at her neck. She slips her hands under my shirt. Her warm palms against my skin is almost enough to make me lose it. I don't think she understands the power she has over me. I push off the bed enough to slip my shirt over my head to give her more access to my body.

Her laughter cuts through the silence in the room. I close my eyes and let it seep into my soul. It's been too long since I've heard that sweet sound come out of her.

"What do you want, Sydney?" I play with the hair that frames her face. Her fingers graze against my bare skin, tracing over the tattoo that covers my shoulder and back, making me squirm.

She lifts her head to kiss me again. "I like this," she says, cradling my head in her arms. "But it wasn't on my perfect day list."

"That's unfortunate." I grind against her. My dick will be more disappointed than I am. Do I want her naked? Absolutely. The feel of her bare skin against mine is a sensation I won't ever forget. I wouldn't complain if she refreshed my memory on a daily basis. "You're always on my perfect day list."

"Have you always been so romantic and smooth?"

"I'm not really."

"Actually, you are. You say the sweetest things and you read my favorite books. I don't think it gets more romantic than that."

"That's me telling you the truth." I kiss the tip of her nose. "You also have good taste in books. I enjoy reading them. I liked knowing we were doing something together even if it was my secret."

"Closet romantic," she declares, kissing me. When she pulls away her mouth curves in a flirty smile. "I'm glad you enjoy reading because that's what we're going to do. But first..." She cups my cheeks in her hands. "Face masks," she says, gently tapping the side of my face.

"Face masks?"

19

SYDNEY

Koa's face scrunches up in confusion. As much as I'm enjoying using his half naked body as a security blanket, I need a minute to collect my thoughts.

He's read every book. And not just read them but annotated them in detail. How did I never notice? I feel like an idiot for never seeing the signs.

"Yes, face masks!" I pop a kiss on his lips—which feels more natural than it should—and push him off of me.

He groans as he rolls onto his back and I slide off the bed. I brought all the necessities for a night of reading. When he asked me what I wanted to do at the library, a night spent wrapped up in my favorite robe and a good book is what I would pick every time. Although now I will be adding *'wrapped up with Koa to the list'* too.

"You are going to love this. Your pores will be so grateful," I say. He grunts and I glance over my shoulder to say something snarky. The words come to a screeching halt in my brain when my eyes land on Koa still spread out on the bed.

His face is wedged in his elbow and his other hand is squeezing and readjusting his cock which is barely hidden behind a pair of gym shorts. My cheeks warm and my thighs clench watching the way the muscles in his abs tighten from the movement.

"You better stop looking at me like that, trouble." He smirks, turning on his side. A vision of me tackling him and sucking on him like a newly created vampire flashes through my mind.

He catapults himself off the bed and his arms lasso me in less than two seconds. "Nothing but trouble," he says, burying his face in the crook of my neck.

"I don't see how I'm the troublemaker here. I'm not the one laying on the bed touching myself. I'd say you're the one who's trouble."

Koa groans into my hair and playfully bites down on my shoulder. "We're doing that later after your face masks and whatever else you have planned."

"Wh-what?"

His eyes darken and his tongue slowly slides over his lower lip. "You. Naked on the bed. I'll watch while you make yourself come. Maybe I'll pull my cock out and show you exactly what thinking about you does to me."

My knees threaten to buckle. Thank goodness for his arms tightening around me.

"Do you want to do that? Do you want to see how hard you make me? How easy it is for me to come when I picture you taking me in your mouth?" He grabs hold of my hips and pushes his cock between my legs.

"What about me?" I raise an eyebrow. I've never been one to hold my tongue around him. If he gets to put me on edge with his dirty talk, two can play that game.

"What about you?"

Placing my hand over his, I slide his hand down until he's cupping my pussy over my pants. His finger pushes against my center. "Do you want to see how wet you make me?" I wouldn't be surprised if can't already feel it through the fabric.

His eyes flutter closed. My nails scrape against his chest, needing something to hold myself steady as he continues to work me over my clothes. "Do you want to see how I make myself orgasm thinking of you touching me again?"

"Damnit, baby." He kisses me, slipping his tongue inside my mouth. Pulling away, he rests his head against mine. "You've always been my trouble. My demise. The first time I saw you, I knew you were going to be someone special in my life."

My eyes close and I let his words sink into my heart. "Don't ever tell me you're not romantic again," I say, before tearing myself away from him.

Opening up one of the bags I brought, I retrieve the reading robe I brought for him. "Here put this on." It's baby blue with moons and suns reading books.

He chuckles as he slips one of his massive arms through the sleeve. "I think it might be my color."

"It looks good on you." I roll my lips to keep from smiling. The sleeves are so tight on his arms one false move will split every seam in the fabric. "I'll be right back," I say, picking up my cozy pajamas, robe, and the premade dry mixture I have for our masks.

Koa bounces onto his bed and lays down with his hands behind his head. He is really testing the durability and quality of my robe. With one last glance at his bare chest, I make my way to the bathroom in the middle of the hallway he shares with Hart.

I change my clothes and slip into my robe. I don't want to give myself too much time to think about what's waiting for me back in his room. Everything between us is moving so fast. We are falling back into place like years of heartache hasn't kept us apart.

Isn't this what you've always wanted? I put my terry cloth headband over my head and fluff my hair. Yes, it is. Looking at myself in the mirror, I take in my smile and the color in my cheeks. He is slowly waking me back up. I'm not sure I could walk away from him even if I wanted to.

Quickly I add a little bit of water into the jar of dry ingredients. I'm still experimenting with the recipe, but this mix of matcha, ground oatmeal, and a little bit of activated charcoal has been my favorite.

I grab my clothes in one hand and my mask concoction in the other and go back to his room. I knock on the door before peeking my head inside the room. "Are you fucking kidding me right now?" I ask, closing the door behind me.

"What? I got started without you," he says, innocently. "Sorry. I only read a few pages."

"When did you start wearing glasses?" He can't be that naive. He has to know that sitting in his bed shirtless—the blue robe is easy to ignore—with an open book in his lap and wearing wire frame reading glasses is a fantasy. *My fantasy.*

"Last year. They're just for reading."

"They look good on you." I exchange my clothes for the book I brought for myself and join him on the bed. "Unfortunately you're going to have to take them off so I can do your mask," I say, sitting on my knees.

"Do you really like them? I only wear them at home. I'm kind of self conscious about them."

A small laugh escapes me. Maybe he doesn't get how hot he looks wearing them. "I more than like them," I say, inching closer to him. "You look very sexy in them." I lift my left leg and position myself so I'm straddling over him.

He glides his hands up my thighs and keeps going until he's able to latch onto my ass. He yanks me closer and urges me to sit down on his lap.

"Thank you, baby." He tilts his chin and gives me a quick kiss.

"Are you ready for your facial?" I ask, removing his glasses. "Don't worry. We'll put you back on later," I say to the glasses, as I reach over to the table and put them down for safe keeping.

"You're cute," he says, kissing my neck this time.

"This might be a little cold." I dip two fingers into the muddy olive green mixture and pick up a nice glob of it. "You need to stay still," I scold. "I don't want to get this in your eyes."

"I'm doing the best I can but it's difficult when you're sitting on my lap like this." His dick twitches beneath me and I have to squeeze my thighs to stop myself from grinding down on him.

"You need to be a good boy and try."

He grabs my wrist before I have a chance to spread anything on his face. Forcing my fingers back into the jar, he scrapes them against the side of the glass, removing most of the mixture from my fingers. Then he places the jar on the table next to his reading glasses.

"How about I'll be a good boy and sit still while you show me how pretty you look when you rub yourself on my cock and make yourself come. Do you think you can do that?"

"Do you think you can actually stay still while I'm using you as my personal scratching post?"

Grinning, he nods and relaxes into the headboard. I roll my hips, dragging my clit across his large cock. He curses and his hands pull at my sides.

Every move I make is eliciting even more pleasure out of me. I throw my head back and moan when his dick gets even harder as I drag myself down the length of him.

"Look at you. Taking what's yours like the queen you are. Fucking gorgeous." He slides a hand under my pajama top, slowly traveling up my torso until he reaches my breasts. His fingers toy with my nipple, making me whimper.

"Are you going to come for me?" He pinches my nipple and kneads my breast in his palm. He's failing miserably at staying still but I'm not going to complain. I love the way his rough hands feel rubbing against my skin.

"Yes," I say, gritting my teeth. I'm so close. It's right there.

"That's it, baby. Let me see you. God, I've missed touching you like this." The raw honesty in his eyes pushes me over the edge, igniting my climax. His lips meet mine and he kisses me like it's a vow.

This feels like a new beginning and a promise of what's waiting for us in the future. I know now I never stopped loving Koa because it's what I was made to do. Loving him is a part of my DNA. It's sewn into the fabric of my being.

"Thank you for giving me that."

"I think I should be the one thanking you," I say, wrapping my arms around his neck. He's still hard beneath me and I want to ask or offer something in return but the smile on his face makes me think he's already satisfied by receiving something his own orgasm can't provide.

"No, that was definitely a treat for me." He leans toward the table and picks up the glass jar. "I promise I'll be still this time," he says, closing his eyes.

Carefully I apply the mask, avoiding his mouth and eyes. He does a decent job staying still. Only flinching from time to time when the cool mixture hits his skin.

"You're all done. Don't smile or it will crack. You can do me now." In a flash he flips me onto my back.

"Gladly." He positions himself between my legs. He delicately paints my face with the green gook. His fingers trace the contours of my cheeks and chin, handling every inch of me with care.

"Now what?" he asks, trying not to move his lips too much.

"We wait." If he didn't need his glasses, I would suggest we start reading. That was my original plan but then he had to go all sexy scholar on me. "I have an idea," I say, pushing him off me.

I sift through my purse until I find my earbuds and phone. "Here." I hand him one of the earbuds. "We can listen to a book while we wait for our masks to finish drying. I have a new audiobook you're going to love."

"You've never steered me wrong before."

"I don't know about that. I've read a few duds. Now stop talking and listen." I pull up the app I use for my audiobooks and hit play.

I lean into Koa's side, doing my best to keep my face off his chest. The warm, rich voice of the narrator talks into my ear while my hand lazily drifts over the ridged muscles on Koa's stomach.

His muscles tighten under my touch. I move my hand lower, circling the outline of his dick over his shorts. I keep swirling my hand around, occasionally grazing the length of him with the tips of my fingers. He grows harder with every lap.

His hand on my ass clenches when I skim his erection from base to tip. "Sydney, please," he chokes out the words. His eyes pierce mine, begging me to touch him and end my teasing. Silently I dip my hand under the waistband of his shorts and take him in my hand.

"Fuck," he moans, as my hand wraps around the base of his cock. I tenderly move my hand over the smooth skin to the tip. I swirl my thumb over the head of his cock, collecting the precum that's already leaking.

The enemy in the audiobook tightens their grip on the heroine's wrist and I do the same to his dick after I free it from the confines of his shorts.

A groan reverberates through his chest. "Fuck, you know just what I like. I've gotten myself off more times than I can count imagining it was your hand squeezing my cock instead of my own. The real thing is a million times better."

His words come out of his mouth disjointed. I don't know if he's struggling because the mask is tightening on his face or if it's because of me and his fight for control.

"Sydney," he draws out my name in a low groan. He cups the back of my neck and pulls me toward his face. "You're everything I've ever wanted," he says, before slamming his mouth against mine.

The dry particles of the mask rub against my chin. It's a minor inconvenience that is a thousand percent worth it to taste him on my tongue. Instinctively my hand works his cock with the same fervor he is kissing me.

Koa pulls away, ending our kiss. His body slumps against the headboard and his eyes roll back in his head as he grunts out his release. I continue to pump him, enjoying the look and the feel of his cum dripping over my hand.

I pause the audiobook with my clean hand and let go of his dick before it gets awkward. I cautiously hold my hand in the air, careful to not drip on anything. Koa tucks himself back in his shorts. Our eyes meet and we both start laughing.

"We must look ridiculous." I accidentally touch my face, getting some of his cum on my cheek. "I wonder if there are any cosmetic benefits to having semen on your face," I joke.

Koa's eyes darken and the muscle in his jaw ticks. "Baby, don't even play with me about painting your beautiful face with my cum. You're going to make me hard again just thinking about it." He kisses me, then says, "Go ahead and get cleaned up. I can wait."

"Okay," I say before scurrying out the room. I wash my hands and then find a cloth to warm so I can wash the mask off of my face. I remove the headband from my hair and try my best to put my bangs back into place.

Koa gives me a kiss on the cheek when he passes me in the hallway. I feel like I'm floating on air. He's right this is how we were always meant to be. I've been a fool to think anyone else could ever take his place in my heart.

I grab my phone off the bed and snatch the earbud he left on the nightstand. It accidentally slips out of my fingers and lands on the floor. "Damnit." Not seeing it anywhere, I bend to the floor and look under the bed. I laugh when I find more books.

"He's worse than me." The spine of the book on the top of the stack catches my eye. It's *The Magic of Fire and Bones*. "He really is reading every book I am." I grab it off the stack and open it up. He has a few sticky notes full of annotations.

My smile starts to dissolve the more I read them. His notes are too familiar. I've heard all of this before from someone else. "He wouldn't," I whisper to myself. I glance at his phone on the nightstand.

Picking up my own phone, I pull up a private message I haven't thought of in days. "Please let me be wrong."

I close my eyes and hit send. His phone dings beside me and my head falls forward. Maybe it's just a coincidence. I'm afraid to look at the notification.

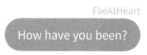

Hesitantly I peek at the notifications on his phone. My heart plummets when I see my messages. "It was him. He pretended to be someone else. Why would he do this to me?" I mumble incoherently to myself as I slowly begin to spiral. "I need to get out of here."

I type up one last parting message before I begin gathering my things around his room and throwing them in my bag. I'm almost ready to leave when I hear footsteps behind me.

"I grabbed us a few snacks," he says.

My body shakes and tears pool in my eyes. I refuse to let him see me cry. I swallow hard and take a few deep breaths to steady my nerves.

"Baby, what's wrong?" He spins me around. "Syd, talk to me. What happened? I was gone less than ten minutes. I come back and you're crying." He wipes the tears off my face to prove his point. *Dumbass tears. I told you not to fall.*

When he's had enough of my silence he glances around the room trying to figure out my sudden change of demeanor. He flinches when he sees the open book on his bed. "Let me explain." He reaches for me but I step out of his grasp.

"No. I'm getting my stuff and I'm leaving."

"I guess that means you're taking me with you because I'm yours too."

"You don't know how much I wish that were true," I say before walking out the door.

20

KOA

Fuck. Fuck. Fuck. Fuck. Fuck.

I scrub my hands through my hair as Sydney marches out the door. Why didn't I tell her earlier? I should have fucking told her the minute she walked into my room, but my dumbass didn't do it.

I rip my phone off the charger and scroll through the messages until I reach the last one.

FaeAtHeart

> Fuck you for making me believe in us again.

I'm not letting her go without giving me a chance to explain why I did it. I need her to hear me out. I snatch a shirt out of my closet and throw on some shoes. Grabbing my keys off the dresser, I race out the door.

I'm grateful the drive to her dorm is short. The more time I spend in my head, the worse I imagine the outcome of this conversation. If she even gives me a chance to tell my side of the story.

I release a deep exhale when I reach her door. It does nothing to soothe my nerves like I hoped it would. I knock a few times but no one answers. It's eerie how silent the hallway is.

I knock harder and give the door knob a try. Of course she remembers to lock the door today. "Sydney!" I knock again. "I know you're in there. Please open up. Let me explain."

The silence is deafening. I lean my head against the door. "I'm not leaving until you open the door. If that means I'm sleeping in the hallway tonight, I will." I press my palm against the door. "Please, baby."

The lock on the door clicks and I stop breathing for a moment. Sydney opens the door and my heart shatters seeing her puffy, bloodshot eyes.

"I opened the door. You can leave now." She pushes on the door to close it, but I move in front of the door jam, blocking her.

"Five minutes. Give me five minutes. Please," I beg.

She spins on her heel and stomps over to the back of the couch. I close the door but leave it unlocked. As much as I want her to be trapped with me forever, I don't want her to feel that way right now.

"I'm sorry," I say.

"Not good enough." Her arms wrap around her middle as she leans against the couch.

"I know it's not. You need to understand that my intentions were never to hurt you. I was going to tell you the truth. I tried to confess a few times."

Her laugh is wicked. "I guess the moment passed and you what? Forgot to mention it before my hand was wrapping around your cock? Fool me once..." she says, her voice trailing off into manic laughter.

"What's so funny?"

"Nothing," she says, sobering. "Just thinking about something Charlie said." Her eyes narrow. "You're running out of time."

"I'm only sorry for not telling you. I should have said something a lot sooner. I'm not sorry for doing it. You have to understand."

"Actually I don't. I don't have to do anything."

My head drops along with my heart. I clear my throat in an attempt to reset my emotions. "I joined the forum three years ago," I confess. Sydney gasps and her eyes widen. "We were eating breakfast and the notification popped up on your phone. It took me a while to figure out what it was, but once I did, I made an account."

Sydney stares at the ground near her feet. I pray she's listening to me and not busy planning my murder in her mind. There is no doubt that she could pull it off with the help of Lauren and Wren.

"I missed you. You were carving out a new life here at school with Lauren. I was running out of excuses to check up on you. I was desperate to feel connected to you in some way. I stayed anonymous until recently."

"Why now? Why that screen name?"

I take a step toward her and she flinches. *Fuck*. I wince and my hands curl into fists. I inhale and exhale a deep breath, forcing my body to relax and find a peaceful center. I don't want her scared of me now, or ever.

"I've left comments anonymously on your posts from the first day I joined. I needed that connection to you. Why now?" I shrug. "Why not now? I've spent a lot of time wishing I could be with you. This made me feel like I was."

"And the name?"

"You said once years ago '*I don't want some average Joe for a boyfriend.*' It was right after your breakup with that idiot Wilson."

"I remember," she whispers.

"That's all I could think of at the time. It was a silly name. The nineteen is for the first day I saw you. I'll never forget that day. It's also the password on my phone and why I wear the number on my back every time I step onto a baseball field."

She inhales a deep breath and tips her face toward the ceiling. "A sweet username isn't going to win you any points. You've had an unfair advantage. You knew you were talking to me and could manipulate the conversation. I told you things I've never said to anyone."

"Unfair advantage." I scoff, pacing the floor. "Do you know what's unfair? Seeing you every day and not being able to talk to you. *Really* talk to you."

I stop in front of her, allowing her warm vanilla scent to finally help me calm down. Not giving her the option to look away, I say, "Unfair is existing in the same world as you and not being able to enjoy all the benefits of being yours. I couldn't hold you, or comfort you. I didn't get to know how your day was or the opportunity to help make it better."

She swipes at the tears rolling down her cheeks. I hate that she's crying right now. Taking a step toward her, I cup her face in my hands. Her lower lip trembles. "You wouldn't talk to me but you would talk to him."

"You could have come to me," she says, removing my hands from her face. "You could have told me how you felt about me. Instead, you snuck around behind my back pretending to be someone else. You claim being near me was difficult because I wasn't yours, yet you still did it. Why? Why not just let me go? We could have both moved on."

"Moving on? That was never going to happen. We all had our ways of coping. You coped by dating other guys to get over me. This was how I coped."

"What do you mean?"

"Mithridatism," I state. I read about it in one of her books once.

"Mithridatism?"

"I tried to become immune to you. I took a little bit of you everyday to build up an immunity. Thinking eventually you wouldn't have an effect on me. That maybe at some point in my life I would have one day I wasn't absolutely desperate for you."

"Are you saying I'm a poison?" Her eyes narrow.

"No. Turns out there was no way I could become immune to you because you were the antidote. You're the cure to everything that is wrong. You're the light in the darkness.

You're the reason I have more good days than bad ones. Tell me what I have to do. We said we aren't going to run anymore."

"Don't you dare throw that in my face." She points a finger in my direction. "That was said before I knew you were lying to me."

"Nothing I said to you were lies. It was all my truths said behind an alias. Would you have listened to me if it had been me? I'm lucky I got you to go out with me."

"Yes, you are," she snarks.

Her sass makes me smile. I take her hands in mine. "I feel like all I've been doing lately is begging you to forgive me and asking for another chance. You are it for me. I'm not going to stop, Syd. I won't lose you again. I lo—"

"Don't say it. Not now." Her eyes close tight and leave wrinkles in the corners. "This is not love." She releases a slow breath. "It's too painful. I can't keep doing this to myself. Today, the date in the park, everything, it was a mistake. We're a mistake."

My heart plummets to my stomach. I feel like I'm freefalling through the sky without a parachute. It's not easy to hear words you said years ago thrown back into your face. "You don't mean that."

"I do. We've become toxic. I think it's best if we call it before we hurt each other anymore. You have your baseball career to look forward to and I have my life in North Carolina," she says, her eyes shining with unshed tears.

"No." I shake my hand. "I've made mistakes. Me." I pound my fist into my chest. "But, baby, you and me." I drop my head to hers. "You and I are not a mistake." Intertwining our fingers, I give her hands a gentle squeeze. "I never believed that."

"I need time," she says, softly. "You need to give me space to think about what I really want. I need to do that without being under the influence of you."

"I'll be gone the next two nights for games. I know it's not a lot of time, but can I call you when I get back and check on you? I don't need your answer. I just want to hear your voice and make sure you're okay."

She nods slowly. "I think that would be fine."

"Good." I kiss the top of her head. "I can't go back to pretending I'm nothing more than a family friend with you." Wrapping my arms around her, I hold her so close you can't tell where I start and she begins. I pull back and cup the side of her neck in my hand. "I know you don't want to hear this right now but know that I do feel a certain way about you. I always have. I pray one day you will let me tell you just how far that feeling goes." I lean down and give her a chaste kiss on the lips.

"You should go," she says, wiping at her face and then wrapping her fluffy pink robe tighter around her middle. The words are a dull knife to my chest.

"Alright. I'll check in with you in a few days. You promise you'll answer?" I ask. She nods as her eyes fill with more tears.

"I don't like leaving you alone like this." I hesitate by the front door.

"I'm fine. Lauren will be home later." She opens the door and I reluctantly walk out.

I stand outside her door, hoping it will fling open after having a quick change of heart. I don't know how much time has passed but she never comes back out.

"Are you okay?" Wren asks from behind me.

"Never better," I reply, faking a smile. Pushing away from the door, I turn toward Wren.

"Wyatt is forcing me to watch the entire *Miss Congeniality* series tonight. If you want to suffer with me while he says every line from the movies along with the actors, I wouldn't mind having backup."

"I don't think I'll be the best company right now." I glance at Sydney's door.

"That's okay. Wyatt isn't either most days." Wren walks toward the stairs, but I'm still hesitating. "Give her the time she needs to come to the conclusion you already know. You can't force it. Her heart will lead her back to you."

Wren waits for me to take the first step before she continues toward the stairs. The whole drive home I keep thinking about what Wren said and hoping she's right.

That Sydney's heart will lead her back to me where she belongs.

"Someone going to tell me why we're here again?" Wyatt asks, staring at the flashing neon light in the window.

"Because Koa needs a little tattoo therapy and we need something to remember our last year at Newhouse together," Hart says, grabbing Wyatt by the shoulders and pushing him through the door I'm holding open for them.

"I've got lots of memories right here." Wyatt taps the side of his head. "I don't need to stick a needle in my arm a million times to remind me what it was like living with the two of you the last four years."

"What about something for Wren?" I ask.

"Do you think she would like that?" he asks, scanning the flash art on the wall.

"*Sí, mí brujita* loves all my ink." Hart lifts one of his tattooed arms.

Wyatt grunts, flinching every now and then when the sound of a tattoo gun starts up.

"What can I do for you gentlemen this evening?"

"Do you have time for a few walk-ins?" I ask. It's our last night in New Orleans. A lot of the guys from the team went out drinking but we didn't find that appealing without our girls with us.

"If you only have time for two tonight, I'll bow out," Wyatt tells the guy with a nervous smile, making him laugh.

"It's your lucky night, young man. We can take all three of you." He smirks at Wyatt.

"Goody." Wyatt grimaces under his mustache.

"I can take one of you now if you're ready," the man says.

"I'm ready." I step forward.

He nods. "I'll let Jude and Scottie know you're waiting for them," he tells Hart and Wyatt. Then he leads me back to his private tattooing area. There's black and white artwork covering the walls and a set of cabinets in the corner.

"Take a seat." He points to the black tattoo chair. He sits on a rolling stool and wheels himself in front of me. "The name is Axle."

"Koa." I shake his hand.

"What do you have in mind?"

I open up my photo album and flip through a few photos until I find the one I'm looking for. "Can you do something similar to this?"

He takes my phone and examines the photo, enlarging it and moving it around. "Same spot?"

"Yes. And the words. I want the words. You can do it in your style, but maybe keep it all the same place?"

"Let me sketch something up and see what you think." He pushes off the floor and glides over to the cabinets. He slides over a sketchbook and grabs a pen from a skull mug sitting in the corner.

I wait patiently while he draws up a rough sketch. Next door I can hear Wyatt talking to his tattoo artist. A loud scream echoes through the room a second after the tattoo gun starts to buzz.

Two minutes later Wyatt ducks his head into my room. "I'm all done," he says, holding up his wrist that is wrapped in a white bandage. "I'll be waiting out here if you need me."

"Son, it might be awhile. There's an ice cream shop next door. Why don't you treat yourself to a sundae? You were a very brave boy today," Axle says, barely keeping a straight face.

I cover my mouth with my hand and choke back a laugh.

"I was a brave boy," Wyatt agrees. Axle opens a drawer and starts digging around. He pulls out his tattoo gun.

Wyatt's eyes go wide. "If you need me, I'll be next door. Please don't need me." He spins on his boot and speed walks toward the door.

Axle chuckles as he places the tattoo gun back in the drawer. "He's a jittery one," he says, then gets back to his sketch.

My nerves are starting to get the best of me too. Not about the tattoo. I knew the minute I saw the finished painting it was going to have a permanent spot on my body. That's why I asked her to snap a photo for me.

I'm worried about my chat with Sydney. I miss her like fucking crazy and I'm afraid she'll ask for more time or be done for good. I'm willing to give her as much time as she needs. I'm just hoping I don't have to.

"What do you think about this?" Axle asks, holding up the sketchpad.

"It's perfect," I say, swallowing the emotions attached to the image he's holding up.

"Sit tight. I'll get everything ready." He leaves me alone with my thoughts.

Less than forty-eight hours and I'll have the answer I've been waiting for. I would be lying if I said it's been easy waiting. I've done my best to respect her request for space but if she thinks I'm going to just sit by and not continue to show her how much I love her, she would need to think again.

Now that I've had her back in my arms, I will never give up on us. I'll keep trying to prove to her we were never a mistake and I'm someone she can depend on.

21

SYDNEY

"Did you find a place to live yet?" Zoe asks. She is one of the co-founders of Blooming Beauty Co. I've been joining them on their weekly business meetings ever since I signed my contract with them.

It's been a great opportunity to see how they operate and get to know the staff I'll be working with in a few months.

Their story is inspiring. Zoe and Jade met in college. Being two of the few Black women in their business class, they gravitated toward each other and struck up a friendship. After graduation they started small with only three products and have grown large enough to compete with the best in the industry.

This is exactly what I want. It's everything I've dreamed about since I was a little girl crushing my mom's blush into a powder and mixing it with coconut oil to make my own lip balm. Now I'm going to be working beside women just like me who are driven, ambitious, and know how to make things happen.

"I have." I smile. The apartment is more than I'll be able to afford long term. I looked everywhere for a studio or a one bedroom but there wasn't anything available for my move-in date. All I could find remotely in my price range is a two bedroom. I'm hoping I can either find a night job bartending or a roommate. Otherwise I will be coming back to Alabama with my tail between my legs.

"If you need anything, you have our numbers," Jade—the other co-owner—says.

"Thank you both. I appreciate everything you're doing for me. It's going to be difficult to say goodbye to everyone at home. You're making me feel so welcome. It makes things a little easier."

Jade and Zoe exchange a look. "You are going to be a huge asset to us while you learn and create your own product line. Our hope is that while you'll be working for us, we will also be creating a collaborative relationship for the future," Jade says.

"When we started we didn't have any help. We had to do all the leg work from figuring out how to get our business license to learning every FDA regulation we needed to follow. It was a lot," Zoe says, shaking her head at the memory.

"It sounds overwhelming." I knew there would be a lot I would need to figure out, but thinking about it is almost paralyzing.

"It was and sometimes still is but the purpose and the passion for what we're doing in the beauty industry is always greater," Jade says wistfully.

"With your knowledge of cosmetic chemistry and creativity, you're going to be a powerhouse. We look forward to watching you grow."

"Zoe, thank you. I still can't believe this is happening." I press my fingers into my cheeks. They are warm from all the praise.

"How is that boy of yours?" Jade asks.

"He isn't our business. You don't get to ask about him." Zoe smacks Jade's arm playfully. When we were discussing my move to North Carolina, they noticed my hesitancy and asked what would keep me here.

Koa was the first and only thing that came to mind. It didn't take much to get me to open up. His proposal for a second chance was so fresh at the time.

Look what that's gotten me. I'm right back where I started. Maybe even worse. I got a taste of how good we could be together and then it was ripped out from underneath me.

"It's fine. He's fine." I don't think they would understand if I said it's been very *'Bella New Moon'* around here the last couple of days. If it wasn't for everything that I have to do in order to start my new life, I would be staring out the window watching the world go by.

"You'll have to bring him to the office sometime. Let him see where you'll be working every day," Zoe says.

"I'll do that," I agree, as if he'll be moving with me when I know for a fact he won't.

"Until next week then. You take care of yourself, Sydney." Jade gives me a knowing smile. She can see straight through my facade. It's probably easy to see I'm barely holding myself together at the moment.

"See you both next week. Thank you." I log off the video call and doom scroll through social media. After adding ten more books to my wishlist, I toggle over to the Fiction Forum.

I've been hesitant to log on since I found out who AverageJoe really was. I felt so angry and betrayed. I shared things I never would have if I'd known it was Koa. "Which was his point." I remind myself of our conversation from a few days ago.

I open up our private chat and comb through the chats with a new lens. Reading all of the messages in Koa's voice has my heart fluttering and my stomach doing flips.

He wasn't subtle with his affections. On more than one occasion he was openly flirting with me. If I read everything line by line, it's obvious he has felt the same burden I have the last few years.

Loving someone when you can't be with them. Knowing you should be with them and there is no one else who understands you the way they do. I don't know how to let go of that feeling.

I also don't know how to move forward. Koa's future is undecided. He's still working out details with his agent over which team he'll sign with. None of which are located in North Carolina last I heard.

A knock on the door breaks me from my thoughts. I have no idea who it could be. Everyone I know would just let themselves in. I look out the peephole and no one's there.

Probably someone accidentally at the wrong door. It happens all the time.

I open the door and glance down the hall in both directions. It's empty except for a delivery man. Sure enough, he left me a package. My favorite kind of package, but I haven't ordered anything recently. I mentally pat myself on the back for keeping my cart empty even with the current climate of my emotions.

With very little grace, I rip open the box like it contains life saving medicine. I would be right. It's not medicine but the contents do mend my heart and feed my soul.

Jumping in place with excitement, I pick up a book I've been dying to read for the last few weeks and flip through the crisp new pages. I glance down and notice a second copy of the same book. "Wait, why did I get two copies? Who is this from?"

After emptying the contents of the box, I find a note at the bottom.

For the next time we get to spend a perfect day together.
Damn him.

I was a fool for ever thinking I could get over Koa Mahina. He was always going to be mine and I was always meant to be his.

"I can't believe it's your last shift." Lindsey frowns as she makes a couple of whiskey sours and passes them to the couple in front of her.

"I'm going to miss working here with all of you." I finish taking the payment from the couple and hand them their receipt.

"No you won't. You already have one foot out of Alabama," she says, her blonde ponytail swinging with every word she says.

"That might be true but I'll still miss you and the rest of the girls." I hip check her as I pass by. Walking the length of the bar, I check on customers' drinks and clear any empty glasses.

I'm a little nostalgic thinking back to my first night working. Lauren and I broke so many glasses and messed up too many orders, but we still managed to keep our jobs.

I know Ray wanted Lauren because she helped with all the dance routines. I didn't bring anything to the table. It wasn't until I started messing around with different liquors and mixes—creating new drinks—that I found my place.

Seeing customers ask for the "Sydney Special" is an ego boost to say the least. Working here has given me the confidence to try new things and not be afraid to fail. It's something I'll need in my next job.

Flipping my wrist, I check the time on my watch. "Drink up fellas," I tell the group of regulars in front of me. "It's almost time for a little show." I wink. I wipe down the bar with a dry cloth and clean up their empty glasses.

The DJ signals us to get ready. I move to my spot at the bar and wait for the music to change. Lauren didn't mention there would be dancing involved with this job until after we had turned in our paperwork.

It has been an unexpected bright spot. Reading a book is how I cope with my emotions internally. Music is how I express myself when I want to share my emotions with other people.

I straighten my cropped Ray's Bar tee and pull at the inseam of my cut off shorts—that sucker likes to fly a little too close to the sun from time to time.

The music switches to one of my favorite songs and I'm all smiles. The five of us walk up the miniature steps we keep behind the bar and work our way to our spots.

We stomp our feet and clap our hands to the beat while a couple of the girls waitressing at the tables make their way to the dance floor. Gazing out to the crowd, I can't stop myself from checking the back corner.

I know he won't be here tonight, but I look for him every night I work out of habit. Koa coming to babysit me was infuriating in the beginning. He made me feel like he didn't think I was capable of making my own decisions.

I see now that he needed to be here for himself. It had very little to do with what I'm capable of. His need to be my protector required him to make sure I made it home safe for his own sanity.

Spinning around a few times on my heel, I stop in front of a customer and extend an arm to remove his cowboy hat from his head. He laughs as I playfully pretend to put it on my head before giving it back.

This is usually the part of the routine when I would glance over at Koa and see how tight he is gripping his beer bottle. The whitening of his knuckles always made me want to shimmy and shake a little harder for the rest of the night.

His text earlier led me to believe he wasn't going to make it tonight but I check one more time anyway. I stumble over my steps, but manage to recover before it's noticeable to others. Koa isn't in the corner, but the sleazy customer who tried to corner me in the storage room is sitting in his place.

I ignore the way my heart is pumping out of my chest and how my hands start to tremble as I work through the rest of the routine. I'm safe here. Nothing has ever happened to any of the girls while we're working.

Sure the place gets out of hand from time to time, but there are several bodyguards on scene. They don't mess around when it comes to the women working here. I wouldn't be surprised if one or two of them have a crush on the girls.

When the song ends, I climb back down the stairs and get right back to work refilling drinks. I don't allow myself to think of the man sitting in the back corner. He is no one to me.

It doesn't stop me from wishing Koa would walk through the door. I'm still not sure if I've forgiven him, but I wouldn't deny myself the opportunity to seek comfort from his presence.

The shift continues without any incident. I gladly let Lindsey help me restock the alcohol and beer for the night.

FOUL TERRITORY

The bar begins to clear out as everyone pays their tab. We work efficiently cleaning the bar top, wiping down chairs, and mopping the floors.

It's a lot of work but we turn up the music and we get everything checked off the list in no time at all. The girls hug me goodbye and I wipe a few tears as I walk toward my car.

There are only a few vehicles left in the lot. Quite the contrast from when I arrived for my shift earlier tonight. I get inside my car and immediately lock the door. Starting the car up, I get my phone plugged in and check to see if I have any messages.

The girls honk and wave as they pass, exiting the parking lot toward the two lane road that leads to the highway.

I smile when I see a message from Koa.

> KOA
>
> Hope your last night goes well. Wish I could be there to see you dance one last time on the bar.

I'll text him later. He's probably asleep after a day on the road. I put my phone on the charger and shift the car into drive. As soon as I start to move I know something is wrong.

I put the car back in park and open the door. Walking to the front of my car, I notice the tire is flat. My heart rate picks up as I make my way around my car, noting every tire is flat.

I glance around the parking lot hoping maybe someone lingered behind, everyone has already cleared out. *Damn it.* How did I manage to do this? I must have driven through some broken glass or something. That's what I force myself to believe. The other option will make me spiral and I can't afford to do that right now. What I need is a ride home and a tow.

I get back in my car and call my brother. He owes me at least one late night rescue after all the times I picked his ass up from a party in high school.

My hands shake as I put the phone on speaker. No one is here. I'm fine. It's just a coincidence. "Come on Nash, pick up." Fear prickles over my skin. What if he doesn't answer?

"Hi, baby," Koa says, answering Nash's phone. I didn't know how much I needed to hear his voice.

The tough facade I've been holding onto starts to crumble and tears begin to fall. My body shakes and snot starts to run down my nose. It has nothing to do with being frightened or worried. It's because I know that he'll be here soon.

Koa will always be there for me when I need him. I just have to stop pushing him away.

22

KOA

Rolling over, I check the time on the clock. Fuck. I slept a lot longer than I planned. The last few days have been emotionally draining and hell on my sleep cycle.

I rub my eyes and let out a long yawn. I was going to head up to Ray's and wait for Sydney to get off work but she'll be leaving any minute now.

I grab a clean shirt and shorts and throw them on before I go downstairs to get something to eat. I'm fucking starving after sleeping most of the evening. I haven't eaten anything since the breakfast we had before we got on the team bus.

Nash is asleep at the dining room table and using one of his textbooks as a pillow. Poor guy. The late nights and early mornings are catching up with him too. I should wake him up and get him downstairs so he can get a few decent hours of sleep before morning workouts.

I'm in the process of folding down his laptop and stacking his notes and textbooks when his phone starts to ring with a familiar song. *Sydney's ringtone.*

I check the time on the microwave clock. She should be on her way home. Why is she calling this late? Maybe she calls Nash every night on her drive home.

Intuition is telling me this isn't a nightly tradition and there is something else going on.

"Hi, baby," I say, acting casual. I don't want to freak her out if she's alright. She doesn't say anything. Is she mad I answered or is something else going on?

"Are you okay?" I ask, full with worry. Her breathing gets heavier and then I hear her sniffling. She's crying. "What's wrong?"

"My tires." She sniffles aggressively. "They're flat."

"All of them?" I question, as calmly as I can.

"Yes," she says, her breathing returning to normal the more we talk. "I must have run over a broken beer bottle or something."

"Is anyone there with you?"

"No. Everyone left already. There is one car in the parking lot. I could go see—"

"No," I say, cutting her off. "If you aren't already, I need you to get in your car and lock the doors."

I pull my phone out of my pocket and call her on my phone. "Switch lines. That's me calling you."

"Okay. Hello." Her sweet voice echoes through my soul. I hang up Nash's phone and leave it on the table.

"Hey, baby." I hold my phone against my chest. "Nash," I smack him on the arm jostling him awake. "I'm going to go get Syd from work. She's having car issues."

"Do you need me to go with you?" he asks, rubbing his eyes.

I shake my head. "I'm good. Go to bed. I'll fill you in tomorrow." Walking out the door, I hold the phone back to my ear. "I'm on my way. Don't open the door or window for any reason. Do you understand me?"

"Yeah. I got it. You're starting to scare me."

"I'm sorry. I don't mean to." I place the call on speaker phone, trying to remain calm as I start my car. I peel out of my parking spot and down the main road that will take me off campus.

I have an eerie feeling. What are the chances that all four of her tires went flat from broken glass in the parking lot? It seems highly unlikely to me.

"How was work tonight?" I ask. I need more information. I don't understand how something like this could happen.

"Really busy. A lot of regulars showed up for my last night. It's probably a good thing you couldn't make it. We needed your table," she jokes, but she's hiding something.

"I'm sure Margo appreciated the extra tips from customers who have more than one beer a night."

"She did but I think she missed seeing your face for whatever reason," she says, then hesitates.

"What? You sound like you've got something else to say."

"He came back."

Her words send a chill down my spine. I know exactly who she's talking about and it makes me hit the gas a little harder. "Did anything happen?"

"No, well, it was weird. He was just sitting there drinking a beer. It was creepy."

If I wasn't so fucking worried at the moment, I would take offense to this statement.

"What kind of car is in the parking lot?"

"I don't know. It's really dark. It's white and it has a black racing stripe down the side."

Fuck. That's the asshole's car. He did this. I know it in my gut.

"Is there anyone in the car? Can you tell?"

"I can't. I'm sorry. It probably belongs to someone who was too drunk to drive home," she says, with a slight tremble in her voice. She's putting on her strong act. Sydney has always been the kind of person to keep it together until the very end.

"Don't apologize. You're doing good." The light turns red in front of me and I want to be mad but this gives me a minute to send a text to Hart.

He's the only person I know who'll be up. He's always up late watching documentaries with Lauren.

Me

> I need you to call the cops and send them to Ray's.

> Sydney's tires got slashed. I'm driving there now. I'll explain later.

Hart

> Give me a minute.

I tap my thumb against the steering wheel waiting for the light and his text. I'll feel better knowing cops are enroute.

Hart

> Done. They're on their way. Text us when you can.

"You're quiet," she says, cutting through all my worried thoughts.

"That's not new information."

"Have you always been quiet?"

"No. My mom always called me her little chatterbox. Once I started, I didn't know how to stop."

"Why did you stop?"

This isn't something I want to talk about over the phone but if it keeps her mind occupied while she waits for me and the police then fine.

"There are two reasons I turned into a quiet kid when you met me. One reason was because of Hart. I hated how other kids treated him when he wouldn't talk. I thought if we were both quiet then maybe the kids at school wouldn't tease him so much. Or if they did, they would have to deal with both of us."

"That's really sweet of you."

"I told you I was a nice guy. I might not always make the right decisions, but I make them with good intentions."

"I never said you weren't nice. I know you're a good guy. I've never questioned that. I've questioned if you were a good guy for me."

"One day you won't have to question that anymore."

"I think you're right," she says, and my heart lights up with hope.

"You do?"

"You said there were two reasons you stopped talking all the time. What was the other one?" she asks, returning to our earlier conversation.

"When I was twelve I moved to Alabama and I met this girl. She loved stories as much as I loved having her talk to me. I figured out early on if I stayed quiet long enough, she would fill the silence with her stories."

"Koa…that's…Koa," she says my name a second time in a deep whisper. It would be sexy if there wasn't a hint of fear in her tone.

"What is it?" I practically shout.

"The lights. The lights on the car. They just came on."

"I'm almost there. Hold tight for ten minutes. Can you do that for me?"

"Yeah. I can do that." The tremor in her voice is destroying me. I'm coming up on the exit. I'll be there soon but it's not good enough. I need to be there now.

"Did he get out of the car?"

"He? How do you know it's a man?" she asks, half hysterical. "Koa, how do you know? It's him, isn't it? He did this to my car."

"The police are on their way. Please—"

"Koa, he's driving over here."

Fuck. I push the gas harder. Why does this place have to be out in the middle of nowhere?

"What's happening? Keep talking to me. As long as you're talking you're okay." *As long as she's talking she's okay.* Maybe if I keep repeating it over and over I'll believe it.

"He's opening the door and getting out of his car."

"Listen to me, Syd. I know you don't like me telling you what to do, but I need you to do this for me. You ignore him. Don't react to whatever he says or does. You don't give him the satisfaction of letting him think he's getting to you."

"What if he breaks the window or something and he can get to me?"

Then he's a dead man.

There's a loud thud followed by a scream from Sydney.

"You listen to my voice. Not his," I say as he curses at her through the car window.

Her agreement is lost among tears and sharp inhales of fear.

"Tell me what happens with Vincent and Aster," I say to distract her.

"Wh-what?"

"Give me the best spoilers. Just like you used to. Does Aster pick Vincent or is she going to break my heart and pick Troy?"

"There is a crazy man banging on my window and you want me to tell you about a book?" she hisses.

"Yes. I want to know everything."

"Bitch, I know you can hear me. Open the fucking door or I'll bust it open," he screams at my girl.

"Tell me about the badass queen in the story, baby" I say, knowing full well I'm talking to the queen in mine.

With a slight tremor in her voice she tells me parts of *The Magic of Fire and Bones* I haven't read yet. As I figured, Troy was out for himself—the one that looks like the good guy never is. Nothing is ever what it seems.

The banging continues on her window. I'm surprised he hasn't punched his fist through the glass yet.

"V-Vincent isn't helping as much as giving orders to her. He acts like he doesn't like her but I think he's secretly falling in love with her. He just doesn't know what to do because he's not supposed to love her."

"I knew it. Why not?"

"Because he was poor and she turned out to be a queen. He wasn't allowed to like her."

As I wait to turn on to the two lane street leading to Ray's, three cop cars come up behind me with lights and sirens, blowing through the light and disappearing down the road.

"I hear sirens. He's backing off and walking back to his car. He's going to get away."

"No, he won't. They will get the road barricaded and stop him before he gets that far."

"But that means you can't get in."

"Nothing can't stop me from getting to you," I say as I pull up behind the cop car.

I roll down my window and wait for one of the officers standing at the barricade to approach my car.

"This road is closed. I'm going to have to ask you to turn around."

"My girlfriend is the woman in the parking lot with the slashed tires. I would really like to be the one to give her a ride home."

He gives me an understanding nod. "Give me a moment," he says, then goes back to his cruiser.

"Sydney, are you there?"

"Yeah."

"Are you okay?"

"Uh-huh."

"The cop is coming back."

"The other unit is coming out now with the perpetrator. Once they've cleared the location, we'll let you through and you can take your girlfriend home."

"Great. Thank you."

"You can follow us down," he says. He walks back to his car and gets inside. He maneuvers the cruiser so it's no longer blocking the road.

The other cop passes in the opposite lane after stopping beside the officer in front of me and having a brief conversation.

I keep my head focused on what's in front of me. This guy doesn't deserve a second glance. The only thing I can think about is getting to Sydney.

As soon as I'm parked, I'm out of my car and rushing over to her. She's frozen, sitting in her car.

"We tried to get her out but she didn't respond," an officer says as I pass him.

"Thanks. I'll give it a go." Even with my gentle approach, she flinches when I make it to her window. I place my palm against the warm glass. It's something we used to do when we were teenagers.

If one of us were grounded and trapped in our bedroom, we would put our palm against the window and wait for the other one to hear our call. It was our way of letting the other person know we were there for them.

Her arm lifts and her palm presses against mine. The lock on the door clicks and I whip it open. For a second I think I should approach her with caution, but I need to feel her in my arms. I know this whole situation scared her more than she'll let on.

Hell, sitting alone in a dark parking lot is scary enough without having some creep watching you across the lot, and then banging against your car and yelling obscenities at you.

Before I get a chance to scoop her up she is unbuckling her seatbelt and climbing out of the car. Silently she collects her book bag and cleans the back seat of her car, throwing miscellaneous items into a large reusable shopping bag. She pulls out her phone and begins to type furiously.

"Let me put these in my car." I take her bags and put them in the backseat of my Camaro. "Is there anything else you need?"

She shakes her head, placing her phone to her ear. She sighs in frustration and then starts scrolling on her phone again.

"What are you doing?" I ask, approaching her.

"Trying to call for a tow. I need to get it to a shop. I need my car."

Reaching for her phone, I say, "Let me—"

"I don't need you taking care of me," she snaps, cutting me off. "I don't need you looking out for me. I can do this myself. Soon I'm going to be living alone in a state hundreds of miles away. You won't be there to swoop in and save the day every time," she says, frantically. *The fuck I won't.* I cover my hand over hers and slowly remove her phone from her hand.

She is independent and strong. I love this about her. It isn't her fault I'm the one with this overwhelming desire to take care of her. I also hear what she's saying underneath her armor.

She feels alone. Her life is changing faster than she can blink at the moment and she's feeling the impact. I want to reassure her I'm not going anywhere. If she thinks I'm not going to try everything I can to get drafted to North Carolina, she would be dead fucking wrong.

"I know you can do this by yourself, but I also know someone who can help." I look up the contact on my phone and hit the call button.

"Kind of late for a call, man," Milo says, tapping away on his keyboard.

"Don't act like you were about to go to sleep. I can hear you gaming."

"You know me well. What can I do for you?"

"I'm going to pass the phone to Sydney. She'll tell you what she needs," I say, my eyes focused on her. She rolls her eyes with a hint of a smile.

"Milo is Gage's older brother. He runs the garage in town with his dad." I hand over my phone.

While she's working out the details with Milo, I seek out answers from the police officers who have been walking around casing the place and noting details from the incident.

"Hi. I was wondering if we were okay to leave or if you needed to talk to her tonight?" I ask the officer who has been searching through the guy's car.

"I would like to get her side of things tonight for my report but she can make a formal statement at the station tomorrow. I'm sure she's ready to call it a night. Ray has cameras filming the parking lot. We'll come back and get the footage from him to see if we caught him on tape."

"Thank you," I say, shaking his hand.

"Here's my number if you need me for anything," he says, passing me a small white card. "Stay close to her tonight. She's lucky he wasn't able to crack her window." The officer nods toward Sydney.

"I don't plan on letting her out of my sight for the rest of my life."

He nods and I take that as my cue to leave and check on Sydney.

"Is everything all set?" I ask.

"Yep. He'll be here early in the morning to pick it up and he's going to call me when the new tires are on."

"He couldn't come tonight?"

"He offered, but I told him it can wait until the morning. It can't get any worse." She pouts, looking at her car one last time.

"Come on. Let's talk to the cops so we can get out of here." I put an arm around her and usher her toward the officer who seems to be in charge. She tells them everything that she remembers from seeing the guy at the bar—in my motherfucking seat no less—and then walking out to her car.

He makes his notes, repeats what he told me about the video cameras, and confirms that Sydney wasn't harmed physically. The bile in my stomach crawled up my throat at the thought.

"We'll be in touch," he says, leaving us to finish taking photos and examining the guy's car.

I open the door for her and wait for her to sit down. "I'll take you to the station first thing in the morning to file charges." I buckle and start the engine.

"I'll get Nash to take me. You have baseball stuff and classes in the morning," she says, staring absentmindedly out the window. She has her arms wrapped so tightly around herself you would think she was cold. I turn down the air conditioning just in case but I have a feeling she's cold with fear.

"Why don't you call Lauren and let her know you're okay? She's probably worried," I say.

"How does she know what happened?" Sydney picks up her phone where I dropped it in the console next to mine.

"I needed Hart to call the police for me. I didn't want you to know how serious the situation was. I was afraid…" I hesitate, searching for the right words to describe how I felt.

"I couldn't handle it?"

I shake my head. "No. You can handle anything. It's more me wanting to shield you as much as I can. I wanted to protect your peace. I don't think I did a good enough job."

"You don't give yourself enough credit," she says, before hitting the call button on Lauren's number.

Hearing the two of them talk brings mixed emotions out of me. It reminds me of when I didn't trust Lauren but at the same time I was glad Sydney had her friendship. Lauren was quiet and didn't ever want to come over to our place when Sydney would visit. It wasn't until she started hanging out with Hart and I got to know her, I realized she had the biggest heart. She's a fighter and cares about everyone. She was exactly who Sydney needed. Who we all needed.

Learning that Lauren was Sydney's first real friend since me, wasn't something I was happy to hear. I've failed her way too many times. I won't do that to her anymore.

I stop at a drive-thru and pick up some food. I don't know if I can eat after all of that or if she's hungry but I would rather have it just in case.

When we get back to my place, I start wondering at what point she's going to start fighting me for bringing here instead of dropping her off at her dorm. She's been quiet since she got off the phone with Lauren.

Sydney helps with carrying the food, while I grab her bags from the back seat. Once inside, she heads to the kitchen and sits down at the table. I follow her lead, leaving her bags by the stairs. I'm glad Nash made it to bed. I make a mental note to update him on everything in the morning.

We eat in silence. I want to ask her how she's doing but I think the answer is obvious. She is processing tonight's events and I want to give her the space to do that.

"How'd your games go?" she asks, as she throws away her trash.

"Good. It's going to come down to the final games against Enzo and Marco."

"They will love that." She starts up the stairs and I trail behind her.

"I'm already getting texts from Enzo."

She laughs, but it's barely audible. "Do you have something I can wear to bed?" she asks, once we're inside my room.

"Of course. Do you want to shower?" I glance over my shoulder, as I grab a shirt from my closet. She nods. "Come on." I place a hand on her back and escort her to the bathroom.

I turn on the water then dig in the cabinet for an extra toothbrush, a new shower cap, and anything else she might need. "I'll give you some privacy, but I'll be right outside the door. If you need me, just yell."

She nods and I leave her to wait in the hall. Ten minutes later, she opens the door and walks out in my shirt. Fuck she's gorgeous.

"I'm going to brush my teeth and I'll be right there. Are you okay?"

"Yeah, I'm fine," she says. I don't believe her, but that's okay. She'll break when it's time and then she can start to heal from this experience.

She's already stretched out in bed staring at the ceiling fan when I enter the room. I turn off the overhead light, leaving only the dim lighting from the lamp on my side of the bed.

Removing my shorts and shirt, I crawl in beside her and wait for her to say something. *Anything.*

She moves closer until her arms are wrapped around me and she's curled into my side. Looking up at me, she says, "I need you to help me forget."

Letting out a deep sigh, I kiss her forehead and then reach for my glasses on the nightstand. "Give me a second," I say, and she moves back, giving me enough space to move around.

I put on my glasses and then bend down and grab a book I have under the bed. "Come here," I tell her. She pulls the covers over us and snuggles deep against my side. "Turn the pages for me?" I ask.

I don't know how long I read. I don't stop until her arm falls limp and the pages stop turning. Tomorrow might be a different story, but tonight Sydney is home. She's safe. And she's mine.

23

SYDNEY

Koa swats my hand away when I reach into the trunk for a bag of groceries. "I can carry something too," I say.

"I know, but I want to do it." He continues to load his arms up with bags until his forearms are straining.

"That means I'm getting the door." I slam the trunk of his Camaro and race up the steps to the front door of his townhouse. I dig my keys out of my bag and unlock the door for us.

Koa side steps through the door, making me laugh. "I don't like that you have *that* key," he says, dropping the groceries on the kitchen island.

I rub my thumb down the jagged edge of the key Nash gave me a week after moving into the house his freshman year. "I didn't know. I wouldn't have used it as freely as I did had I known it bothered you so much."

I drop my bag and my keys on the table by the door and move into the kitchen. I start unbagging groceries, trying to not think about all the times I've come over and let myself into their home without knocking when Nash invited me over. Being around Hart, Koa, and Nash reminded me of home. It was my Sunday thing I did while Lauren went to see her "family".

Koa tips my chin with his finger, forcing me to look at him. "I said I don't like you having *that* key. I want you to have my key. A key that I've given you. Not your brother." He drops his hand from my chin and goes back to unloading and organizing our grocery haul.

"That's ridiculous. They're the same key," I state.

"They might be the same key but they don't have the same meaning."

"It's going to be irrelevant in a few weeks anyway. Once we graduate, we will be handing our keys over to Gage and Eli."

"Nothing is irrelevant with you," he grumbles.

I chuckle and place all the cold items we purchased in the fridge. I have a feeling we won't need those for a while.

This morning we went to the police station and I gave my statement. I was nervous walking into the building. I didn't know what to expect or how I would feel reliving all the events. Being able to hold onto Koa's hand like a lifeline made it easier.

Apparently this guy was a repeat offender. Ray's wasn't the first bar he's been arrested at and I wasn't his first target. He won't be seeing the outside of a cell for a while. That made moving through the rest of the day a lot easier.

Koa has been by my side for most of it—walking me to classes and eating lunch with me. It wasn't any different than our usual routine, but it felt different.

Instead of cold stares and grunts, he engaged in conversation and held my hand. We still haven't talked about everything. *About us*. I'm giving myself at least twenty-four hours to let him suffocate me with all his attention. Then we can have a real conversation about what we need to do in order to move forward or part ways. There is a deep pang in my chest thinking about that option.

"I think we've bitten off more than we can chew. All of this looks above our pay grade," I say surveying all the ingredients we need to make a chicken pot pie and forgetting about the pain in my chest.

"That's what the recipe is for. How hard can it be?"

"Famous last words," I sigh.

Koa searches for the recipe on his phone. He zooms in on the text and squints. "We need to start with prepping all the vegetables." He opens a few drawers until he finds the one with the cutting boards.

"How long have you lived here?" I ask, teasing him.

"I have a meal plan," he says, swatting my ass playfully. "I haven't made anything in this kitchen except bowls of cereal and protein shakes."

I push all the ingredients to the side and he places the two cutting boards down. I take the celery and carrots over to the sink and quickly wash my hands before doing the same to the vegetables.

Koa places a giant knife in front of me then heads to the sink to wash his hands. "Do you know where the first aid kit is? I don't want to be bleeding to death while you're checking every cabinet for a bandage." I tighten my grip on the knife and get used to the weight of it.

"Yes, I know where those are." He opens the cabinet under the sink and places a small first aid kit on the counter. His eyes go wide when he notices the large knife in my hand. "Maybe you should start with peeling the carrots."

"You don't think I can handle the slicing and dicing?" I casually hold the knife out with the tip pointed in his direction.

"I don't know if having sharp objects accessible to you is in my best interest until after we've talked." He opens one of the drawers in the island and sifts around until he finds the vegetable peeler.

"What do you want to talk about?" I select a carrot to start peeling.

He removes the skin from an onion and then cuts it in half. Wearing a dish towel on his shoulder, he carefully chops the onion into uneven pieces. Chef Koa is hot. Maybe not as sexy as *'reads in bed wearing glasses Koa,'* but it's close.

"What?" he asks. "Are you judging my technique?"

"I wouldn't dare. You're doing great. They're getting smaller. Mission accomplished." I grin wildly at him.

He stares at me in awe. "I haven't seen that smile in a long time."

I chew on my lip as I peel a carrot, occasionally glancing over at Koa. He grins every time he catches me looking at him. My skin heats on my chest and up my neck. This reminds me of how we used to steal glances at each other from across the room.

"I haven't been alone with you like this in a long time," I say, keeping my eyes on the carrot in my hand.

"I want to talk about us," he says, answering my earlier question as he transfers the annihilated onions into a pan but doesn't turn the stove on yet. We are going to 'sauté' them—apparently that is a fancy word for pushing them around in a pan.

"I thought about us a lot while you were gone." Picking up the knife, I raise an eyebrow in his direction. He swallows hard, his eyes bouncing from the knife to me. "The chat situation felt like graduation night two point oh. Different incidents but the same outcome."

He chops celery while I take some of my aggression out on innocent carrots. "My feelings were once again a second thought. It didn't matter what I wanted as long as you got what you wanted. Not to sound like a selfish brat, but what about me?"

His knife clatters on the counter. He steps behind me and spins me around. Holding me on my waist, he smirks when he notices the knife is still in my hands.

"Baby, can we put the knife down?" He removes it from grip and places it behind me. "What did you want?"

"I wanted you. I wanted to wake up the morning after we slept together and have you feel the same. But you didn't. You said it was a mistake. After the best night of my life, I couldn't believe those words came out of your mouth. Then you ignored me the rest of the day while you hung out with

Nash. How do you think that made me feel?" God, I'm so fucking tired of crying.

"I wish the word mistake never left my mouth that day."

"Me too."

"I left your room in the middle of the night. It wasn't an easy thing to do. I could have stayed wrapped up with you forever, but I wasn't trying to get caught by Papa Pierce. When Nash and I woke up in the morning, I knew he was suspicious."

"Of course he was." I roll my eyes.

"He asked me if there was something going on between us." His hands slide from my waist to my hips. "I said we were friends. Knowing what I do now, I think Nash was pushing me then to tell him the truth. All he wanted was for me to step up and tell him how bad I wanted you. I didn't do that."

"It wasn't his choice to make. He had no right interfering in our relationship. Why did you say that being with me was a mistake if you didn't feel that way?"

"You caught me off guard in the hallway. I was going to your room to talk to you about my conversation with Nash. You had this shy smile on your face. Fuck, you looked beautiful. I said it was a mistake. The words tumbled out of my mouth without thinking about you hearing me. But the mistake I was making was telling you we couldn't be together."

Oh God. I squeeze the back of his neck. I thought maybe I played a part in our breakup, but I didn't want to believe it. "I did this to us. I said we should be friends. I agreed with you because I didn't want to look like a fool. I should have waited for you to say something. I should have fought harder for us."

I heard the word mistake and immediately felt hurt and got defensive. I should have marched into Nash's room and told him to get over it and that I wasn't going to lose Koa again.

"You didn't do anything wrong. I'm the one who should have said more. I should have corrected you but I didn't. I let you walk away and that is an error I won't make twice."

"I would have done it too," I whisper.

"Done what?" He tilts his head and his eyebrows scrunch together.

"I would have done anything to get closer to you. If that meant talking to you like an undercover spy in a chat room, I would have done it."

"It wasn't quite like that," he chuckles.

"I guess what I'm saying is I understand. I get it."

"What does that mean for us going forward?" His hands slip around to my ass and he pulls me closer against him. I inhale a deep breath of his cologne and I freefall. I take the leap and dive into the deep end.

"I don't think there's anything else left for us to do," I say. His head falls forward. I slide my hands down his chest and over his shoulders, loving the way the hard planes of his body flex under my touch. "Except get it right this time."

Koa smiles back at me with watery eyes. I push up on my toes and press my lips against his. Tightening my grip around his neck, I pull myself closer and eliminate any space between us.

He sweeps his tongue between my lips, tasting my new peppermint gloss. When he does it a second time, I part my lips and allow him access. He pushes against my ass until I'm flush against his body and rubbing against his erection.

"How hungry are you?" he asks. I glance around at the mess we made. There isn't anything that will go bad in the next hour...or two.

"I can wait."

"Good because I'm fucking starving for you," he says, lifting me off the ground. He cuts off my yelp with a fierce kiss and I wrap my legs around his waist.

He swiftly walks through the living room and up the stairs without ever removing his mouth from mine. He kicks the door to his room shut and locks the door.

I'm not surprised by his show of athleticism and dexterity, but I am turned on by it. He lowers me to the bed, kissing down to my chest until he hits the top of my breast.

Leaning back on his knees, he looks down at me with eyes full of lust and desire. He's looked at me like this once or twice before but never with so much intensity.

I slide my hands up his forearms while his hands run up and down my thighs. Neither one of us are acting like we're in a rush, but we are desperate to keep our hands on each other at the same time.

"Now that I have you here I don't know where to start." His eyes roam from the top of my head, to my breasts, over my pussy, and down my legs.

"We made it to first base downstairs," I say. "Maybe we should give second base a try." I lift my shirt over my head. Koa's laughter over my silly analogy dies on his lips when he sees my bare breasts. Bras are overrated. I rarely wear them unless I have to. I think he approves.

"Look at you, trouble. Fucking gorgeous." He lifts his shirt over his head and tosses the fabric off the side of the bed with mine. He levels his head to my body, and kisses, licks, and tastes me until he reaches my chest.

His mouth latches over my breast and he swirls his tongue around my nipple. I wrap my hand around the back of his head holding him in place. Switching to the other breast, he gives it the same treatment while fondling and caressing the one he just abandoned.

I move my hands down his back until I reach the waistband of his shorts. We are both wearing too many clothes. He grabs my hands and raises them above my head.

Laying flush against me, I feel every hard inch of him. I can't stop myself. I lift my pelvis and rub my pussy down the length of him. Damn, he feels good.

"Fuck," he hisses. "We need to set up ground rules." His lips kiss up the side of my face. "No touching me from the waist down."

I pout. "You are taking half the fun out of it."

"You can touch me however you want up here." He pushes his hand against his chest.

"I've touched your dick before and you didn't complain. Pretty sure you begged for it," I say, rolling my hips again.

"Trouble," he groans. "Don't test me." His grip tightens on my wrists but not enough to hurt. "That was different."

"How?"

His head falls on my chest and he groans. "I have been waiting for this moment for a long time. One false move and it's over." His cheeks flush. "I want to take my time savoring every millimeter of your body. If you start touching me, I will lose control."

"That sounds like something I might like."

"Next time." He smirks.

"Fine. Any other rules for me?"

"I want you bare. Nothing in between us anymore. It's just us from now on. Are you comfortable with that?"

"Yes. I trust you. I'm on birth control. I'm clean." The thought of going through our sexual history right now seems the opposite of sexy or romantic. I don't want to discuss the two guys I slept with in my crusade of getting over Koa.

I definitely don't want to hear about all the women he's been with since me. The thought alone fills me with dread. I would rather swim in a pool of snakes. In case you're wondering, I would really fucking hate to do that.

He nods. Maybe he's thinking the same thing I am. "Good." He kisses me and starts playing with my breast again.

"Wait," I say in between kisses. "What about you?"

"I'm clean." He moves down my neck. "You always smell so sweet for being such a little troublemaker."

The way he moves over my body with his tongue and lips has me withering. He unbuttons my pants and pulls them off. My underwear follows shortly after another round of kisses and bites through the lace fabric. "Are you going to let me have another taste? I haven't stopped thinking about how much I love having your cum coating my tongue."

I pop my thighs open, letting him see how wet I am for him. Niagara Falls is drier than my vagina. He runs his fingers through my slit and collects my juices. Placing his fingers in his mouth, he closes his eyes and groans as he savors my taste.

I've never felt so turned on yet vulnerable at the same time. Other than when I fooled around with Koa, this is the first time I've been so exposed and open with a man.

I had my own set of rules with the others. Clothes stayed on, never in a bed, and no talking. It makes sense why I was never able to get over Koa. I wouldn't let a man get close enough to try.

Emotions fill my chest and clog my throat. I swallow them down, hoping he's too busy staring at my pussy to notice I'm about to cry.

"Baby," he says, laying himself over me. He brushes my hair off my face and wipes a tear off my cheek. "This isn't like last time. I'm going to prove it to you. Every day, and in every possible way. Starting now with my tongue on your pussy. Does that sound good?"

I nod and he kisses me with a sweet smile on his face. "Good girl."

He slides back down my body and places open mouth kisses on my thighs and hip bone. Finally he licks me up my center and my back bows off the bed.

He slips a finger inside while he sucks my clit. It burns as he adds another finger, scissoring them and stroking them against my walls. "Fuck you're tight, baby."

I let out a low moan when he begins to caress one of my breasts in his palm. "Koa," I plead with him. "More. I need..." My words trail off when my eyes land on him. His eyes hold mine captive, while his mouth does devious things to my pussy.

His fingers pump faster, dragging over my g-spot every time. I bite down on my lip and hold back a moan as my hands fist the comforter.

"Stop biting your lip. I want to hear you scream my name when you come. Don't fucking think about being quiet," he says, working his fingers in a slow and deliberate rhythm.

I arch my back and press my clit harder against the tip of his tongue. "Koa," I say, in between whimpers and moans. I say his name over and over as I chase my orgasm and a few more times as I come down from the high.

He stands and discards the rest of his clothes. If I wasn't already flat on my back, I would be now. He is fucking gorgeous. Broad shoulders, hard muscles, tattoos, and his large cock he's palming in his hand. I want it all.

Climbing on top of me, he kisses me tenderly. "Go easy on me, baby." He lines himself up at my entrance and pushes himself forward. His neck strains and he blows out a breath.

He pulls out and watches where we're connected as he works himself another inch. "You're doing so well. Look how much your pussy likes my cock. You got me glistening," he says, and my body shudders.

I hook my arms under his and wrap them around his back. I want to feel as much of his skin on mine as possible. Sweat beads collect under my bangs but I refuse to let go of his warm body as he continues to thrusts his hips.

"Are you going to come for me again?" he asks.

"I don't know that I can."

"Baby, you can do anything." He kisses me and the taste of me on his lips makes my clit pulse remembering his tongue was there a few minutes ago.

His eyes soften as they meet mine. "I love you, Sydney," he says, slowing his rhythm. "I have for years. You don't have to say it back but I need you to know that I do." He kisses the tears that roll down my cheeks.

His admission has me squeezing him tighter as stars explode behind my eyes and everything goes black for a moment. He ducks his head into my chest and lets out a feral groan while he reaches his release.

"I love you too," I admit to him finally. I kiss him again, weaving my fingers through his short hair and pressing my breasts into his chest. "I don't think my heart knows how to do anything else but love you."

"Thank you for loving me again. I promise I'll never hurt you again."

"I know you won't. I don't think I was the only one hurting."

"You weren't," he admits. "Let me get us cleaned up and then we can talk." He pulls out and we both groan. "I can't wait to be inside you again." He kisses my forehead and then rushes off to the bathroom.

We clean up quickly and grab a bite to eat. We even cleaned up our mess in the kitchen. I guess we'll have to learn how to cook another day.

"I like this," he says, when I lay my head against his bare chest.

"Me too. Can I ask you something?" I lift my head and balance my chin on his pec.

"You can ask me anything."

"Hmm...where have I heard that before?" I tease him, remembering he said that exact phrase to me once online. He just rolls his eyes. "It might ruin the vibe."

"What do you want to know, trouble?"

I nibble at my lip, debating how badly I want to know the number of people Koa has been with. "How many sexual partners have you had?" I blurt out.

"Including you?" he questions. I nod. "One. You are the only person I've ever seen. You are the only person I've ever wanted. You were my first and you'll be my last."

I drop my head. He's never been with anyone. He stayed faithful to me the entire time even though we weren't together. And I…

"Don't do that," he says, lifting me onto him like a blanket. "I don't give a fuck who you were with in the past. I knew they meant nothing before you even got with them because you were always going to end up here."

"You seem pretty confident."

"I am. If you look close enough, you would have seen it all along too. Really look," he says, pointing to his tattoos.

"I felt it. Loving you was too easy but I had to ignore it to protect myself," I say then start looking at his tattoos on his chest and arm.

He sighs and kisses my forehead. "I hate that you went through that."

"Trouble," I read his tattoo out loud. I never thought twice about this word being tattooed over his heart. For years I saw the tattoo thinking it was about turning eighteen and being rebellious. "It was for me."

He nods. "They all are." He places my palm on his chest. I trace over the lines of the tattoo that coil around my nickname.

"What is all of this?" I ask, examining the decorative lines of his tattoo that covers his pecs and doesn't end until it reaches his left shoulder. Upon closer inspection they look like leaves lined up end to end in various shapes and sizes to create a geometric pattern.

"What do you think it is?"

"It looks like leaves."

"Willow tree leaves. One for every week since we were together the first time. I added to it every year," he confesses. Water instantly fills my lash line. I inhale a deep breath hoping it can stop the wave of emotions I'm feeling. "While you were fighting hard to forget, I was doing whatever I could to hold on."

"I'm sorry."

"Don't be sorry. You were hurting because of me."

"And you were hurting because of me." I kiss the tattoo over his heart.

"But we're together now. No matter what, remember?" he asks, twisting his right arm to show me his newest tattoo.

I gasp noticing the upgraded version of my body paint job from our date. I graze my fingers over the stars that seem to shimmer in the sky with whatever technique the artist used. I swallow hard. "You did it."

"What did I do?"

"I don't remember why I ever stopped loving you."

24

KOA

Sweat flings off my arm as I throw the ball back to Wyatt. He's ready for this game to be over. His arm is getting tired but he refuses to tap out. As long as he's throwing strikes, no one will ask him to either.

We need one more out. Then it's our last chance at bat. We have to get a run on the board to take the win home. We're currently tied three to three against Alabama State thanks to some solid pitching and base hitting from both sides.

Enzo steps up to the plate with a smug smile on his face. "Mahina," he says, like he's my worst enemy instead of one of my closest friends.

"Morelli."

He digs his cleats into the dirt and readies his swing. I signal Wyatt to throw a fastball. Enzo has been swinging at everything today. I line up outside the strike zone to throw Enzo off and make him believe Wyatt is going to throw his slider.

Wyatt releases the ball and I quickly adjust my stance to catch it. As I suspected, Enzo swings a hair too late. I smirk under my mask.

"Almost had that one."

"I'll get the next one. You act like I haven't gotten a few hits off him already today."

"One of which you popped up just for me to catch. Thanks for making me look good."

"Yeah, yeah. Will you call it already? I kind of miss the grumpy catcher behind the plate. You've been talking a lot more shit since you got with Syd."

He's not wrong. I'm happier. I'm playing better. Everything is falling into place. I only have one, maybe two, more hurdles to jump before the next phase of our lives can begin.

I signal Wyatt for his slider. I want to see if we can get Enzo to reach for it. Wyatt agrees and I hold my glove up in the center of the plate. I drop it just in time to catch the ball in the bottom corner.

"Damn it." Enzo steps out of the batter's box and shakes his arms loose. "Call it again."

"I'm not going to hand you the pitch you want." I signal Wyatt to give him another fastball but he shakes it off. This time I try for a curve and he agrees.

Enzo swings and I watch in horror as the ball flies out of the stadium. He throws his bat and starts running the bases. I lift my mask and step away from the plate giving him room to tag it when he runs down third base.

"Better luck next time. Maybe you can wear my jersey at the championship game," he says with a wink.

"Asshole," I mutter, as he disappears into the crowd of his teammates celebrating.

Hart approaches Wyatt and whispers something in his ear. Wyatt nods then glances over at Wren in the stands. She dips her chin and that must mean something to him because suddenly he's ready to go.

Before I pull my mask down, I sneak a quick look at Sydney. For the first time in the four years I've been playing at Newhouse she's wearing my jersey. It shouldn't make a difference but it's a visible confirmation she's here for me. Having the most beautiful girl in the stands cheering for me makes winning the game irrelevant because I've already got the prize.

Last one. One more out. We can do this. The next batter steps up to the plate. He's been striking out all day. Just like Enzo, he's been swinging at everything too. He wants to be the hero for his team. I have a feeling Enzo's home run is going to feed his complex even further.

I tell Wyatt to throw his slider. This guy is going to swing regardless. We might as well give him something he can't reach.

As predicted he swings and the ball drops to my glove. Wyatt repeats the pitch two more times and adds another strikeout to his list. Now it's our turn to flip this game in our favor.

I'm helpless sitting in the dugout as Marco strikes out one of our batters, another one grounds out, and our last hope swings hard and hits a pop fly out to center field ending the game.

"Fuck." My head drops.

Hart slaps me on the back. "We had a good run."

We did. It was a good season. It was a good year.

"Are you okay, Wyatt?" I ask. He's sitting on the bench staring out at the field.

"That was the last game for me. I'm never playing again. I really wanted to bring home another championship. I can't believe it's over now."

"Are you having regrets?"

He shakes his head. "Nah. I'm going where I'm supposed to be." He gave up a career in the majors to go back home and help his family rebuild their farm. He'll be leaving for Rivers Bend right after graduation.

"Let's go get our girls." I tap his leg and we leave the dugout.

Walking out to the parking lot, there is only one person I'm looking for. As soon as she sees me, she's running. Fuck, if that isn't a good feeling.

"Hey, trouble," I say, when I catch her in my arms.

"I'm sorry. You played well." She gives me a quick kiss.

"It was a good game. It just didn't go the way we wanted." I put her back on the ground. Then take her hand in mine.

"What's everyone going to do now?" I ask once we reach the small gathering of our friends. "Anyone want to get something to eat?" I ask, looking directly at Sydney.

She glances over at her friends with a big smile on her face. She asked the group the same thing at the beginning of the season. I don't know if her invitation was meant for me, but I wanted it to be.

Instead of telling her that, I got after her about her job again for no reason. It's what I did to keep myself from showing all my cards.

"Get out of here you two. We'll catch up with you later back at the house," Lauren says.

"You don't have to tell me twice," I say, tugging Sydney toward my car. "Where do you want to eat?"

She drops her head against my shoulder as we walk. "How does Chinese takeout sound and we eat at home?"

"As you wish," I say, opening the car door and letting her climb inside.

"How many more times do you think he's going to text? It's been two days." Sydney asks. Enzo's been texting nonstop since they won the game against us and made it to the playoffs.

"Low ball number? A hundred." I shrug. He gets off on rubbing the win in our faces. I don't blame him. We did the same to him last year. "It's payback." I continue massaging her calves as we watch our movie. I like her sitting on the couch with her legs draped over my lap much better than curled up in the corner by herself.

Correction, I'm watching a movie. She has a book open on her lap. I'm not sure if she's really reading it though.

"Can you turn your phone off?"

I wince. "I could but I'm expecting a call." My agent is supposed to call me today to let me know if he was able to work out a deal with the Carolina Cardinals organization. I didn't want to mention it until I knew for sure if it was happening.

I think Sydney has accepted the fact that we'll be doing this thing long distance for the first few years while she works with the women at Blooming Beauty and starts her business on the side.

"Have you heard anything new?" she asks, then nibbles on her lip while she flips a page in her book. Pretty sure she didn't read a word of it.

"Not yet. That's what I'm waiting on. I have options." The only benefit of sacrificing your life to the sport you love is being good enough to have multiple teams interested in you.

"I can visit you on the weekends," she says. "We'll make it work."

"Baby, there will be no weekend visits because I am going to be living with you." I made my decision the minute she decided where she was going to be.

"You don't know that. And how do you know I even have room for you? I don't know if you've realized this but you have a lot of books. I saw all the stacks under your bed. They're not all going to fit in my new apartment."

I love her like this. Smiling, open, teasing me. This is the Sydney I met ten years ago. This is the girl who captured my heart.

"My books? I remember hauling box after box up to your dorm last year. I'm pretty sure you have more than me. But you know what?" I tickle her foot, making her giggle.

"What?"

"Since I'll be moving in you won't need a roommate. We can turn that second bedroom into a library. Wall to wall bookshelves and a big comfy chair. Would you like that?"

"You know I would. I like the idea of living with you more. I'm trying really hard not to get my hopes up about it. As much as I'm willing to travel and do video chats, I would much rather have you with me every day."

"What kind of video chats?" I ask, ignoring everything else she said. My brain short circuited at the thought of watching Syd coming undone on video. That would be the only perk of being away from her. She rolls her lips tight and pretends to go back to reading her book. "Oh come on, trouble. Don't leave me on the hook like that."

I remove the book from her lap and place it on the floor. Pushing her over a little, I lay beside her, trapping one of her legs between mine. She squirms as she looks up at me through hooded eyes.

"We were really good online. Don't you think?" She pushes one of her hands up my chest and wraps it around my neck while her other hand rests on my thigh. I'm glad this is something we can tease each other about now.

"I think we are really good everywhere." I press my lips against her and get lost in all her softness. My hand travels up her leg. I'm very appreciative of the skirt she's wearing today as my thumb toys with the edge of her panties.

Dragging my thumb down over the cotton of her underwear, I don't stop until I reach the middle of her pussy. "Soaking wet." I press my thumb against her clit. Sydney whines and her breaths quickens. "Do you like the idea of showing me how you can get yourself off while I watch?"

"I like the idea of you," she says, pushing her clit harder against my thumb. "I like the idea of you telling me how you want me to touch myself." She moves a hand to her stomach and slips it under her shirt.

"Fuck, trouble. You look so beautiful right now." I push her panties to the side and slide a finger down her slit. Then dip it inside her pussy.

"I like the idea of you saying filthy things. And you telling me how pretty I look while you make me come with your words," she says, pinching her nipples. Fuck, she's turning me on right now. I need to get her upstairs and naked on my bed.

"Do you know how many ways I've imagined making you orgasm?" I ask, slipping a second finger inside her. "When you were dancing at The Armory, I thought how easy it would be to pull you to a dark corner and watch you fall apart while everyone danced around us." I scissor my fingers faster, causing her fingers to dig deeper into the back of my neck.

"I thought about doing something just like this at least a thousand times. Every time you would curl up in your corner of the couch I wanted to slip my hand under the blanket and see if your pussy was wet for me. Would you have liked that?"

"Yes," she moans.

"Are you going to come for me, baby? Show me what I've been missing all this time. That's it." I capture her lips with mine as she mewls and whimpers. Her pussy tightens around my fingers and her clit pulses under my thumb as she climaxes.

My phone starts ringing and I smirk against her lips. "You should get that," she says, breathlessly.

"We aren't finished." I pull my fingers out of her and suck them clean. "Definitely not done with you," I say, kissing her so she can taste herself on my lips.

Sitting back up, I reach for my phone laying on the coffee table. "Hello," I answer, then put the phone on speaker.

Sydney sits up and straightens her clothes. I take her hand in mine and she kisses the tattoo on my arm before leaning her head there.

"Hi, Koa. How's it going?" Tony—my agent—asks.

"Good. Might be better depending on what you're about to tell me. Have you heard anything?"

"I have. It's looking like it will be Colorado," he says. Sydney smiles but there are already tears collecting in her eyes. "I know this isn't what you wanted but the offer is good. You would be the second pick and they're going to pay you well."

"What did Carolina say?" I asked him to inquire and see if there's a possibility of them picking me up if I'm available.

He sighs. "It would be a gamble. They didn't say no, but they also didn't say yes. They aren't going to lock themselves into anything until after the draft is over."

I scrub my free hand down my face. This isn't the news I wanted to hear but it's what I expected.

"So, I decline the offer from Colorado when or if it comes and wait for Carolina."

"Koa, you can't do that. You take the deal with Colorado if they offer," Sydney says.

"No," I tell her, shaking my head.

"I have to agree with your girlfriend. Even if Carolina comes up with a deal when you're a free agent, it won't be as good of an offer as being the second pick in the draft."

"I'm not playing for the payday. I play because I love the game. I won't be happy doing what I love if the *person* I love isn't with me for the ride." I squeeze Syd's hand.

"You know I have nothing but your best interest at heart. It's my job to make sure you understand all your options. It sounds like you are set on your decision but I'll encourage you to keep an open mind until the draft. Sydney, maybe you can talk to him."

"Thanks Tony. I'll talk to you soon," I say, effectively ending the call before Sydney can reply to him. I fall back against the couch and sigh.

Sydney pulls one of her legs on the couch and turns towards me. Her fingers trace over the veins in my hand. "You need to take the offer. You're a top draft pick. That will be life changing."

"My life changed the day my family moved into a house on Grove Street. It changed again when you skated into my life.

And it changed again the moment you took me back. Do you see a pattern here, baby?"

"I do but that doesn't change anything. We'll still be together whether you're in North Carolina or Colorado."

"You still don't get it. All of my life changing moments belong to you. I can't have more of them if we aren't building that life together. Side by side in North Carolina."

"I don't want you to regret it. If you don't get to play for the Cardinals in North Carolina, I don't want to be the reason you miss out on your dream. I'll never forgive myself for that."

"Regret," I scoff. Picking her up, I place her on my lap so she's straddling me. I need her to hear what I'm about to say. "You are the dream I've been chasing after most of my life. My dream is coming true every day we're together. The only regret I'll have is not being by your side while you chase yours."

"Even if that means not playing baseball?"

I nod. "I have a political science degree from a top university. I can get a job teaching and coaching high school baseball." I run my hands up her thighs until I get to the curve of her ass.

"And you would be happy doing that?" she asks, tilting her head.

"The happiest I've been in my life."

She nods. "Do you know what this means?" She grins, rubbing her hands up my chest and leaning toward me like she's going to kiss me.

"What?" I ask, hoping her mind is as dirty as mine.

"I'm getting a library!" she squeals, throwing her hands up in the air and bouncing on my lap, making me laugh.

"Hell yeah you are! Come on, baby." I stand with her in my arms. "I think getting a library calls for a celebration." I pat her ass and carry her upstairs.

People may think I'm crazy for passing on a multi-million dollar contract to play baseball. Even crazier would be passing up the opportunity to spend the rest of your days and nights with Sydney Pierce.

25

SYDNEY

Charlie yawns dramatically. "I'm so bored. Are we really going to spend one of our last nights together watching a movie? We've already done this a hundred times."

"We voted," Wren says.

"I did not vote for this," Charlie declares.

"We can do facials," I suggest. "Paint our nails for graduation."

"Do you remember the time we all put on our sluttiest clothes and went down to The Armory?" Charlie asks.

"I don't remember ever doing that," Lauren replies.

"Me either," I say.

"Exactly!" Charlie stands on the couch cushion. "That's because we've never done it. Tonight is the night, ladies. Come on, Wren. Let's go get a scrap of fabric to cover ourselves with."

"I'll pass," Wren says, turning her attention back to the movie.

"Oh, no, you don't. You are moving hundreds of miles away from me. Give me this one night," she says, tugging on Wren's arm.

"This is emotional manipulation." Wren glares at her.

"Is it working?" Charlie asks.

"Yes. Fine," Wren agrees. "But only for a few hours."

"Lauren, Sydney, what about you?" Charlie asks, holding on tight to Wren.

"I don't see how we can say no if Wren is going. Meet back here in ten minutes?" I ask. She nods and pushes Wren towards the door.

"This night just got a lot more interesting," Lauren remarks, picking up the bowls of chips and popcorn and bringing them to the kitchen. I gather up our glasses and turn off the television.

"Are you cool with going out?" I rinse the glasses and put them in the dishwasher.

"Of course. Charlie's right. We haven't had a true girls' night out with all four of us. It will be fun. I'm just having a hard time coming to terms with the fact that this is it. We're about to close the door on this part of our lives and I'm not ready."

I wrap my arms around Lauren and squeeze as hard as I can. "Our door never closes. No matter where we live. Do you understand? Years can pass without a word and I will still be there for you."

"If you don't call me every day, I will be on the next flight to Charlotte to make sure you're doing okay. I know you're going to be a big boss babe out there but don't forget about me."

"I could never. You're my sister."

"I love you, Sydney. I don't know what I would have done if you weren't my roommate freshman year. I came here alone and because of you, I'm leaving with a family." Lauren sucks in a breath and wipes at her eyes.

"I love you too." I give her one more squeeze. "We should get dressed before Charlie comes back over. Do you know what you're going to wear?"

"I have a little something hiding in the back of my closet I haven't had an excuse to wear yet," she says with a devious smile.

I laugh all the way to my room. I think I have a dress in the back of my closet like that too. I slide hangers around until I find one of the bodycon dresses Koa snubbed for Nash's party.

This pink mini spaghetti strap dress is perfect for a girls' night out at The Armory. I strip out of my sweats and one of Koa's shirts I stole from him the last time I stayed the night at his place and slip on the dress.

Once I've got the girls in place, I take a quick look in the mirror. Definitely need a different pair of underwear...or maybe no underwear. That would be a fun text to send Koa later.

I shimmy out of my underwear and fling it in the direction of the hamper. I pull my hair out of the silk wrap I have it in and fluff out my curls. They still have some life left in them. I add a little blush to my cheeks and gloss to my lips to finish off my look.

I grab my favorite black pumps from the bottom of my closet before meeting Lauren in the living room.

"Damn, girl," she says when she sees me. I do a little spin and booty shake for her. "We need to take a photo."

"Fine, but don't send it to Hart. You know they will spoil our night out if they see us looking like this." Lauren's wearing something similar to me but in green. Instead of her skirt being tight on her thighs it has a little movement to it. And despite her short stature she's wearing sneakers instead of heels.

We manage to get in a few photos before Charlie and Wren come back over dressed to kill.

"Wren, I don't think I've ever seen you in something so delicious," I say as we walk out the door.

"Get your fill. This is a one night only event." She smooths out the bottom of her form fitting sky blue dress.

My eyes flit around our surroundings as we walk across campus to The Armory. I like to think of myself as a strong woman but the situation at Ray's shook me.

I was a sitting duck and anything could have happened. If Koa hadn't reacted as quickly as he did and got Hart to call the cops, that guy would have had more time to break my window.

I've been able to block out most of the nasty things he was saying about me but I haven't forgotten everything. I'm grateful this bad memory is also woven together with the way Koa spoke to me, took care of me, and the way he held me all night.

It will take time but I hope one day I will be comfortable going out after dark without feeling like I have to look over my shoulder every two seconds.

Pop music floods The Armory and my mood is instantly lifted. We head straight to the bar and get a round of drinks and start a tab. Once we have our drinks, we walk to the back room where the dance floor is located. This is where we thrive.

"I'll grab us a table," Wren says.

"You have to dance too. I'm not going to let you get away with sitting at the table all night." Charlie crosses her arms over her chest.

"Sure. Fine. Let me at least have a drink first," she replies. "Now go dance. I've got the first drink watch." She shoos us away.

"Don't have to tell me twice," Lauren says, taking my hand and leading me out to the dance floor with Charlie following close behind.

We manage to carve out a space between all the bodies. There are people everywhere. It shouldn't be surprising. We aren't the only ones trying to savor the last few days at Newhouse and creating as many memories as possible.

Charlie, Lauren, and I form a small circle, taking turns dancing in the middle of the group. When Lauren steps into the circle, I'm once again impressed by my best friend's dance skills.

"She's really good," a random guy says beside me.

I nod in agreement. Two guys have joined Lauren in a little dance battle of sorts. It's fun to see everyone watch her with shocked looks on their faces. Charlie and I continue to dance together while we keep an eye on our girl.

"Who were those guys?" Charlie asks Lauren when she joins us.

Lauren glances over her shoulder. "They're on the step team here. Not bad, right?"

"Not as good as my girl," I say, bumping my hip with hers.

"Do you think we should check on Wren?" Lauren asks, nodding toward our table.

"Two more songs," Charlie says. "Then we can finish our drinks and drag her out here with us."

Another upbeat pop song fills the room and we immediately start moving our feet. I swing my hips as I dance behind Lauren. Charlie's eyes widen at something happening behind me. I'm about to ask what's going on when a strong arm wraps around my waist and draws me against their hard body.

I inhale a breath and I submerge myself in the ocean of Koa's scent while his hands slide up and down the curves of my hips and thighs.

He pulls my hair off my neck, exposing my ear. "You look like you want to make one of my fantasies come true," he says, then leaves a trail of kisses down my neck and over my shoulder.

I turn in his arms and his hands drift down to my ass. Draping my arms over his shoulder, I enjoy the desperate way Koa is looking at me.

"I'm surprised to see you here," I tell him.

"It wasn't my idea but I'm glad I came. I would have been really sad if I missed you wearing this dress." His eyes dip to my cleavage.

"You didn't seem very impressed with this dress when I was thinking about wearing it for Nash's party."

He pulls me closer to him and slips a finger under the thin strap on my shoulder. "That's because I knew I wouldn't be the one taking it off of you that night. I have a personal affliction with a lot of your clothes."

"I don't like that you're suffering." I glance over at our table. Lauren and Charlie have joined Wren, Wyatt, Nash, and Hart. They probably wouldn't mind if I called it an early night. "Maybe we should say our goodbyes and put you out of your misery."

Holding tightly to my hand, Koa turns on his heel and briskly walks through the crowded dance floor.

"What are the four of you doing here?" Charlie asks, suspiciously. I snag my drink and take a slow sip waiting for someone to fess up.

Charlie glares at each of the guys, trying to get one of them to crack. Then she narrows her sights on Wren and Wyatt. Both of which have their phones sitting out in front of them.

"You texted him," Charlie accuses Wren. "And you just had to come, didn't you?" she asks Wyatt.

"I'm just a man," he says, holding up his hands. "If you got this text, you would have come running too." He passes Charlie his phone. She reads over his texts and pouts.

"Ugh, fine. Why do you have to be so hot, Wren?" Charlie asks, passing Wyatt's phone back to him.

"It's a curse," she replies.

"I know you want to, but you can't leave yet. We have to at least finish our drinks and Wren owes me one dance," Charlie says.

"One drink and then I'm taking you to meet some of my friends," Nash says, throwing an arm around Charlie's shoulders.

"What kind of friends?" Charlie asks, looking up at my brother.

He smirks, knowing he has her on the line.

"The show me a night I won't soon forget kind of friends?" she asks.

"Yes. Those kind. Which reminds me," Nash drops his arm from Charlie's shoulders and leans on the table. "You three," he narrows his eyes on Wyatt, Koa, and Hart, "went and got tattoos without me."

"They did?" Wren questions. "You did?" she asks Wyatt.

"I'm surprised you didn't notice since you like looking at my body so much," Wyatt teases her.

"Where is it?" Wren asks skeptically.

"Right here." Wyatt holds out his wrist.

"Those two tiny dots? They look like freckles," she says. Everyone at the table snickers at him.

"No. It's you and me." He points to the dots. "I call it '*a bird's eye view.*' Kind of perfect right?"

"That is not a tattoo," Wren claims.

"I beg your pardon, it most certainly is. It is a permanent mark on my skin and it isn't going anywhere, birdie. Neither are you," he says, wrapping his arms around her.

Koa stands behind me and pulls me tighter against his chest. I lift my drink and take a sip, enjoying all of my friends chatting and laughing around me. I'm going to miss this.

We order another round of drinks while reminiscing over the last four years. We even manage to get Wren on the dance floor for a few songs.

"I'm taking her home now," Wyatt says.

"Can I take you home too?" Koa asks, kissing my bare shoulder.

"Yes, please," I reply. Then kiss him.

"But we were having fun." Charlie pouts.

"Let them go. We don't need them," Nash says. "We'll have more fun on our own. I think it's time I introduce you to those friends I was telling you about."

"Fine. I can't let this dress go to waste because all of you have boyfriends now. It's really hard being the last one standing in singlehood," Charlie says.

"Come on. You're too pretty to pout." Nash takes hold of her hand. "Text me when you're home. We'll take care of the tab," he says, before escorting Charlie away from our table.

"Don't worry about Charlie," Wren says, getting up from her chair. Wyatt immediately grabs her and pulls her to his side. "She will be the center of attention and forget we even left."

As we walk by the bar, I glance over toward the bar, and sure enough, Nash has managed to make Charlie the main attraction. I send him a quick text to keep an eye on her and make sure she gets home okay.

"Everything good?" Koa asks, once we get to his car.

"Yeah. It's perfect."

And for once, I feel everything really is and will only get better from here.

26

KOA

"Do you want anything to eat?" I ask, once we get home from the bar.

"Not really," Sydney says, grazing the handrail on the stairs that lead to my room and taking a step up. "I think I'm ready for you." She takes another step up the stairs.

"Is that so?" I ask, following after her. She sends me a coy look over her shoulder.

"Yes."

"I'm not going to be gentle this time." I wouldn't say I've been holding back with Sydney. There have definitely been a few times we've had sex where it's been quick and dirty. Last night in the shower comes to mind. I wouldn't mind doing that again real soon.

"What does that mean?" she asks, entering my bedroom. She stands in front of my dresser and removes her jewelry.

"It means you've been torturing me all night in this scam of a dress and your pussy is going to pay the price." I stand behind her and skate my hands up her thighs and slip them under the thin pink fabric of her dress.

I keep going until I reach her hips. I expect to feel at minimum a string to her underwear but there's nothing.

"About that," she says, giggling. "I was going to text you."

"You were going to text me," I murmur, reaching around and sliding my hand over her bare pussy. "What were you going to tell me?" I ask, pressing against her clit.

"I-I don't know. Koa," she moans, gripping the edge of the dresser and pressing her ass against my cock. "A picture maybe. Something that would convince you to come over and see me."

"You still aren't understanding." I remove my hand from between her legs and spin her around.

"Understanding what?"

"I always want to see you." I grab the bottom of her dress and start slipping it up the curve of her hips and ass. "I always want to be next to you." I lift the dress exposing her breasts and over her head. "Convincing me is futile."

"But you don't even know what I was going to say." She lifts the bottom of my shirt over my head. Her hands move to my belt and she removes it briskly, making it slap the dresser before it falls to the ground.

"What were you going to say in your text, baby?" I ask, giving her a brief kiss. It takes all my control not to put my hands on her with her naked in front of me.

She peels my pants and briefs down my legs, springing my cock free. I've had a semi since I saw her dancing at The Armory. Her eyes widen and she lowers herself to her knees.

"You'll have to use your imagination since you took my dress off already," she says. The last thing I'm going to do is imagine Sydney wearing clothes right now. "I thought maybe if you saw me on my knees waiting for you, you would want to come give me what I want."

Her hands dig into the muscles in my thighs. Clearing my throat, I ask, "What is it you want?"

She looks up at me with hooded eyes. Her breasts hang heavy, begging for my hands. She's a fucking goddess on her knees.

"Let me show you," she says, wrapping her hand around the base of my cock. Now I'm the one needing to use the dresser as a crutch to keep myself upright.

Sydney runs her tongue from the base of my cock to the tip and back down again, teasing me. I grow harder with every pass of her tongue until I'm twitching in her hand.

She smirks and swirls her tongue around the head of my cock, moaning as she laps at the precum leaking. A quick glance at me through a curtain of bangs is the only warning I receive.

"Goddammit, trouble," I croak, when she hollows her cheeks and pulls me to the back of her throat. I gather her hair in my hands. I want to see her lips run up and down the length of my cock. "This is better than I've ever imagined."

She moans and squirms on her knees, making her tits bounce. I grip her hair a little tighter but still allow her to control the pace. Saliva drips down her chin and her eyes begin to water. The image makes me feral.

This isn't how I want to come. I pull out of her mouth, making her whine. "Get on the bed, baby," I say, helping her up from the floor. "I'll let you finish that later but right now I want to see your pussy dripping with my cum."

"Have you always had such a dirty mouth?" she asks, laying down on the bed. She is resting back on her elbows with her legs spread waiting for me. She nibbles down on her lip and her dark nipples pebble in anticipation.

"Only for you. Flip over. I want you on your hands and knees with your ass up." Her eyes flit from my eyes to my cock in my hand. I pump myself a few times, attempting to release the tension.

She slowly rolls over and stretches her arms out in front of her. A low whimper releases from her as her breasts graze against the top of the comforter. "Like this?" she asks, glancing at me over her shoulder.

I nod slowly, taking my time to appreciate her ass that is on full display. I prowl towards the bed. Once I'm close enough, I grab her by the hips and pull her to the edge.

I palm her ass in my hands and massage the plush muscles. "I have watched this ass walk away from me for years. Tonight, I want to see it coming back to me."

Stepping closer, I push my cock down her ass and through her slick center. Sydney groans when I slip a finger inside her. "Do you think you're ready for my cock?"

"Yes. Koa, please," she begs.

"Are you going to come for me first?"

She shakes her head. "I want your cock. Not your fingers."

Fuck, I like it when she tells me what she wants. I've been dying to hear her beg for me like this. I line up at her entrance and start easing my way inside. I'm not convinced her body is prepped for me. As much as I want to punish her for that dress, I don't want to hurt her.

"Koa, I need more." Her hands dig into the comforter as I pull out and push in another inch.

"Relax for me, baby." Every time I push back in, she tightens around me like a vice. It feels phenomenal but I'm not going to get all the way in at this rate.

I slide my hands up her waist and around the front of her chest. Lifting her from the mattress, I press her back against me and she melts into my chest.

Her arms wrap around my neck and I kiss her bicep. I slide one hand down to her pussy and start working her clit and the other I place at the base of her throat.

"That's it," I say when she relaxes enough to take all of me. "This is how it was always meant to be. You and me." I tilt her chin so she's looking at me. "Can you feel how good we are together?" I ask, pumping into her harder.

"Yes. Don't stop. Please don't stop. I'm so close," she says, with a low moan.

"I'm not going to," I say, picking up my pace and tightening my grip around her neck. "I'll never stop." I dip my head and capture my lips with hers.

She cries out against my lips as she finds her release. I hold her tight and thrust into her until my spine is tingling and darkness clouds my eyes. "Fuck," I shout, filling her with my cum.

I pull out and watch as my cum drips down her thighs. I run a finger up her leg, collecting the cum, and then push it back inside her pussy.

Sydney looks at me over her shoulders with a quirked brow and I smirk back at her. "Someday we're going to need every drop. We might as well learn to stop being wasteful now."

She stands from the bed and walks over to my closet. "Is that what you want? Kids? A family?" she asks, pulling down a shirt and throwing it over her head.

"When it's time, yes, that's what I want." I grab a clean pair of briefs and put them on. "What about you?"

"I want a family too. How will we know when it's time?" she asks, twiddling her fingers.

I shrug. "I think it'll just feel right. Once we're settled and your business is off the ground and doing well. We'll know." I wrap my arms around her and she does the same to me.

"Do you think I could do both? Be a mom and run a business?"

"Baby, you could run the world and be an incredible mom. But we don't have to worry about that now. You've got to flip the beauty industry on its head first."

"Thank you for believing in me. I'm glad you're going with me. I wouldn't want to do this without you. Even when we weren't together, I've realized now that I've always had you with me. You never gave up on us. I love you, Koa Mahina. I have from the first moment I met you and I always will."

"I love you, too, baby," I reply, holding back tears thinking about how far we've come and our future together.

I crowd Sydney from behind and inhale her sweet vanilla scent. It still feels like a dream waking up with her in the mornings. She's been staying over here almost every night since we got back together.

The nights she's been staying at the dorm I find myself driving over there in the middle of the night. When I do start traveling again for baseball, those nights away are going to be brutal.

Sydney stirs, pressing her ass into my cock which is well aware of her presence. "Morning, baby," I say, roaming my hand down her legs and back up her chest.

"Good morning." She yawns and stretches. Fuck, that feels good. "Don't even think about it," she says. "I've got to at least pee first." She tilts her head back and kisses my jaw.

She taps my arms and I set her free. "Hurry back." I'll be waiting. I flip over on my back and put my hands behind my head. My cock is fully erect now, tenting the sheets.

Her eyes fill with desire and she runs her tongue over her lower lip. "Five minutes. Don't move. I'll be right back," she says, holding up a finger. Then scurries out the door.

Fuck, I love that girl. I can't wait until graduation is over and we can move on to the next phase of our life. I should probably start packing. I don't have a lot at the townhouse. Most of my stuff is still at my parent's house. I'll have—

My thoughts get cut off by a loud scream. I shoot off the bed. I throw my door open and enter the hall. Hart is leaning against the wall outside the bathroom.

"You heard it too?" I ask.

He nods. "They're both in there," he says, pointing to the bathroom door.

"He said that?" Lauren asks. "That's so hot."

"And then he..." Syd's voice trails off. She must have realized how loud she was being. Lauren gasps and they both start giggling.

I cross my arms over my chest and chuckle. "This is our future," I say. "The two of them screaming and laughing together at our expense."

"I think so," he agrees with a smirk.

"I wouldn't want it any other way."

"Me either," he says, smiling back at me.

I've been so concerned with getting Sydney back, I haven't had time to let it sink in that my best friends are all going in different directions.

"Don't even think about it, man," he says, reading my mind. "I'll be seeing you on the field again before you know it. Lauren isn't going to let go of the family she just got either."

"You're right. It's just hard to say goodbye."

"Then we won't." He slaps my shoulder. "Come on. Let's find some breakfast. They are going to be in there awhile."

"I'll meet you down there. I need to throw some clothes on."

I hope Hart is right and this isn't goodbye but see you later.

27

SYDNEY

I straighten the tassel on my graduate cap again. I've only fixed it ten times since I've been waiting in the crowded tunnel.

Is this what it's like for Nash before every home game? The nerves, the adrenaline? We've been waiting in the underground tunnels of the football stadium for at least twenty minutes.

I'm ready to walk onto the field and take my seat. It's already been an emotional day. From the moment I woke up this morning I've had a slideshow of memories playing through my mind.

From moving in freshman year, meeting Lauren for the first time, our first frat party, late night study sessions, sleepovers with the girls, and everything in between that got me to this moment.

"Please welcome Newhouse University's graduating class," the dean of students says into the microphone. The students around me straighten their spines and prepare to walk.

Koa glances at me over his shoulder and winks. He's about twenty people in front of me. I smile back and hide my nerves.

The marching band begins to play the Newhouse U fight song. I have to swallow back the tears. This song isn't just for the football team on game day. It's our motto here at Newhouse: to fight until the end. To show up until the job is done. To give it your all until you have nothing left.

Walking out onto the turf, the sun and heat is almost too much to bear after being in the dark tunnels for so long. I search the stands for my family. They texted me earlier with their location. I spot them easily sitting next to Koa's mom and dad, and do a little finger wave in their direction.

My mom is already crying into a tissue and my dad is clapping with his chest puffed. They've always believed in me. When I told them my major they were skeptical, or maybe they were realistic. They knew it wasn't going to be an easy road. But I did it.

We file through the white chairs setup on the field until we find our assigned seat. Koa squeezes my hand when I pass by him.

I find Lauren, Hart, and Wren a few rows ahead of me and Wyatt behind me. I spot Charlie where she is sitting on stage and blow her a kiss. Hiring all of those cute tutors paid off because she's our valedictorian.

The dean of students as well as a few other faculty members, and prestigious alumni address our graduating class offering congratulations and words of wisdom for our future. I tune them out and let my mind drift to what's next for me.

Koa and I are loading up the moving truck in a few days. It's bittersweet to leave behind all the places that got us here.

I'm going to miss summers reading under the willow trees on Grove Street.

I'm going to miss Sunday afternoons spent listening to my brother and his friends arguing over dropped passes and missed calls by the referees while watching football games at the townhouse.

I'll miss living with Lauren and being able to run down to the hall to her room when I need her. I think that is going to be the hardest one.

It's strange how you can be so excited about what's next and still grieve everything you're leaving behind.

The dean introduces Charlie and there is a mix of wolf whistles and clapping from everyone.

"Good afternoon family, friends, faculty, staff, honored guests, and my fellow graduates. Today we are celebrating four years of hard work. After all the hours of studying and cramming information into our brains, we made it to the end. We have achieved the goal. Mission accomplished."

Charlie's eyes roam over all of us, stopping to smile at me, Wren, and Lauren. "A degree is not the only thing I will be leaving here with. Like some of you," her eyes land on Lauren for a moment, "I came to Newhouse looking for a fresh start.

"I came to school prepared to make friends and have a good time. Instead, I'm leaving with a lifetime of memories and a family. Newhouse University is one of the best schools in the country because of you.

"Each and every one of us have our own unique set of skills and qualities. All of which we have been able to show off in our safe space at Newhouse among people that we love," she says. I tilt my head back and try to stave off tears.

"As we close this chapter and move on to the next, I have one thing I want to ask you to do. The world will try to dim the light you have found here. It will try to hold you back. I ask that instead of dimming your light to blend in with others, you choose to stand tall and teach others how to shine as bright as you do.

"I will be leaving here today with an immense amount of gratitude and hope in my heart. Congratulations to each and everyone of you! On to our next adventure!"

I stand, along with all of my friends, and clap for Charlie. I'm so proud of her. I don't know much about her home life. She never talked about her family much. I can't help but wonder if she is hiding something behind her flirty and fun personality.

The department heads line the stage and begin calling our names. Row by row my classmates walk across the stage and receive their diploma.

Once Wren walks down the steps she looks somewhere behind me with a big smile on her face. No doubt she is looking at Wyatt. She directs the guy behind her to start a new row, making me laugh.

Hart and Lauren join her in our newly saved seats. I wait patiently for my turn and scream as loud as I can when my man walks the stage and shakes hands with all of his professors.

He smiles back at me as he walks to his seat. I'll never get tired of seeing that smile. It's been gone for so long. If only I had known, that I held the power to bring it back.

I have to believe in the timing of everything. Our break let us grow and mature. It gave us space to miss and appreciate each other. Koa has always been a big part of everything I do even when I couldn't see it for myself.

Standing from my seat, I follow my line to the stage. I glance over at my family again and down to my friends. "Sydney Pierce," the dean announces my name as I pass by, grabbing my diploma.

As I walk down the steps, Koa is there waiting for me.

"Congratulations, baby. I'm so fucking proud of you," he says, giving me a quick kiss.

"I'm proud of you too. I love you."

"I love you too." He kisses my cheek.

I hug Lauren and Wren when I get to our seats. "We did it," I whisper-shout, bouncing on my feet.

Wyatt is the last of our friends to walk the stage. He stops in front of Charlie and offers her an elbow. She gladly accepts and they join our group.

We shuffle around so Wyatt can stand with Wren. I sling my arms around Charlie. "Your speech was perfect. I'm glad you're a part of my family."

"Thanks, Syd. I wouldn't have made it through this past year without you. I'm going to miss you."

"I'm going to miss you too," I say, giving her one last squeeze.

The last few rows of students file across the stage and the dean of students takes to the podium again.

"If I can ask everyone to please stand," he says. The stadium erupts in loud cheering. It echoes through my chest causing my eyes to well with emotion. Koa smiles softly and kisses my cheek.

"Graduates, you can now turn your tassels." Another outburst of screams erupts as we move our tassels to the other side of our cap.

"It's been an honor to have each of you here with us at Newhouse the past four years. Congratulations to this year's graduating class of Newhouse University."

I take my cap off my head and fling it into the air with a squeal. Koa grabs me by the waist and lifts me into the air.

"Are you ready, baby?" he asks.

"For what?"

"Whatever you want." He slides his hand around the back of my head and pulls me in for a kiss.

"I think we should keep up with our tradition," I reply.

"What's that?"

"Let's celebrate the same way we did our last graduation night except this time I'm keeping you in my arms forever and never letting go."

28

KOA

"Baby," I call out for Syd as I enter our apartment with my arms full of groceries. It's only been a month since we moved in. It's taken us some time but we are slowly making it our own.

I was able to get a lot of our stuff unpacked and organized when we first moved in while Sydney focused on work. I'm so fucking proud of her. I didn't expect our guest bathroom and kitchen to turn into a science lab but I love watching her work and coming up with new products.

Working with Jade and Zoe has fueled her passion. She comes home from work with new ideas and concepts for her business. I'm back to being the thirteen year old boy hanging on her every word.

"Baby," I yell again. *What is she doing?* I unload the groceries and put everything away that I won't need for dinner. We're still figuring out this cooking thing. We've managed to make a few basics like spaghetti and tacos edible. Although, even those get burned or overcooked on occasion.

I walk through our living room, passing our couch that has more blankets than available seating, and admiring all the plants she has managed to add in a tiny room.

My girl can't cook but she can keep plants alive. They seem to multiply overnight. Every day I come home from practice or workouts and find new plants she's 'rescued' from the nursery and at least two or three cups with plant clippings.

I go to our room and check the bathroom, but both are empty. Walking back to the hall, I open the door to the spare room. We haven't been able to do much with this room yet. We've ordered bookshelves and a chair but everything is still in boxes.

My plan was to work on it while I waited to hear from the Cardinals. However, the call ended up coming a lot faster than we anticipated. I haven't played a game yet but I do practice and dress for them.

As predicted, the contract wasn't as good as the one I passed on with Colorado. But I got the better deal with the life Sydney and I are building together.

Which is proven once again when I see what Sydney is doing. "Fuck me," I mumble to myself.

Sydney is on her knees leaning over an open box of one of the bookshelves and reading the instructions. Her ass is on full display in tiny bike shorts.

Dinner and everything else might have to wait. I readjust myself and walk into the room. She has headphones on, no doubt listening to an audiobook.

Before I can get too close, she removes her headphones and looks at me over her shoulder. "Hi," she says, standing and slipping her arms under my shirt and around my back.

"How did you know I was in here?" I ask.

"I can feel you when you're near me. I just know." She shrugs. Lifting to her tiptoes, she kisses me. My hands go to her ass and I give it a pat and a quick squeeze.

"Do you want me to help you put these together?" I ask, glancing around the room.

"I don't think so. The last time you 'helped' me with my bookshelves they fell apart."

"That wasn't just me," I remind her. "Your brother was also to blame for that mess."

"Oh, sure, blame the best friend," she teases. "How come he didn't help fix it then?"

I snag her by the waist again. "That's because your brother doesn't care about making you happy like I do. I don't like seeing you upset about anything."

"You're too good to me," she says. "I'm going to work on this. Unless you want my help with dinner."

I chuckle. "No, I'm good. I'm just doing steak, potatoes, and salad."

"Sounds yummy."

"Come get me if you need me to hold a board or something. I don't want you to hurt yourself," I say, kissing her forehead.

She waves me off. "I've got it." She goes back to reading the instructions and I admire her ass one last time.

Turning on some music, I busy myself in the kitchen marinating the steaks and preparing the vegetables. Sydney joins me a half hour or so later and slams her palm on the kitchen island.

"Extra pieces," she says with a grin. I throw my head back laughing. "Do you think manufacturers do this on purpose to mess with your head?"

"Probably, baby. Did it feel sturdy?" I ask, adding the tomatoes and cucumbers I've diced into a large salad bowl.

"Enough to put your books on the shelf and test it out first." She winks and steals a cucumber from the bowl.

"I see how it is." I shake my head.

"Oh," she shouts, waving her hands and jumping from foot to foot. "I forgot to tell you. Jade invited us to this big industry party. I told her I needed to check with my roommate and see if he's free."

My eyes narrow on the way her lip curls on one side. She knows exactly what she said. It isn't the first time she's said that evil word. I dry my hands on the towel I have thrown over my shoulder and drop it on the counter.

Rounding the island, I place a hand on either side of her, boxing her in. "Call me your roommate one more time," I say, bringing my face closer to hers.

"What are you going to do about it...*roommate*?"

I glance around the kitchen. The steaks are resting, the salad is done, and the potatoes are in the oven. As long as I turn the oven off...

I grab Sydney by the waist and throw her over my shoulder. "I warned you, baby," I say, walking to the oven and flipping it off.

"The potatoes are going to burn." She tries to wiggle herself loose but I just hold on tighter.

"It wouldn't be the first time." I slap her ass enough to make it sting and walk us to our bedroom.

"What are you going to do?" she asks when I toss her on the bed.

"Remind you what kind of roommate I am. Now strip."

"Are you ready for today?" my teammate, Caleb, asks as we take the field for the start of the game.

I nod. This is it. My major league debut. I can't believe this is really happening. Hours of practice, nights spent outside while everyone was asleep, sacrificing almost everything to get to this moment.

He slaps me on the back and walks out to first base. I follow behind him, savoring every moment. Spinning as I walk, I take in the crowd.

My parents, brother, and Sydney along with her parents have seats near the dugout. I wave over to them, but I don't see Sydney. I know she's here. She's texted me a selfie every five minutes. First it was with the Cardinal mascot and then it was with a big plate of nachos. She said she was sending that one to Lauren for some reason.

I want to see her but I don't let it bother me. Knowing her, she is standing on top of someone in the front row trying to get a better photo. Maybe I should tell her they have professional photographers. She doesn't have to capture everything herself.

The announcer begins to introduce the starting lineup. I hold my breath until I hear my name. I stand behind home plate, taking a minute to etch this memory in my brain and my heart.

"Making his major league debut, behind the plate is number nineteen, Koa Mahina," he says over the loudspeaker. I raise my hand and wave at the crowd before lowering my mask. *Fuck, I made it.*

"To make his debut even more memorable, we've asked his girlfriend to throw the first pitch. Please welcome Ms. Sydney Pierce to the field."

My heart begins to race as Syd walks up to the pitcher's mound. She looks gorgeous as always with her legs on display in denim shorts and my jersey knotted at her waist.

I wanted her here to witness what she helped me accomplish but to have her be a part of it like this makes it even more special.

Holding my gloved hand out over the plate, I open and close it to signal that I'm ready for her.

She nibbles on her lower lip before winding her arm back and throwing the ball in my direction. I stand and run forward to snag the ball out of the air. The poor thing didn't even make it halfway to the plate.

Sydney doesn't seem to care as she laughs wildly into the warm summer air.

She runs toward me and leaps. "Nice catch," she says, as I hold her up in my arms.

"The best one I've ever made."

SYDNEY

TWO YEARS LATER

I stand in front of the mirror in the guest room in Koa's parents house—after today, my in-laws' house—and slip the small diamond stud earrings onto my ears that once belonged to my mom. She wore them on her wedding day too.

"You're stunning," Lauren says, from behind me as she fluffs my veil.

"Thank you, but you are the one who is glowing." She's currently five months pregnant with a little boy. I surprised her earlier this week with a little baby shower while we were all in town.

"I can't wait to see Koa's face when you walk down the aisle in this gown. He's going to cry."

"He's not going to cry." I shake my head. I do love my dress—it is white lace with a high slit and plunging neckline. The skirt and train flow freely when I walk. It's the dress of my dreams.

"I will be crying enough for everyone," she says, grabbing a tissue.

There is a light knock at the door. It clicks open and Wren pops her inside followed by Charlie.

"Everyone is settled outside. I think it's time," Wren says, checking the list on her phone. She planned most of the wedding along with the help of Wyatt's sister-in-law.

"It's gorgeous by the way. Not as gorgeous as you but I think you'll be happy with the way everything turned out." Charlie applies another layer of gloss to her lips.

When Koa asked me to marry him last Christmas, I already had our entire wedding planned. It's been planned since we had our first adventure together in his backyard. Maybe not in full detail, but I knew I wanted to get married to him here where it all began.

Our first date in college was my inspiration. I wanted to recreate the lights in the trees and all the magic I felt flowing through the air that night. We even have a face painting station setup for the kids. Wren already had to warn Wyatt once that he's not allowed to paint his face—or anything else—until after we take formal pictures.

"I can't wait to see it." I helped with the planning and the layout, but the execution was all my family and friends.

"Do you have room for a few more in here?" my dad asks, stepping inside the room with Nash and my mom.

"We'll wait for you outside," Lauren says, gathering the flowers and exiting the room with Charlie and Wren.

"My God, if you aren't as pretty as a picture," he says, holding my hands and lifting them wide.

"Thank you, Dad."

My mom embraces me and the tears begin to well. This is the woman I have looked up to all my life. She has taught me to be brave and strong. To always fight for what I believed in and do the right thing regardless of the cost.

"I'm so proud of you, Sydney," she whispers into my ear.

"You sure you want to marry him? I've got my keys. We can get out of here. It's not too late," he says, smiling. My mom slaps his arm.

"You know I want this. I love him."

He sighs. "I know you do. I was kind of hoping I could hold on to you a little longer."

"You are the reason I know how I'm supposed to be loved and how a man should treat me. You love Mom so well." I smile at both of them as they stand holding onto each other.

He takes the handkerchief out of his coat pocket and dabs his eyes. "You promise me he loves you as much as I love your mama?" He kisses the top of her head.

"I promise," I say, kissing his cheek and wrapping my arms around both of them. I want to tell him I think Koa loves me more but then we will be here all night while he lists the ways he loves the woman standing beside him.

"We should get you married then. That boy of yours hasn't stopped fidgeting since he got dressed," Dad says.

I nod, but notice Nash over his shoulder leaning against the wall. "Give me a minute." I nod towards my brother.

"We'll be in the hall." My dad leads my mom outside the room, squeezing Nash's shoulder as he passes him.

"You look beautiful, Sis. Koa's not going to be able to handle it."

"That's what I keep hearing but I think you underestimate my future husband."

He walks over to me admiring the clips and jewels in my hair. "I don't underestimate him. I know him. I've seen his face every time you've entered a room and every time you've left one since you were twelve years old. I've watched his fists clench more times than I can count because he was dying to touch you." He smirks at the memories. "And I saw the way you completely altered his personality when you gave him a second chance."

He picks up the box of tissues off the table and hands it to me. "I can say without a doubt that he is going to lose it because today he is marrying his dream girl."

"I love you, Nash, but I'm kind of mad you're making me cry."

"I love you too. Let's get you hitched," he says, leading me out the door where Lauren and the girls are waiting.

They help carry my train and my dad takes my arm as we walk down the stairs. "Where's Mom?" I ask, once we get downstairs.

"Wyatt escorted her to her seat. She's in the front row waiting for you," Wren informs me. I nod and swallow back tears.

"You can keep crying if you want," Lauren says, fixing a few of my curls that have migrated out of place. "Your makeup is top of the line. It's completely waterproof. Trust me. I put it to the test every day." She winks.

We're all wearing my brand Glamour & Grace. I named it after my love of fantasy and all things fae. Their ability to glamour themselves is similar to the magic of makeup.

We walk outside and wait off to the side out of sight. The sun has set and the backyard is lit up with hundreds, if not thousands, of fairy lights. We have put them in every tree and along the fence line.

Guests sit at round tables strategically placed around the back yard with a walkway of white rose petals down the center leading to the altar.

One by one Charlie, Wren, and Lauren make their way down the aisle. The instrumental version of one of our songs begins to play. "That's our cue," I tell my dad. He locks his arm with mine.

Step by step I walk toward my future husband.

Koa stands in front of our willow tree. We've pulled back the branches and added white hydrangeas to an arch to create a whimsical backdrop.

His gray suit is fitted over his broad shoulders and the purple tie is the perfect pop of color. I can't take my eyes off of him. He shamelessly wipes at his eyes, and one of my own tears manages to escape. I'm afraid I won't be able to hold it together much longer.

I didn't think walking toward him would make me so emotional. We've been living together for two years but there's something about having him promise to love me forever in front of all of our family and friends that has me disintegrating.

"Hi," Koa greets me we're close enough to touch.

"Hi," I whisper back.

"Take care of my little girl," my dad says, shaking his hand. He kisses me on the cheek, then he takes my bouquet and passes it to Lauren before placing my trembling hands in Koa's.

The officiant addresses our guests and welcomes all of our family. We decided against a traditional ceremony. That has never been our style.

"Koa and Sydney have both prepared their own vows. Koa, if you'd like to go first."

He squeezes my hands and exhales a deep breath.

"You look beautiful, baby," he murmurs, making me smile. "I thought a lot about this moment and what I wanted to say. Nothing seemed like enough. Do I promise to love you? Until my last breath. Protect you? With everything that I have. Cherish you? I will get on my knees every day and show you how much," he says, making Wyatt snicker. I shake my head. "I love you more today than I did yesterday and I will love you even more tomorrow. That isn't a promise but a guarantee."

"I love you too. I have since the moment we met. Even when I didn't want to love you, I loved you with all my heart." I squeeze his hands to let him know I'm teasing. It isn't often we bring up the time we weren't together but we both know it's a part of our story and it got us where we are now.

"The kind of love we have doesn't just exist in this world. There is no beginning and no end. It transcends other dimensions and realms. We were always going to find each other again because you are my best friend, my other half, my fated mate," I tell him.

Koa tightens his grip on my hands and smiles. A lot of our friends may not understand why I would mention realms and dimensions but he does. Because he knows me. He understands me. He always has.

With shaky hands we exchange rings and say *I do*.

"Congratulations, Mr. and Mrs. Mahina. You may kiss your bride," the officiant announces.

Koa wraps a hand around my waist and cups my cheek. He pulls me tight against his chest and presses his lips into mine. My hands wrap around his neck and I push my fingers into the hair at his neck. This kiss brings me back to our first kiss in the photobooth but this time he's claiming me as his wife.

Our friends and family clapping and cheering brings us back to reality. I break the kiss and giggle at his disappointment.

Music starts back up again and we walk down the aisle hand in hand. This time as husband and wife. Koa doesn't stop walking until we are completely out of view from our guests.

"My wife," he says, pulling close to him again. "You are absolutely stunning. This dress..." his voice trails off as he kisses down my neck and over my cleavage.

"You like it, husband?"

"Say that again." His eyes snap to mine.

"My husband," I repeat. He slams his mouth over mine so hard I have to hold onto his forearms to steady myself.

"How long do we have to stay here? I want to be alone with you." He drops his head against mine.

"Only a few hours and then I'm yours for the rest of your life," I say.

"I like the sound of that, Mrs. Mahina," he says, with a smirk.

"Me too, Mr. Mahina," I tease, as I walk away. He growls then chases me back toward all of our wedding guests.

THANK YOU

Koa and Sydney have my heart. They are my most anticipated book/couple to date. Since the first time they were introduced to us in Easy Out, we could all feel the tension and attraction between them. I had no idea where their story was going to go. The two of them completely ran the show. I'm just glad I was able to be here for the ride.

These books do not get written without a lot of help. I can't do this on my own.

My Family. They are my everything. I am so blessed to have so much support. They not only push me to keep going but inspire me. Sydney and all of her cosmetic experiments all of the bathroom were inspired by my daughters.

Kelsey. My ride or die. This is going to be a fun year. I'm so glad I get to spend it with you. Thank you for all your hard work and your never ending support.

Danie. You are so amazing! I am so lucky to have you helping me and for our friendship. I appreciate everything you do so much.

Author Friends. I am blessed to be surrounded by so many talented people who are willing to help me when I have questions and cheer me on. Being an author is very difficult and sometimes very lonely. All of you make everything better.

Yinn. You keep me sane. You make me laugh all day. I love having you to bounce ideas off of. Thank you for being my official complaint department.

Beta Team. Thank you so much for taking the time to read the book and give feedback. I hope you read Foul Territory for a second time and see how impactful your feedback was. You truly made this book better.

Katie, Megan, Lauren, Maeghen, Jessi, Tara, TL, Denice, Tracey, and Karin thank you all for going above and beyond. You all are so special and I appreciate you very much. I could go on and on about all of you but we would be here all day.

Stephanie, Jasmine, Kaila, and Jessica, thank you so much for being sensitivity readers/beta readers and offering your insights on the book. I appreciate you being open to sharing your thoughts and feelings to help me shape their story even more.

Sam at Ink & Laurel. You're amazing. Thank you so much for bringing my vision to life once again. I'm so obsessed with the way their cover turned out. I can't wait for the next one.

Kristen at Kristen's Red Pen. We did it! Thank you for being so insightful and always making me reconsider certain scenes from a different perspective. And since you made me delete them out of the book, I'm adding them here lol. Baby, baby, baby, baby, baby, baby, baby, baby, baby.

Lemmy and the team at Luna Literary Management. You are a creative and marketing genius. I am continuously blown away by your talent. Thank you for your support and encouragement throughout this process and for putting together the best ARC team a girl could ask for. I kept everything I said in Strike Zone because it is all still true. I LOVE YOU! And I can't wait to see what this year holds for us.

Newhouse Nation! You are the best ARC and Street team a girl could ask for. You make it worth it. And to my readers in Newhouse Nation, I am filled with joy and gratitude when I think of the community we are building. Your love and support means so much to me. I feel like I won the lottery with all of you.

To anyone new who picks up this book. Thank you. I don't care if you love it or hate. I appreciate you taking a chance on me, Koa and Sydney.

ABOUT THE AUTHOR

Ginger Walls is most known for her Newhouse University series. She writes steamy contemporary romance with a mix of humor and heartbreaks. Her characters go through real-life struggles with strength and a side of vulnerability. You will laugh, cry, and swoon your way through every page.

When Ginger isn't writing she enjoys reading books about motorcycle clubs and seven-foot-tall aliens. She also enjoys listening to music and spending time with her family.

Follow her on social media (@gingerwallsauthor) to stay up to date on her upcoming book releases or the latest antics from her family.

AVAILABLE NOW

The Summer List
Pieces of You

NEWHOUSE UNIVERSITY

Easy Out: Newhouse University Book 1 (Hart & Lauren)
Strike Zone: Newhouse University Book 2 (Wyatt & Wren)
Foul Territory: Newhouse University Book 3 (Koa & Sydney)
Newhouse University Book 4 (Nash)
Newhouse University Book 5 (Eli)
Newhouse University Book 6 (Gage)
Newhouse University Book 7 (Ozzy)

WHAT'S NEXT

Are you missing our OG Newhouse crew already? Don't worry! They will all be making future appearances in some of the series have planned.

Grab your boots and cowboy hat. We are going to Rivers Bend, Alabama and visiting Songland Farms while the Rivers' family rebuilds their legacy.

You can also look out for books on the Carter, Emilio, and the rest of the King's Crew and all the kids going to Westfield Prep in the future.

Keep up to date with everything in the Newhouse Nation Readers Group on Facebook.

JOIN NEWHOUSE NATION

Made in the USA
Middletown, DE
07 February 2025

70956470R00266